KEEPING *Kylee*

JAN ROMES

Cover Design: Tugboat Design
Formatting: Tugboat Design
www.tugboatdesign.net

To Bill, always!

KEEPING *Kylee*

TEXAS BOYS FALLING FAST SERIES - BOOK TWO: QUINN

Chapter One

Yes, he was scum.

Or maybe his ex had called him sludge.

Scum. Sludge. Whatever. Both fit.

Quinn Randel leaned against the bar and took a sip of gin and tonic, refusing to let his split from Tori Caye completely ruin his mood. Their relationship had been bumpy for almost a year, so it wasn't a complete surprise that she'd called it quits. Still, her timing sucked. Shortly after arriving at the church to take part in Ty Vincent and Maggie Gray's wedding, Tori delivered an ultimatum. 'Set a date for *our* wedding right now or we're through'. His truthful reply that it might be years down the road, finished them off. Tori slid her engagement ring from her finger and flung it at him, grazing the high part of his cheek. Six hours and several drinks later, instead of mourning the breakup, he was scoping out the moves of the barmaid whose silky blonde curls tapered to her abundant chest.

He was scum all right.

Without taking his eyes off Kylee Steele, Quinn removed his tie and shoved it in the pocket of his tuxedo jacket. A raw and potent charge of sexual energy had sparked the moment he and Kylee set eyes on each other and it was still going strong. The powerful tug wouldn't let loose. They would stare at one another until Kylee was distracted by someone wanting a drink.

Minutes later, they went back to the unspoken conversation taking place between them. Quinn made sure his eyes constantly conveyed, "Niiiice" and he interpreted her replies as 'Back at ya'. He snickered at the likelihood that there was no conversation and that it was just the gin talking. One thing he was certain of though, they'd exchanged plenty of hot looks.

Kylee wandered to the opposite end of the bar but she was still slanting him glances.

Quinn swirled the ice cubes in his glass and finished his drink. He loosened the top three buttons of his stiff-collared white shirt and shifted to get a better look at the voluptuous barmaid. He could watch her all night. God she was gorgeous! She had the most amazing green eyes. When the light hit them they shimmered like… "Emeralds." He unwittingly finished the thought out loud and coughed to disguise a smile.

Ty Vincent shook his head with disapproval. "No, Quinn."

Quinn grinned at his best friend. "What?"

Ty scolded with a stern look and a tactful low voice. "Kylee is not for you."

"Kill joy."

"And then some." Ty nodded toward the dance floor where Tori Caye was dancing to the bands' rendition of Hot Blooded by Foreigner. "Take some time to adjust to being single again before you set your sights on someone else. Your ex is right there. She did the dumping but she's kept you on her radar all night, which means, it ain't over."

"Ohhhh, it's over."

"The relationship might be done. Making you suffer for everything that didn't go right while you were a couple, hasn't even begun. Save yourself a boat load of drama by not being so obvious with your interest in Kylee, or anyone else, this soon." He nudged Quinn with his elbow. "I doubt Tori would have a problem impaling your groin with her foot."

Quinn snorted a laugh but Ty was right. Any *normal*

woman would've left in tears after severing a two-year engagement. She wouldn't be laughing it up on the dance floor with her girl friends. He cursed under his breath and held up his empty glass for Kylee to refill.

Ty sifted air through his teeth. "Speaking of the devil…"

Quinn turned in time to see Tori closing in fast with her hands commandingly placed on her hips. She stopped less than an inch from him before glaring over his shoulder at Kylee. Her murderous squint came back to him in a hurry. "Really, Quinn?"

He eased back a step and dropped his hands in front of him to protect his crotch in case Ty was right about the shoe thing. "What?" He knew the question would ignite her short fuse but he didn't care. Tense lines etched Tori's flawless complexion and there were flecks of angry fire in her amber eyes. If she was upset about him slobbering over Kylee, that was her problem. She was the one who cut the flimsy string that had held them together, not the other way around. Quinn was close to refreshing her memory.

Tori mocked him by repeating the question. "What?"

Quinn was hit by a disturbing thought. In the three or so years that he and Tori had been together she never once got upset if he flirted with another woman, as long as the woman was wealthy or affiliated with their circle of friends. She referred to it as harmless networking. Kylee Steele wasn't wealthy and was in no way connected to anyone they ran with. Technically, there was a small connection. She was Sam Bright's employee and Sam was a good friend. Tori's turned up nose said it wasn't enough; Kylee wasn't one of them.

"Do I look stupid?" Tori zipped her irritation back and forth between Quinn and Ty like she dared either of them to say yes. "You've stayed anchored by the bar because of those 36C's."

"I've stay anchored by the bar because I intend to drink

myself into a drunken stupor." Quinn lobbed a silent appeal to Ty for support but received nothing more than a smirk. "Thanks buddy."

Ty put his palms up. "This is between you two." His somewhat-amused expression turned serious. "If you make a scene I'll have security toss you out." The comment was directed at Tori but Quinn knew if they went at it, he'd be kissing the sidewalk too. "I'm off to find my wife," Ty said. He pointed to Tori, then to Quinn. "Behave."

As soon as he was gone, Tori started in. "You're an ass." She harrumphed loud enough to draw a few sideways glances from some of the other guests.

"Not breaking news." Quinn didn't hold back. "Everyone knows I'm an ass, including me."

Tori shocked him by slithering possessively against him and clawing the front of his Hugo Boss tux with her long, intricately painted fingernails. "You're ruthless." She made an embarrassing purring sound. "It's so damned sexy."

From the corner of his eye, Quinn saw Kylee shake her head. He half-turned to meet her eyes. For a few seconds, it was just the two of them; blocking out the mayhem, refreshing that powerful tug. Tori put a hand on each side of his face to move his attention back to her. Once she had it, she wrapped her arms around his waist to lock him in place.

Dammit!

"Let go," Quinn said stiffly, trying to wrench Tori away but she tightened her arms.

"I've decided that even though we're through, I need to save you from yourself."

"You can't decide anything that involves me." His voice went up a notch. "I sure as hell don't want to hear you say I'm sexy. As far as saving me from myself, guess again. I'm a lost cause. Remember?"

"We've known each other forever, Quinn." She removed

the vise of her arms and began messing with the lapels of his jacket. "We went to the same private schools and partied together in high school and college. Since we were always in each other's space, it made sense when we finally hooked up. We have a long history. What I'm trying to say is that even though we're no longer lovers, we're still friends. Friends look out for each other." She continued without taking a breath. "I can't let you scrape the bottom of the barrel with a rebound attraction."

A fast-burning fury scorched Quinn from the inside out. He brusquely removed her grip from his jacket, finger by finger.

"I'm trying to keep you from making a big mistake." Again, Tori slipped an icy stare over his shoulder.

A low growl formed deep in his throat. "What I do from now on is my business, including my mistakes." He immediately regretted his poor choice of words when he heard a sharp intake of air behind him. Kylee was not the bottom of the barrel or a rebound attraction. She certainly wasn't a mistake. She was… His thoughts kinked from a combination of anger and uncertainty. He had no idea what Kylee was or wasn't. All he knew for sure is that it was easy to get lost in those remarkable eyes and he had an overwhelming desire to kiss her sweet pink mouth.

Tori refused to let him key on anything but her. "Dance with me."

With slow, calculated moves, he shook his head. "Not happening. I hate dancing."

"Dance with me," she strongly reiterated, "or I'm going to make things uncomfortable."

"You mean more than they already are?"

"There are things that need to be said. What better place to say them than on a loud, crowded dance floor?"

Tori didn't know the meaning of the word no because her

parents said yes to her every whim. It was the same for him. If he wanted a villa in Tuscany or a garage filled with Bentleys, his parents would make it happen. Quinn finally expelled that long, cavernous growl. Tori must've mistaken the sound as a white flag of surrender and circled his wrist. He muffled obscenities as she pulled him onto the dance floor.

Quinn held up a finger. "One dance. That's it. Say what you have to say in a hurry because I'm not staying for two."

Damn. A slow song.

* * *

Kylee had fought the warm feeling that lathered her from head to toe from Quinn Randel mentally removing her clothes. For reasons she couldn't explain, she'd allowed it to go on. Quinn would order a gin and tonic, make small talk, and engage in licentious gawking. She'd been powerless to stop it; the gawking anyway. Dang he was hot! And he'd made *her* hot all over.

She fanned herself with a laminated drink guide. Her hands were shaking, palms were sweating and she was biting her bottom lip so hard she expected to pierce the tender skin any second.

Nancy Reeger, Ty and Maggie's maid of honor, ordered a Long Island Iced Tea. "I'm freezing and you're fanning yourself?" She held out her arms to display goose bumps.

The temperature outside hovered around a hundred degrees and when Kylee arrived to the reception hall ahead of the wedding party and invited guests, it had been uncomfortably warm and stuffy. To try to cool the hall off in a hurry someone dialed the thermostat for the air conditioning down to where the place now felt like a walk-in cooler, to everyone but Kylee. She quirked a smile and handed Nancy her drink. "This should help."

Nancy purposely bumped Quinn with her hip. "I hope so or I'm going to have to borrow Quinn's jacket."

Kylee shifted in place when Quinn kept his eyes locked with hers even though he spoke to Nancy.

"It's yours if you want it. I'm the best man and it's my job to take care of the maid of honor." A shameless smile dimpled the corners of his mouth.

Nancy mocked him with a raspy chuckle. "Watch out for this one. He's too smooth for his britches."

Ty Vincent stood beside Quinn, taking it all in. "True that."

Kylee had no choice but to grin. "Noted."

Nancy raised her drink. "To warming up."

Kylee tapped her water bottle against Nancy's glass. "To cooling off."

They shared a laugh and Nancy bee-bopped to the dance floor with her drink in hand.

From beneath lowered lashes, Kylee tried to figure Quinn out. He was one of Dallas's most notorious womanizers even though he was heavily linked to Tori Caye. Tori was one of Dallas's most stunning yet mean-girl debutantes. Kylee was perplexed that Quinn was wasting time giving her the eye when he had Tori in his life.

Kylee puffed out a small breath. She would never understand men. They were complicated and frustrating and she was of the strict opinion that every last one of them qualified as a pain in the butt. Her father was a huge pain who broke away from the family to start a new life with a much younger woman. Asher Hutten, the man who fathered Kylee's three-year old daughter Gabbi, definitely was a pain. Without reading all the things printed in the newspapers about Quinn Randel, her instincts pegged him to be a pain too; a dangerous one with blue-grey eyes capable of stripping her naked with just a glance. All three men were well-known skirt-chasers. Two of the three had already turned her life upside down. Quinn's remarkable blue-grey orbs said he'd do it too if given the chance. The steamy looks passing between them promised paradise between the sheets, nothing more. She quietly scoffed, "Been there, done that. With Asher." Maybe she should be upfront with Quinn and let him know that he stood an ice cube's chance at the equator of hooking up with her. No way could she risk her heart and sanity with another meaningless liaison, especially with someone who would toss her aside before he put his clothes back on. Kylee tried not to stare but the man lassoed her attention the second he entered the reception hall. It was hard *not* to stare at the infamous millionaire. Quinn Randel was drop-dead handsome. There was no other way to describe him. Mischief and lust radiated from his every pore. And those lips…

It was nerve-wracking to be excited over someone whose magnificence was only on the surface. Quinn was arrogant, privileged, a man who had the capacity to make a difference in the world but was too busy to notice anything outside the perimeter of his social circle. He wasn't worth the brain space to fantasize over. Given that, why was she splitting her focus between his eyes and his mouth? Instinctively, she ran her tongue over her lips. Either wittingly, or unwittingly, Quinn mimicked her.

In an attempt to stop behaving like a love-starved ditz, Kylee swept her attention away from his mouth only to land on his stylishly cut every-strand-in-place blondish-brown hair. Perfect hair. Of course it was perfect. Everything else was spectacular; it only stood to reason his hair would be too. She had a strong urge to lean across the granite countertop of the bar and rearrange all that perfection. Even with tufts of hair going every which way, he'd still look yummy.

Her moral compass pricked her with its pointy arrow – Quinn Randel belonged to someone else. To boost the message, her conscience jabbed her again with another compelling thought – the fantasy is always better than reality.

All right already! I get it!

A scratchy noise of disenchantment at the tug of war going on in her head rolled out with no chance to stop it.

The smile lines at the corners of Quinn's eyes deepened like he could read her mind.

Kylee shifted from foot to foot while she pondered how she would be able to help someone else understand and cope with the things bothering them when she couldn't get some semblance of control over the things wreaking havoc in her own backyard. She was studying to become a psychologist, for crying out loud. It was a slow undertaking, but at some point she'd have her PhD and license to practice. Hopefully by then she'd have a good understanding as to why she continued to fall prey to hot guys with bedroom eyes who would leave after they scratched their itch.

Turning her back to Quinn, she engaged in small tasks to try to block him out. She straightened a stack of drink napkins, wiped a drip of grenadine syrup from the side of the bottle, refilled crystal dishes with mixed nuts and opened another bottle of wine to let it breathe per her boss's instructions at the beginning of the reception. When one bottle got low, she was to open another to allow the wine to become more expressive.

Kylee could still feel the heat of Quinn's gaze boring into her. She casually moved to the opposite end of the bar to collect empty beer mugs. From her peripheral she watched him bend forward to follow her movements.

A small light bulb popped behind the bar, both literally and figuratively. She startled from the sound *and* from the information that sank deeper into her psyche. While she replaced the decorative bulb she hashed over what she'd been subconsciously rejecting – that the excitement rushing over her wasn't excitement at all. What was really happening was a type of meltdown from overload. She had a lot to contend with, mostly self-inflicted. Working full time with occasional overtime hours on top of raising a very sweet, very active three year old daughter was a bit much. Plus she'd been cramming classes into a very tight schedule. Instead of excitement, she was starting to malfunction. This weird and sudden longing for the millionaire flirt, was her minds' way of trying to loosen or sidetrack her stress before she short-circuited. Kylee frowned. No matter how she tried to spin the information, it amounted to a sordid heap of hooey. Yes, she was strapped for time and had an excessive schedule, but she'd always been a person who worked better under pressure. This attraction for Quinn wasn't added stress, nor was it complex. The only thing going on was an ardent enthusiasm for physical fulfillment. It had been awhile since she'd been intimate – three years and nine months, to be exact – and her body wanted what it wanted. It. Wanted. Quinn. Although, if he was interested in a tryst, which he wasn't, who had the time?

Someone hollered that they wanted a Gibson. Kylee searched the laminated cheat sheet she'd been using as a fan. Gibson: a dry martini with a cocktail onion instead of an olive. While she made the drink, she swung her interest back to Quinn.

Big mistake!

Quinn's eyes locked with hers and held her immobile, for how long she wasn't sure. The warmth simmering in her veins turned into searing heat. A trickle of sweat rolled down the front of her to pool in her cleavage.

"Uh, miss, my drink?"

Kylee curved around to the kind elderly gent who was giving her a big smile like he was privy to what was going on. Maybe he was an intuitive old coot who could clue her in because she didn't have a tight grasp on what was happening. She placed his drink in front of him.

One silvery brow arched high before he slid a fifty dollar tip in her direction. "There ya go, beautiful." The distinct Texas twang more commonly associated with West Texas was as charming as he was.

Kylee's eyes widened at the generous gratuity. "Thank you so much."

"My pleasure, doll." He took a sip of his Gibson, winked and hobbled away.

Kylee ran her fingers over the crisp bill with the picture of Ulysses S. Grant. Without tips, she'd be in a world of hurt. She used them to pay her half of the rent and for childcare for Gabbi. Occasionally she utilized them to buy an outrageously expensive book for school. Between her wages and tips, she made ends meet but she had to give careful consideration to each dollar spent. Actually, she could only make use of ninety percent of her tips. The other ten percent went to Dallas's food banks and pantries. Regardless of her monthly bills, she faithfully dropped a check in the mail as thanks for helping her through a tough time. A few months after Gabbi was born her pocketbook took a direct hit. Her bucket of rust with four wheels died an untimely death, forcing her to drain her savings account. With those funds and her weekly paycheck she bought another oxidized heap of aluminum and steel. To add insult to injury, her yearly car insurance premium was due and she had to renew her license plates. Of course, bad luck was on a rampage. The building superintendent tucked a note in her mailbox that stated there would be a hike in rent. It was financial gloom to the nth degree. Had it not been for the food bank, she wouldn't have been able to feed Gabbi. They eased her panic and she would forever hold those folks close to her heart.

Kylee flinched when a weighted glass clunked on the bar. She instantly recognized the huge gold watch on the wrist of the Casanova who held the glass. Slowly lifting her head, Kylee met the blue-grey mischief in Quinn Randel's eyes. "What would you…" Her inner-ditz emerged and she could barely finish her question. "…like?"

The wicked gleam in his eyes suggested he wanted more than alcohol. "Gin and tonic. For now."

Kylee's lower body clenched in response and she didn't have to look in the mirror behind her to verify that she'd turned a tell-tale shade of hot pink. "Okay," was the only thing she was capable of saying.

Quinn's mouth offered a come-here grin.

A chill cut into all that warmth and seduction when Tori Caye made a sudden appearance. Tori looked like an agitated cat. Her eyes were narrowed, pupils wide, claws extended.

Kylee shrank back a step. She could deny under oath that she'd been flirting with an engaged man, but she'd be found guilty. With every curve of her mouth and every sweep of her lashes, she'd egged him on. And the woman in Quinn's life was going to scratch her eyes out.

Tori cut to the chase with Quinn by saying that even though they were no longer a couple she couldn't allow him to make a big mistake by scraping the bottom of the barrel.

Mistake? Bottom of the barrel? A bristle of anger and resentment rushed up Kylee's spine. Maybe she wasn't born with a silver spoon in her mouth or wasn't in the one percent of the population who could boast they had more money than they knew what to do with, that didn't elevate Tori over her or anyone else. Kylee squared her shoulders and lifted her chin. She might not have a lot of money, but she was a hard worker with her eye on the prize – a nothing-to-sneeze-at degree that would help make a good life for her daughter. She wanted to fire back at Tori. Because she'd been making eyes at the angry blondes' fiancé, she had to keep her mouth shut. Kylee fisted her hands so tight her nails dug into her palms.

Wait…

Did she hear right? Tori and Quinn were no longer a couple?

It didn't matter. The news didn't absolve her guilt. She'd broken the hands-off-my-man covenant that was assumed between women. And for what? For a guy who wanted one thing and one thing only.

Quinn made a growling noise and it yanked her from self-recrimination to remember what else had been said. Tori wanted to save Quinn from making a big mistake and he went on the defensive by saying they were his mistakes to make. They both meant…her.

Kylee gave them a hostile glare and grabbed the sink sprayer. If she hadn't heard her boss's voice in the background she would've blasted both Quinn and Tori with water. She slowly loosened her grip on the nozzle. "Sweet," she mumbled under her breath. "I'm the bottom of the barrel *and* a mistake."

It was time to get some distance from the madness before she got fired for drenching two of Dallas's *finest.*

Kylee made her way to the small storage room behind the bar. The second she was on the opposite side of the door, briny tears threatened to spill. Shaking her head adamantly, she commanded them to stay put.

A few tears leaked in defiance.

Kylee brusquely shoved them from her cheeks. She wouldn't cry over two elitists who had nothing better to do on a Saturday evening than mess with her. She muffled cuss words and refused to allow her emotions to take control. She didn't cry over *guys.* Not anymore. When Asher had made it clear he wouldn't accept responsibility for the child he helped create, she'd cried until her eyes practically swelled shut. Afterward, she vowed never to cry over another guy as long as she lived. Yet, here she was, close to blubbering like a darn fool.

Something on the calendar that hung on the wall across from her caught her eye. "Ahh." The flirting. Getting worked up over a guy she'd never seriously consider sleeping with. It. All. Made. Sense. In two days Mother Nature's cruel monthly gift would arrive. All those feelings and bad behavior was nothing more than pesky chemical messengers secreting into her blood stream, causing havoc with her body and her good judgment. She wasn't fascinated with Quinn Randel. Not really. It was hormones running amok. Kylee braced against a storage rack to brood and hash over what had taken place. Quinn hit on her. She let him. Of course, Tori's verbal smack-down of Quinn and less-than-subtle warning to Kylee that he was off limits even though she was no long paired with him, put things in perspective – Quinn was out of her league. In the recesses of her mind, she knew nothing would ever happen between them, but for a little while they were just two people setting each other on fire.

Quinn and his ex-girlfriend could both go to… Kylee curbed the urge to be nasty. She didn't wish either of them any ill will. In a nutshell, she was to blame for thinking it was okay to make eyes at him.

Sam Bright came through the swinging door, making her jump. "Everything okay?"

Kylee smiled to cover her mood. "Here they are." She held up a jar of maraschino cherries.

Sam studied her for a long moment, his expression unreadable. "We have thirsty customers."

"I'm on it, boss." Kylee pushed past him. She hesitated at the door and took a deep breath. She had to keep her emotions in check. There was just one teeny tiny issue that would make things difficult – she didn't have an invisible suit of Kevlar to protect her against the pleasure of Quinn.

* * *

Quinn pasted on a scowl but inside he was laughing. Every

time Tori tried to snuggle closer he put more space between them like she had cooties. It was fifth-grade behavior, but he'd told her he didn't want to dance yet she'd insisted.

"Will you stop being a dork for a few minutes?" Tori tightened her arms around his neck.

"Then stop trying to tell me what I should or shouldn't do."

Tori caught him off guard and lurched forward to squash her breasts against his chest. "You're pretending to be attracted to the barmaid to get back at me. Right?"

Yes. No. Hell, probably. "Why do you say that?"

"Duh. She's not your type. Not by a long shot." Tori squinted with annoyance. "You go for women with really long hair. Hers falls just below her shoulders. And you're a fool for amber and brown eyes, not green. Sure she has big boobs, but so do a lot of women."

Quinn shook his head. "You break up with me and now you're telling me who I should or shouldn't be attracted to. Lady, your elevator is stuck on the thirteenth floor."

Anger flashed through Tori's expression again. "I think you've forgotten who I am, Quinn." At warp speed she said she knew him better than he knew himself. She also didn't hesitate to remind him that she was an heiress who had enough money to buy the city of Dallas, if it was for sale.

Blah. Blah. Blah.

"Stay away from the barmaid. She's clueless." The bossy eyebrow he'd come to know, lifted. "She'll mistake all that charm and cockiness for genuine interest."

Kylee wasn't clueless. She was… There was no need to defend Kylee, either consciously or subconsciously. She was beautiful and intelligent and… His mouth went dry when he pictured her ample body. Plump breasts. Shapely bottom. Gorgeous mouth. A lightly sweet perfume that made his senses go crazy.

Tori rapped the side of his head with her knuckles. "Helloooo."

"I heard you." Quinn gritted his teeth. He hated that Tori was right. Despite all the luscious things about Kylee Steele, he couldn't pursue his interest. They were from two different worlds. She *was* the type of woman who would want more than a wild night of lovemaking. She'd want his heart and everything else that came with him. In exchange for a good romp? He shook his head at the thought. No woman would get that much of him, even one with amazing eyes. "She's Sam's barmaid, nothing more."

"She's also a mom who's going to school in her spare time." Tori laughed like motherhood and Kylee bettering her education were foolish things to do.

Kylee was a mom? With all the finesse of a rhino in a light bulb factory, Quinn twisted around to locate the blonde goddess. He spied her coming from the back room. She was all smiles.

"Oww," Tori complained next to his ear.

"What?" Quinn's patience with his ex was about the size of a grain of salt.

"You stepped on my toe, ya big oaf."

"I told you I didn't want to dance."

Tori thinned her eyes to the point they were almost closed. "Are you deliberately stepping on me?"

"I'm an oaf, but I'm not a deliberate oaf." Quinn turned Tori so he could continue to watch Kylee without being obvious. *Come on. Look this way*, he prompted as though his thoughts could telepathically connect with hers from across the room.

Kylee seemed unaware of anything but people wanting something to drink.

He watched a hound dressed in a long sleeve white shirt with the cuffs rolled up, black jeans and cowboy boots bend across the bar and tuck a strand of Kylee's hair behind her ear. To her credit she frowned and walked to the other end of the bar. Even though she was ignoring the hound, Quinn still wanted to push the guy's nose so far into his head he would need a truck with a log chain to pull it out.

In the span of a few seconds, a handful of thoughts jammed into Quinn's brain. Why did he care whether someone else paid attention to Kylee? He had no intention of hooking up with her. She was just someone to pass the time with. So why did it bother him that she had a kid? Why did he want to stomp across the floor and make a spectacle of himself by taking her in his arms? His mind was a mess but one thing was crystal clear – he wanted to give Kylee a piece his mind because moms weren't supposed to flirt or look that damn good. The second he heard she had a kid his interest should've bottomed out but it didn't. "Good for her," Quinn finally said.

"Huh?"

"It's cool that she's a mom."

"We've already moved on from that part of the conversation." Tori studied him with a measurable look of suspicion. "She's going to become a psychiatrist or psychologist or whatever the heck they call shrinks. I also heard that the guy who got her pregnant bolted the moment he found out. She probably tried to trick him into marrying her."

"Don't say that," Quinn said, a little too forcefully.

Tori drew back like he'd taken a swing at her. "Why do you care what I say about her?"

Quinn groped for a reason. "It feels wrong to trash someone who has a kid."

"Getting soft on me, Quinny?"

"Stop calling me that. I hate it." Tori used the nickname when she wanted to get under his skin.

"Then stop fussing over someone who probably has a stomach filled with stretch marks." She stuck out her tongue.

The music stopped and the band leader announced it was time for Maggie to throw the bouquet. "All you single ladies, drop what you're doing and get out here."

Tori let out a whoop. "I'm catching the bouquet." She batted her eyelashes. "I'm rethinking this breakup." She pointed to her and then to Quinn. "If I catch the bouquet, we could be the next couple to walk down the aisle."

Quinn rolled his eyes. The woman had serious memory issues. The reason they were no longer together was because he wouldn't commit to wedding plans; well that and there was no longer any real affection. He wasn't sure there ever was. "You mean walk the plank."

"You're a riot." She blew him a kiss and shoved her way through the crowd.

He wasn't joking. Getting tied down to one person for all eternity equaled being shoved off a plank into a watery abyss of great white sharks. He smiled irreverently. If he had to choose between marriage and being devoured by a predator with sharp teeth, the choice would be easy.

Kylee drew her silky blonde brows together when he bellied up to the bar again.

"Can I get another gin and tonic?" He expected her to tell him to get lost or that she was cutting him off because he'd already had too much to drink. Instead, she produced the gin and tonic. "Aren't you going to try to catch the bouquet?"

Kylee's eyes rounded in surprise. Truthfully, he was as surprised by the question as she was since he'd said it without any forethought.

"I'm the hired help. Remember?"

"Not to me you're not." Again, words were coming out like he had no control over his thoughts or his mouth.

"Riiight."

Quinn let his gaze leisurely roam over Kylee. "You really should get your..." He teasingly cleared his throat.

"...feet...out on that dance floor."

"Why?" Her brows were still tightly drawn.

Quinn took a sip of his drink. "You deserve to catch the bouquet."

Kylee released her frown. "You have BS down to a fine art." She came through the half-door that cordoned off the bar from the patrons. There was an after-this-leave-me-alone quality to her voice. "Happy?"

Quinn shook with a laugh. "I'm getting there."

She wrinkled her nose.

Two semi-inebriated guys next to him commented that they couldn't wait to catch the garter. Thanks to also being semi-inebriated, Quinn had no filter on his mouth. "Fools." If he remembered correctly, whoever caught the garter was to pair up with whoever caught the bouquet. He said, "Fools", again.

He turned back to Kylee but she was gone.

A crowded gathered in front of him, blocking his view. Quinn stretched to try to look around them.

The band leader counted down. "Three. Two. One."

A commotion on the dance floor made Quinn leave his perch and make his way through the wall of people to see what was going on. Tori stood with her arms crossed, looking more than a little pissed. Kylee was next to her holding a bouquet of short-stemmed red roses, looking like she wanted to throw up. Quinn laughed, almost spilling his drink.

In a surprise move, Kylee shoved the flowers into Tori's grubby mitts and stomped past Quinn on her way back to the bar. He watched her pour a shot of whiskey and throw it to the back of her throat.

The bouquet of red roses was suddenly shoved under his nose.

"Look what I have." Tori thrashed the flowers around in triumph like she was the victor. "I've decided that we're not broken up."

"You can't step back into my life as if nothing happened."

"I just did."

"I'd advise you to step back out."

Tori's smile splintered into frustration. "I don't know what I see in you, Quinn Randel." Her voice, while not freakishly loud, was still penetrating and barbed. "The only person you care about is you. You're a first class jerk." She went into a red-faced rant that he wasn't worth sharing the same air space and people pretended to like him because he was filthy rich, and no woman would truly love him because he wasn't lovable.

True. True. And True. Quinn let her lash out because he *was* a jerk. There was a good chance that's all he'd ever be. He blamed genetics. The Randel men, for as far back as he could remember, were a hearty-stock of narcissistic bastards. It took strong women to deal with them and their legacy. Quinn's mom was the strongest woman he'd ever known. She possessed a special skill that could take him and his father, down a notch when they got out of line. She did it without raising her voice or reducing them to rubble. Quinn snickered in spite of his mood. When the good Lord made Vera Randel, he broke the mold. There wasn't another woman on earth who could take what they dished out.

Tori propelled the bouquet onto a nearby table, gave him a hard look and stomped off in her spiky shoes, cussing like a longshoreman. Instead of seeking comfort from her girl friends, she took refuge with Jake Garrison. Quinn contemplated rescuing his friend but decided to watch how things played out. Of his three close friends – Ty Vincent, Trigg Sinclair and Jake – Jake was the quiet one. He was an all around nice guy who would listen to Tori's long-winded spiel about how Quinn had stepped on her heart…and toes…with his shiny black Ferragamos.

Quinn's curiosity waned in a hurry. He decided to close the book on Tori and go outside to get some air. In a few long strides he was at the side entrance. Before he stepped out a hand landed on his back. He groaned expecting round-two from his ex. Instead, he was surprised to find Maggie bearing down on him with probing blue eyes.

"Quinn," she said softly, "I know Tori and I didn't hit it off, but I'm still sorry to see the two of you call it quits."

Quinn automatically wrapped Maggie in a hug. "I'm the one who should be sorry. We were a little cool to you when we first met."

Maggie's long lashes fluttered across her eyes. "A little cool? You were icebergs." At his wince, she grinned. "All's forgiven."

"It wasn't anything you did, Maggie. It's just that we protect our own." The way her eyes widened he realized there was an embedded slam in what he said. "That came out wrong. I meant that we're a tight group. Always have been. I know you're head over heels in love with Ty and wouldn't hurt him for the world, but there are women out there that only have one thing in mind – easy street. We didn't have a feel for you yet."

"I get that you safeguard each other, but I'm not here to seek your apology. I wanted to see if you're okay."

"I'm fine."

Maggie lowered her voice. "Ty says the reason you and Tori broke up is because you're dead-set against marriage and having a family." He started to say that Ty was spot on, but Maggie put a finger across his lips. "Shh. Shh. Don't speak." Quinn started to laugh and she gave him a bossy look that made him clamp his mouth shut. "What I've observed about you in the past week is contrary to Ty's take on things."

"Meaning?"

"You care about Ty. If you're so anti-marriage you would've done some swift and sneaky maneuvering to make sure we didn't get married. Am I right?"

Quinn was tempted to tease her by saying that she and Ty had gotten married so fast they didn't give him time for any sneaky maneuvering. "You make him happy, Maggie."

Maggie leaned in and quietly ribbed him. "Ah! Ha! I knew it. You're not against marriage. Admit it."

"I don't need a woman to make me happy." He glued a goofy smile on his face and pointed to it. "See. This is me being happy without a woman."

"You look like the Joker."

Quinn cracked up laughing. "Ty has no idea what he's in for with you."

"He knows."

Quinn kissed the side of Maggie's head. "He's a lucky man."

"If you stop being a bonehead maybe you'll get lucky too."

"Doubtful."

"Hands off, hound dog." Ty pulled Maggie away from Quinn and into his arms.

Maggie blinked up at her husband. "Quinn and I were having a heart-to-heart conversation."

Ty sent Quinn a pretend look of jealousy. "What she really means is that she's putting her nose in where it doesn't belong. It's what women do when they're worried about someone."

"No one needs to worry about me because I'm fine. Better than fine." His gaze traveled across the room to Kylee. To stay fine he had to forget about those green eyes and that hot body. A woman like her could make a guy adjust his way of thinking. He didn't want to adjust anything. He was happy being single and planned to stay that way, despite Maggie's opinion.

Chapter Two

Did he get hit by a van or a Mac truck? Pain raced across Quinn's forehead and his temples throbbed. The rest of him ached like he had the flu. He carefully rolled from his stomach to his back and sucked in a deep breath, hoping the extra oxygen would jumpstart him. Realistically it would take more than added air to get him going; it would take a few double espressos. Keeping his eyes closed to block out the tiny slices of sunlight sliding between the wooden slats of the window shades, he reflected on how he'd come to feel like he'd been run over and squished into the bubbly tar of a roadway. Consuming too much gin and then switching to beer probably had something to do with it. He popped open an eye to read the amber digits of his alarm clock setting on the nightstand inches from his head. Six-thirty. A.M.? With all the alcohol in his system he should've been down for the count at least until noon. He rolled to his side with a moan. The muscles in his neck were sore, possibly from craning it all night to keep track of Kylee Steele. He grimaced at the stupidity of his actions, but he had to admit all that lust and gin had been spectacular.

Quinn pulled to a sitting position and grabbed the framed photo he kept next to the bed and ran the tips of his fingers across the picture; something he did every morning without fail. With a heavy sigh he laid it close to his chest until his cell phone plinked with an incoming text message. He leaned over, carefully returned the picture back on the nightstand and snapped up his phone. At the same time, his stomached roiled with discontent. Maybe he really *did* get hit by a van. Or maybe Tori beat the snot out of him. Quinn brushed his palm over the prickly stubble on his chin. He refused to get back together with the sharp-tongued vixen and before the reception was over they had it out one more time. Ty was constantly tailed by paparazzi and he shared with Quinn his hunch that Tori had been loose-lipping his whereabouts to the tabloid and newspaper vultures. Quinn confronted her with the allegation and the damnedest thing happened – Jake protected Tori like he would slay any and all dragons for her. Quinn still couldn't figure out what that was about.

Quinn shifted on the bed and released a lengthy exhale. Something significant had been missing from him and Tori's relationship. Actually, there were two big things that had been non-existent. Commitment and fire. He could've fixed one, but not the other. A couple either had fire or they didn't. He thought of Kylee straight away. Now *there* was fire. Doubtful she'd admit it, but it had been there scorching the air between them.

He finally checked his phone.

The message was from Ty. *Hey, buddy, are you still alive? LOL.* Ty also said that he and Maggie were belted in their seats aboard a Delta flight that would whisk them away on a spontaneous honeymoon. *Heading to Reno. When we get back we need to celebrate because I've just been named CEO of my granddad's company.*

Quinn let out a whoop of joy for his friend but followed up with an "Oww" when his head felt like it was going to explode. He needed a blast of caffeine soon. *Awesome, Ty! I knew it would happen sooner or later, just didn't think it would be the day after you tied the knot. How great is that? You deserve it. I'll set up the party.*

Thanks, man. Nothing too elaborate. Maggie doesn't go for all the bells and whistles.

No worries. I know exactly what we'll do.

Have to go. We'll be back Thursday night. Talk soon.

Enjoy Reno.

Quinn threw his legs over the side of the bed with a mix of emotions. He was happy for Ty. In a way he hated to see his friend accept the helm of Vincent Oil. The position was loaded with responsibility and would suck up all of Ty's free time. It was bound to happen to all four of them at some point. Trigg's dad had been nagging him to take on a greater role in the family's cattle business and Jake's parents had recently pushed him into the Vice President of Marketing position for their magazine empire. Quinn rubbed the back of his neck. His friends were fast becoming movers and shakers, whether they wanted to be or not. And then there was him. He'd fought the idea of responsibility, accountability, liability, and dependability. Why would anyone want those headaches? His grandfather had willed him more money than he would ever spend and he was making a hefty sum as Chief Financial Officer for his dad's chain of cleaning companies. His dad was also a major investor in a telecommunications company and like Trigg's father he had a thriving cattle business as well. Quinn wasn't interested in telecommunications and the only way he liked cattle was on a plate, medium-rare.

Like a flick to the forehead, the revelation that he didn't like much of anything came from out of nowhere. He tried to laugh off the disclosure with "I like sex." His subconscious needled him with the truth – liking sex was normal, but it wasn't enough. He could con everyone around him that he wanted to be nothing more than a philanderer, but he couldn't con himself. He tossed his phone back on the nightstand.

* * *

Kylee flinched awake from the small foot that landed in her eye. She smiled automatically. Gabbi was stretched out sideways in the bed with both feet aimed toward her face. That was the way of it with three year olds. They started out snuggled up next to you and in the morning, their feet or cute little bottom was parked against your face.

She covered a yawn to muffle the noise. Her thoughts drifted to the night before. When she got home from working at Ty Vincent's wedding reception, she'd collected Gabbi from the sitter's apartment next door and then laid awake going over everything that happened. In a lot of ways it had been a really good night. Mostly good. Actually, the jury was still out as to whether it could be construed as good. Something extraordinary had happened – Quinn Randel did what no other guy had been able to do for quite awhile; he roused her desires from their hiding place. The re-emergence made her nervous and was sure to complicate an already crazy life. She was secretly happy to have them back and to feel like a woman again.

Rising up on one elbow, she studied the contented face of her daughter. Gabbi had been a surprise addition to her life; one she welcomed from the moment the doc said she was pregnant. She winced at the memory of the brief relationship with Asher Hutten that resulted in her becoming a mom. She was twenty three at the time and ready to start college. Most people her age had already graduated and were working in their chosen fields. She had a delayed start due to lack of funds. At freshman orientation, she met Asher. He was a pharmacy student with one more class to graduate. He was a hunky handful of clichés – a tall drink of water, as handsome as the day is long, smooth as silk, fine as wine, and a fate worse than death. He was beyond charming and she fell for him the second he spoke. They were a couple for six weeks. For five and a half weeks of those six, she fought his attempts to get her in bed. She'd explained that she couldn't afford to get pregnant. Her parents had started off on the wrong foot by getting pregnant with her and she didn't want to follow in their footsteps. Asher pretended to understand. He said kids weren't in his foreseeable future either but he continued his sexual pursuit. One night after studying for a test until two in the morning, she had no fight left. Asher got what he wanted…and what he didn't want. They used protection but somehow she got pregnant. Kylee was scared to the core but not unhappy. Asher was livid. He shouted like a lunatic that he'd taken precautions. He suggested she take the easy way out. Kylee told him where he could shove his suggestion. No way would she terminate something so precious. Asher said it wasn't fair that she keep the baby. Kylee told him to get out of her apartment before she hit him with a lamp. She hadn't seen him since.

Going forward alone had been difficult. She scrapped college, got a job working for Sam Bright and didn't look back until last year when the urge to go back to school wouldn't let her alone. Every choice she made affected Gabbi in some way. It had taken a few months of nail chewing and battling uncertainty before she decided that getting her degree was for the greater good.

Last night, her tightly guarded life almost slipped away. She let Quinn Randel's sexy blue-grey eyes mess with her head…and her body. She almost did the unthinkable and gave in to those raging hormones. What if she had? Then what? She imagined it might've been a glorious night of wild passion and when the sun came up she and Quinn would've parted, never again to set eyes on each other. When all would've been said and done, he'd continue living his wealthy, pampered existence and she'd carry on raising her child and working her tail off at the bar and in school. End of story. Kylee closed her eyes and folded her arms around her. Even one night of protected bliss carried a high risk of pregnancy and she was in no position, either mentally or financially, to bring another child into the world. Good thing nothing happened.

A low knock made Kylee ease out of bed so she wouldn't wake Gabbi. She shuffled to the door and smashed her eye against the peek-hole. Holding two cups of coffee in a cardboard drink carrier was Angie Stonehill, her best friend, co-worker and roommate. She slid the chain from the lock and turned the deadbolt. She put her finger to her lips to indicate Gabbi was still asleep.

"I stayed at Charlie's last night and just realized I forgot my key," Angie whispered and handed Kylee a venti-size cup of Starbucks medium house blend. Charlie was Angie's on-again off-again boyfriend. Right now, they were on. "He didn't have a drop of coffee in his apartment so I left." She removed the lid from her cup and blew away a burst of steam. "So how was the Vincent wedding?"

Kylee took a much needed sip before answering. "It was good. I made a lot of tips. One guy gave me a fifty."

"You're kidding! I wished Sam would've asked me to work with you." Angie slurped her coffee and gestured for Kylee to keep going. "Did they have those little crab puffs that I love so much? Any hot guys hit on you?"

Kylee was about to enjoy another taste of coffee but mid-sip Angie's last question made her miss her mouth and coffee splashed the front of the faded Gary Allan t-shirt she used as a nightshirt. She smoothed the droplets into the shirt so they wouldn't fall onto the carpet. "Yes, they had crab puffs. I ate some for you."

"Well thank you very much." Angie sat on the couch and patted the cushion next to her. "How about hot guys?"

"There were a few." Kylee averted her eyes from Angie's.

"Spill it, sista," Angie prompted.

Kylee pointed to the coffee spill on her shirt. "I did."

"You know what I mean. Something juicy happened. Tell me."

Kylee perched on the couch with her legs tucked under her and the steamy cup of coffee safely cradled in her hands. "Two words: Quinn Randel."

"Quinn Randel?" Angie made a face. "I said hot guys not pompous asses."

Kylee jiggled with a laugh. "I know, right?"

Angie blinked at Kylee over the rim of her cup. "What did His Royal Highness do now? Try to feel up every woman at the reception?" Quinn and his buddies frequented Sam's bar usually during the late-evening early-morning hours which was Angie's shift. Angie knew all about Quinn.

"I don't think he groped anyone, at least not with his hands." Kylee squirmed under Angie's amused look. "He spent most of the night giving me the eye."

A tight V formed between Angie's eyebrows and she curled her upper lip. "Be careful with that one. He's as tempting as they come, but he's trouble." Her voice rose significantly higher and Kylee said, "Shh."

"Kylee, he's worse than trouble. He's a fleabag that's probably trying to get as much panic-sex as he can."

Kylee laughed while letting Angie's opinion soak in. "Flea bag? Panic sex?"

"Yeah, he's a dog and not the cuddly type. Some dogs engage in panic sex because they can't handle the fact that once they tie the knot they'll only get to sleep with one bitch…erm, female dog…the rest of their lives."

Kylee shifted on the cushion. "When you put it like that who wouldn't panic?"

"I'm serious. He's the world's biggest mutt."

Kylee offered a cheesy grin at Angie's accurate description of Quinn, but she followed up by swallowing a clog of guilt. "I'm not sure but I think Quinn and Tori may no longer be engaged. I may have caused a rift between them. If I did, I didn't mean to." She tapped the side of her Styrofoam cup.

Angie pushed Kylee with her foot. "Don't be silly. What could you have possibly done to put His Royal Highness and the Queen of Dallas, at odds?"

Kylee muffled her reply. "When he flirted, I flirted back."

"Come again?"

"When he flirted, my brain went sideways and I flirted back. I shouldn't have but I couldn't help myself. He was just so..."

"Sleazy?"

Kylee chuckled at Angie's unique way of getting her point across. "He might be sleazy, but he made me feel good for a few hours. He has remarkable eyes and a sexy..."

"We might be from the poor side of town, chick, but we have class. We don't poach unavailable men; especially those with a reputation for being a dog." Angie grabbed her iPad from the lamp table and tapped the app for Candy Crush.

Kylee sighed. Angie was right. They had little money but big consciences. It was wrong to enjoy the attention of unavailable dogs. "Thanks for setting me straight, Ange'"

* * *

Quinn drummed his fingers on the bar and looked around. Sam appeared to be the only one working. Then again, it was Sunday and two in the afternoon. Maybe his help didn't come in until later.

An uncapped bottle of beer landed in front of him. "Try this and tell me what you think."

Quinn checked the label marked dark ale. He took a slug, forced himself to swallow and made a face. "Not to my liking."

"Mine either." Sam dumped the rest of the beer down the drain and produced a bottle of light beer. "Some wedding, huh?" Sam's grin was inquisitive. The man had a special knack for making his customers comfortable so they would drink up and open up at the same time.

"It was damn great, if you ask me."

Sam snapped a bar towel at Quinn. "I did ask you."

"Ha. Ha. You're on your game, funny man. You know it was a great party because you were there." Quinn downed a healthy swallow of *good* beer. "Ahh."

"Hair of the dog?"

"Sort of. I woke up with a monster headache thanks to too many gin and tonics and a dozen bottles of beer, and from acting the fool until they booted me out of the reception hall so they could lock up."

Sam held up a finger to say he'd be right back. He pushed his way through the swinging door that led to the kitchen and returned with a case of beer. He began stowing the long-neck bottles in the beer cooler behind the bar and glanced over his shoulder to continue the conversation. "For a guy who claims to hate dancing, you burned up the dance floor."

Quinn cracked a smile. "That's where the fool part comes in." After numerous maddening discussions with Tori he joined Ty and Maggie on the dance floor to try to forget about his anger and possibly forget about Kylee.

Sam snorted a laugh. "It looked like you were having seizures instead of dancing."

"You're on a roll." Quinn pushed the bottle of beer away. It wasn't conquering the fur that had grown on his tongue overnight. "I could really go for a strong cup of coffee."

"No problem." Sam poured coffee into an over-large ceramic cup and scooted it to Quinn. "Made fresh ten minutes ago. It's piping hot."

Quinn took a cautious sip and smacked his lips. "I've been drinking way too much alcohol lately." He smirked when he realized he was telling that to a man who sold alcohol for a living.

"Do you suppose it has anything to do with Tori?"

Quinn studied Sam, maybe for the first time ever. Sam was tall, muscled, always wore faded blue jeans and a white t-shirt and had an eagle tattoo on his forearm. He had a bouncer-like quality to him, which came in handy when people misbehaved in his bar. Underneath that gruff exterior, lay the heart of a therapist. Kylee seemed to be the same, only a much softer version. She was a barmaid studying to be a psychologist. The whole working in a bar and listening to people thing must go hand in hand. Hmm. He wouldn't mind having a real conversation with Kylee to find out. Although, getting past those eyes and those breasts to have a conversation, wouldn't be easy. The noise of Sam clinking bottles while putting them in the cooler distracted the fantasy. "Tori and I are no longer an item."

"I heard." Sam finished filling the cooler and shoved the empty case under the bar. "Is it because she can't stop nagging about getting married?"

Quinn shrugged. "It's a combination of things." He was in no mood to discuss his ex."Ty thinks she's the one leaking his personal information to the press. I confronted her about it and all hell broke loose for awhile. Since you seem to have the 4-1-1 about most things, you probably already knew that."

"Yep. Heard that too. Do you two hate each other, or what?"

"Surprisingly we don't. After she chewed me out for thinking she was capable of doing something like that, she calmed down and we had a conversation that we should've had a long time ago. She admitted that she loved me but wasn't *in love* with me. I said I felt the same way. I think that was our problem all along. We liked the idea of being a power couple, but it wasn't enough. Her parents finished us off, so to speak. They badgered her about getting the wedding underway. They transferred their anxiety to her, she tried to transfer it to me and things fell apart. Quinn shook his head with amazement.

"The Cayes wanted something for us that deep down neither of us wanted. I don't have to worry about it anymore because she's now pestering Jake."

"I saw her hanging on him. I thought she was doing it to get back at you."

"There was probably some of that going on too, but I saw something in her eyes that makes me think she's really interested in him."

The corners of Sam's eyes crinkled. "She was hitting the wine pretty hard. Maybe that genuine interest was alcohol-induced."

"Or maybe it's that whole opposites attract thing." Straight away he thought of Kylee. They were as different as two people could be. Was that the allure?

Sam refilled their cups and shared some personal information too. "Now that Ty and Maggie have tied the knot, Raven's pushing me to get married. We've dated for eight months and she thinks she's ready to be a wife." He tapped the handle of his cup. "I'm not up for hurrying things along."

"Maybe she's the one, Sam."

"I don't know. There are things I love about her and things I don't."

"That's normal." Quinn raised and lowered his eyebrows. "Raven's gorgeous."

"Yep. She is. That doesn't necessarily make her wife material and I'm not going to settle down with someone who's close to being the one."

"That's deep, man."

"Whatever." Sam slid a cork mat under Quinn's coffee cup.

"How is it that you know so much, Bright?"

"I pay attention. You should try it sometime."

Quinn slurped a sip of his coffee and mouthed off like he always did. "Why would I do that?"

"You just might learn a thing or two, that's why." Sam automatically topped off Quinn's cup and then his own.

"Another deep thought? Or are you referring to something specific?"

"Make of it what you will."

"You've been reading Kylee's psychology books, haven't you?"

Sam grinned and gave him the finger.

"Enough about that. I actually came in to ask a favor. Ty was named CEO of Vincent Oil this morning so I'm throwing a party for him next weekend. I want to hire your bartender service. You and Raven are invited."

"Just a sec." Sam rang up the tab for a couple who'd been sitting in a back booth and now seemed eager to leave. "Thanks, folks." He waited until they took their exit before he came back to Quinn. "That's awesome about Ty. But we can't make the party. We have to go to a wedding in El Paso." He arched an eyebrow at Quinn. "I'm thrilled to see your ugly mug, but you could've taken care of it over the phone." His eyebrow lowered but he began nodding his head up and down. "I know why you came in person. To see Kylee. Right?" Sam didn't wait for an answer. "No use denying it. I didn't miss your tongue hanging out for her last night."

Quinn tried to laugh off the claim. "Bite me." He adjusted himself on the bar stool.

A serious fleck lit Sam's eyes and Quinn knew the lighthearted banter took a swift turn.

"Leave her alone, Quinn. She's a sweet gal with a lot on her plate, including a child."

There it was again – a well-placed pylon meant to block his interest. Ty had told him to back off. Tori did the same thing by pointing out that Kylee had a kid and possibly stretch marks. Now Sam was trying to protect her too by also mentioning that she was a parent. "I know all about Kylee."

"No you don't. You might know the basics, but you don't know who she is or what she wants out of life."

Did everyone think he was a complete tool? "And you do?"

"Like I said, I pay attention."

"Then by all means, fill me in."

Sam rinsed his cup in the sink and stashed it in a plastic tub. "If Kylee wants you to know she'll tell you. I imagine hell will freeze over before that happens."

Quinn narrowed his eyes. "Why's that?"

"Because she's smart enough to know you're a player."

He wasn't a player.

Okay, maybe he was, but the only thing he was guilty of was sweet talking the ladies. He never once stepped out on Tori. So that made him what? Only half a player? "If you pay attention like you say you do, you'd know I'm not out to hurt Kylee." Quinn sighed. "I can't explain it, Sam. Yesterday I couldn't stay away from her and today I can't stop thinking about her."

Sam crossed his arms. "She's a good gal who works hard. Too damned hard. Sometimes she comes in with dark circles under her eyes from staying up all night studying for a test. I've never met anyone so driven. At the same time I see a fragile woman who might not bounce back if her heart gets broken. Get my drift?"

"All I want is an opportunity to be around her so I can figure out what this is that won't let go of me."

"I can tell you exactly what it is. You want what you can't have. Plain and simple. It can't be anything else since you've never even talked to her." Quinn started to balk and Sam gave him a pointed look. "Asking for a gin and tonic doesn't count."

He and Kylee had talked last night. When the band took a break he hung out at the bar and drew her into small talk. They discussed the heavy winds from the hurricane that pounded Dallas earlier in the week and the unrelenting heat gripping the

South. They also talked for a little bit about the Rangers game from the night before. If some jackal hadn't butted in to get a whiskey sour they would've talked a lot longer. Quinn also counted the unspoken dialogue that volleyed back and forth between them all night. "Maybe it is wanting what I can't have, maybe not. I want a chance to find out. Let me have her for three days. I mean, let me hire her for three days."

"Friday, Saturday *and* Sunday?"

"It's a weekend shindig at that new resort." Quinn snapped his fingers like it would help him remember the name. "You know, it's in the foothills off Route 105. I'm renting the whole place including their chef, but not their bar service. I want your bar service. More specifically, I want Kylee."

"A hundred percent no. I won't even consider it."

"Don't make me come across the bar to wring your neck. I want Kylee."

"People in hell want sweet tea."

"Kylee obviously needs money or she wouldn't be working so much. Let me have her for a weekend. I'll pay your rate and I'll give her a hefty amount too. I promise I won't move in on her unless she makes it known that she wants it to happen."

Sam set his mouth in a grim line. "No good can come from having her at your beck and call for seventy two hours."

"Don't make me beg, Sam."

"I'll run it past her." The conversation stalled when two guys clad in biker gear and bandanas came in and ordered chicken wings, hush puppies, cole slaw and Lone Star beer. Sam produced their beer right away and then flew to the kitchen to get their food order underway.

Fifteen minutes later, the biker dudes were munching away on chicken and Sam propped against the back counter to resume the discussion. "If Kylee says no, then it's a no. Understand? No trying to pressure her. Since this is a special request it's going to cost you a lot more money than you offered. There's my rate and ten thousand for Kylee."

"Done," Quinn said, without batting an eye.

"Let me finish. She can't very well leave her child home for three days. The little one comes along with a nanny."

"Sure. No problem." Quinn tried to keep from frowning.

"The nanny gets five thousand."

Quinn rolled his eyes. "Anything else?"

"That ought to do it. Don't get your hopes up because she'll probably say no."

Quinn slid from the bar stool. "Call me after you talk to her. For the record, you want her kid to come along as insurance that I'll leave her alone, right?"

"You're not as dumb as you look."

"You're a prick." Quinn smirked on his way to the door.

"So I've been told."

Quinn stepped outside and squinted for more reasons than just being hit in the eyes with the blinding sun. He'd put it out there that he was interested in Kylee and he was hiring her to be in his personal space for three days. He knew he was playing with fire, but he couldn't help himself. He shrugged and slid on his sunglasses. At least there *was* fire, something he hadn't felt in awhile.

* * *

"It's for you." Kylee propped the full laundry basket against her hip and tossed the phone on the couch where Angie was painting her toenails with bright red polish.

Angie jerked and polish went on her skin instead of her toe nail. "Can you tell whoever it is that I'll call them back in a little bit?"

"It's Sam."

Sam meant work. Angie couldn't insert the tiny brush back in the bottle of polish fast enough.

Kylee retrieved her zipper pouch of quarters from the kitchen cabinet and started for the door. Three floors below was the laundry room. If she hurried she just might find a few open washers. She tried an hour ago but the place was packed with other renters trying to catch up on their laundry too. Before she stepped into the hallway she heard Angie say, "Uh huh. Uh huh. Yeah, it really doesn't surprise me either. Okay. Sure. Why not." Angie hollered, "Kylee, wait." She held the phone out.

Kylee whispered, "What does he want?"

Angie lifted her shoulders like she had no idea, but she didn't hide her impish grin.

Earlier over lunch, she and Angie discussed all the extra hours they'd been working and decided if they wanted to keep their sanity they had to tell Sam no once in awhile. Kylee wanted to spend more time with Gabbi and she was falling behind in her school work. She had a twenty page essay due on Tuesday and hadn't written the first word. Angie wanted more time with Charlie. The sad state of their bank accounts, however, wouldn't allow them to cut back. Kylee had a tuition payment coming up. Angie had her eye on a different, more dependable car. If Sam asked them to work they had little choice but to accept.

Kylee placed the laundry basket on the couch. "Hey, boss, what's up?"

"How's your Sunday going?"

Please don't ask me to come in today. "Having a blast," she said, trying to sound upbeat. "Angie and I cleaned the apartment. Now we're about to tackle laundry. If we don't get it done, we'll be running around in our swimsuits because they're the only things clean."

"My customers would probably dig it; the health department not so much," Sam teased. "Don't worry. You won't have to resort to wearing your swimsuits. Darn it."

She'd caught a break. "Excellent."

"I need to run something by you. Angie didn't especially warm up to my offer, but she didn't say no. I'm hoping you'll say yes too."

Kylee glanced at Angie who didn't reveal anything except that she was amused. With the phone in the crick of her neck she talked to Sam and began picking up the hundred pieces of Legos Gabbi left scattered on the floor. "Don't keep me hanging."

"I need a barmaid and a nanny for Friday through Sunday."

"I'm glad it's not during the week. I have to…" She started to tell him about the essay that she planned to get busy on after she was done with laundry, but stopped because it was irrelevant. The second part of Sam' request seemed odd. "You want me to be a nanny too?"

"I don't want you to do both, Kylee. I want you as the barmaid and Angie as the nanny. I know it sounds strange but hear me out."

Kylee heard a clunk. "Sam?"

"My new phone isn't big enough for my meaty paws. It slipped out of my hand and found the floor. The reason I talked to Angie first is because if she gave me thumbs down there'd be no point in asking you to bartend."

Kylee gave Angie another quick look only to find her laughing behind her hand. "Details please."

Sam gave it to her straight. Quinn Randel was hosting a weekend getaway and asked to hire her services."

"Yeah. No," Kylee said off the cuff. "I'm not playing barmaid for Quinn for one night let alone a whole weekend."

"He'll pay you ten thousand dollars."

You could've knocked her over with a broom straw. "Ten THOUSAND dollars?"

"You heard right. Ten thousand for you and five thousand for Angie to play nanny."

Some people wouldn't blink at that amount of money but the thought of five figures in her checking account was incredible. The moment of exhilaration was short-lived. "For ten thousand dollars all I have to do is make drinks? Smells fishy, Sam. Are you sure it's not an orgy? We're talking about a guy with too much time and money on his hands."

A thud made Kylee's head snap around. Angie had fallen off the couch laughing. Kylee purposely frowned.

"It's not an orgy. Ty Vincent was named CEO of Vincent Oil and Quinn is hosting a celebration in his honor."

"Hmm."

"It's not an orgy," Sam reiterated.

"Ohhh-kay. It's not an orgy. Who does Angie have to babysit all weekend?"

"Gabbi."

Kylee was hit by more shock and a bit of joy at the same time. "Gabs can go along?"

"She can. But she and Angie have to stay out of the way. Say yes because I have to go."

"Ten thousand dollars." Kylee heaved a breath of acceptance. "I'm probably going to regret it, but I have to say yes."

"Awesome. I'll send you an email with directions."

Kylee hung up the phone and wandered to the couch in a daze. She dropped down beside the laundry basket with a hand on her forehead.

"Your flirting made an impression."

"He wants me in his bed."

"At least it's not an orgy."

"That's not helpful."

Angie put her feet up on the coffee table. "On one hand, you're overdue for some lovin'. On the other hand, it's the royal hound."

"Again, not helpful."

Chapter Three

Driving by Kylee's apartment complex to see where she lived wasn't what he set out to do on his way home from work, but somehow Quinn found himself on her street. Never in his wildest dreams did he actually think he'd get a glimpse of Kylee. By some miracle or twist of fate, there she was, walking hand in hand with a little girl in pigtails.

Quinn ducked, which was a stupid thing to do since he was in a convertible.

Kylee and the child made their way through a maze of cars in the parking lot until they came to an older model silver metallic Malibu with a rusty dent in the back bumper. The little girl laughed when Kylee hoisted her in the back and strapped her into a car seat.

Quinn lowered his sunglasses and peeked over the rims for a better look. The corners of his mouth instinctively tipped into a smile. He caught his reaction in the rearview mirror and displeasure rumbled in his throat. He didn't key on people's interactions with their kids. There was no point. He wasn't having kids so why pay attention to anything they did, or get wrapped up in happy scenes that involved them? It was a cynical position; one he relied on.

A small giggle reached his ears.

There was absolutely no sense in chasing after a woman

with a child. Yet here he was, sweating profusely from having the top down on his Corvette Stingray convertible with his pulse thumping through his veins because Kylee was right there.

Removing his foot from the brake, he gently gassed the engine to make a discreet escape. The thing about Corvettes is that they were built to be noticed, not only for their sleek design but also the sweet sound of the engine. He had his modified to sound like a bad-ass car.

Kylee closed the car door and looked in his direction.

Quinn had no idea if he'd been spotted. Regardless, he had to get out of there. He yanked the steering wheel to the left instead of to the right and found himself in an alley filled with ruts. Stones pinged against the undercarriage of the car and at one huge rut it scraped bottom. He called himself an idiot for more reasons than just his poor decision to bump down a long, narrow alley to make his getaway.

The expensive car all but jumped onto the roadway when it reached the end of the beaten path. Quinn scanned the unfamiliar territory. Some of the houses were in dire need of a coat of paint and new shingles, some needed to be torn down. To make the area even more daunting, some vehicles were missing tires and up on blocks. Right away he thought of Kylee and her daughter's safety. This wasn't exactly the seedy part of Dallas but it still wasn't the best. He scolded himself again. Kylee Steele and her daughter could live wherever they wanted. They were not his concern.

By the time he got to the first traffic light he reminded himself twice that this was nuts. He didn't chase women, they chased him. In fact, he'd been dodging a few since Sunday's newspapers declared him available. Every day those rags printed an update. Monday's society page read – *Will Quinn and Tori work it out?* Tuesday's caption – *Quinn Randel: Sexy and Single*. This morning's headline – *Who Will Win Quinn's Heart?*

Yes, he was no longer attached to anyone, but he'd be the

one to decide if he was available. No, he and Tori would not work things out. Was he sexy? If you were into self-centered bastards, then yes, he was sexy as hell. As far as who would win his heart, that remained to be seen. Maybe Kylee already had it. Maybe not. To steal Sam's line – it was too soon to tell.

Being single was weird. Since he was no longer killing time with Tori, he began showing up at the office. All week he'd gotten up early, stopped at Starbucks for two doubleshot espressos and shocked everyone by coming into work. Plenty of reporters had trailed him to the tall skyscraper that housed his father's business. Did they report that he was focusing on his job? Not one word. All they cared about was who he might be sleeping with. The goons needed to get a life and leave his alone.

Quinn checked the cars' navigation system and barreled his way back to I-635. Merging onto the entrance ramp, he gunned the engine, appreciating the sound of raw power. In no way would he ever own a car that would accommodate a kid's car seat. He snorted a laugh. Where did that thought come from? A kid's car seat in a Corvette? Now that was funny.

Sliding Metallica into the CD player, he cranked up the volume to drown out thoughts of car seats. It was time to sound the gong on women with kids and get back to a bachelor state of mind with the wind in his hair, the hot sun at his back and sweet freedom.

He weaved in and out of traffic like he owned the interstate. Of course, the strobe of red and blue lights in his rearview mirror would soon say otherwise.

Shit.

Tomorrow's headline: *Quinn's Downward Spiral.* He laughed without a trace of humor. Next, they'd say he was headed to rehab.

* * *

For a second there… Kylee quietly groaned so Gabbi wouldn't ask what was wrong. She rubbed her forehead above her eyebrow trying to convince herself she was seeing things. All the worry about the coming weekend had her brain in a funk. She considered the possibility that lack of sleep was messing with her as much as anything. Between work, classes, taking care of Gabbi, and anxiety for allowing the pleasure of Quinn's flirting, she hadn't slept much. She'd researched sleep loss for one of her classes last semester and found that it could dumb-down a person by impairing judgment. It was also known to cause irregular heartbeat and high blood pressure. She certainly had impaired judgment and irregular heartbeat going on where Quinn was concerned. Maybe impaired vision was a side effect as well.

She thinned her eyes from what was really going on. While she was prone to nervous tension, she wasn't prone to hallucinations. Her eyes weren't playing tricks on her. The flesh and blood hotness that had been staring directly at her from a convertible had indeed been Quinn Randel. He was set to see her on Friday. Couldn't he wait? A weird excitement rushed over her and Kylee nipped it in the bud right away by calling him a stalker.

Gabbi distracted her thoughts. "McDonald's, Mom."

Twisting around to look over the seat, she touched Gabbi's sneaker. "Is your belly growling?"

The smile on her daughter's face was priceless. "Yes. For McNuggets."

"How about Subway? You love turkey, lettuce and pickles." They'd inevitably end up at McDonalds like they always did on their Wednesday girls night out, but Kylee enjoyed the negotiation. Gabs was three going on thirteen and the things that came out of her mouth blew Kylee away.

"Apple slices are you good for you, Mom. McDonalds has apple slices. I'll share." Gabbi's smile stretched wide to reveal pearly white baby teeth.

"You win. McDonalds it is." Kylee stretched to pat Gabbi's knee. "What do you think about going away this weekend with me and Angie to a place that has a pool?" She assumed it had one; most resorts did. "I've been asked to work there for a few days. While I work, you and Angie can play Candyland and Uno. When the adults are inside, you and Angie can swim."

"Can I bring the Little Mermaid DVD?"

Gabbi would die without that DVD. "We'll bring it along."

"Will there be horses?"

The question drew an automatic smile from Kylee. Gabbi had developed a fondness for horses awhile back after a ride on a gentle Appaloosa at a ranch owned by Angie's cousin. "I don't think they have horses, sweetheart." She made a mental note to do a Google search of the resort when she got home.

"I love horses and I love you, Mommy."

"Horses are awesome. And I love you too, Gabs. Forever." They knuckle-bumped.

Kylee felt the tension leave her shoulders. Everything she did, including the uncomfortable gig that would pay ten thousand dollars, was for Gabbi.

* * *

Weston Randel popped his head into Quinn's office, again. He'd been stopping by every half hour or so, like he couldn't believe his eyes. "You don't know how happy it makes me to see you here, Son."

Quinn set aside the quarterly reports he'd been studying and leaned back in the leather chair. His father's comment wasn't said to make him feel guilty, yet it's exactly how he felt. As the company's CFO he should've been elbow-deep in figures on a daily basis, but he hadn't taken any real interest until this week. He normally pawned his work off on two ladder-climbing eager beavers who would do just about anything he asked. Monday all that changed. He woke up with a sudden desire to repair his image. Maybe it was temporary psychosis. Or maybe the urge was real. "I have some catching up to do."

Weston Randel came into the room and moved to the wet bar. He poured himself a swallow of brandy before taking a chair across from Quinn. "I've been meaning to talk to you about your breakup with Tori. I wanted to have this conversation last night at the museum but you were occupied with Olivia." Against his better judgment, Quinn caved to his mom's request to attend a charity event at the Nasher Sculpture Center with Olivia DiSalle, the daughter of the chairwoman for the fundraiser. Olivia was also recently available due to a split with the guy she'd been seeing for six months. Quinn didn't mind paying big bucks to sip champagne and look at artwork since it was for a good cause, but he wasn't overly thrilled to do it with a date. They didn't exactly hit it off. Olivia was attractive but too uptight for his taste. On the flip side she probably considered him too loose. The night before, his mom paired him with Tawny Billington at the opera. To keep his mom happy he allowed the matchup. Tawny was funny, comfortable to be around and easy on the eyes, but there was no spark.

Quinn waved away the discussion. "Let's talk about something else. The weather. The Rangers. Cucumbers. Anything but Tori."

"Cucumbers?" Weston pulled at the knot in his silk tie. "Whether you like it or not, we need to discuss Tori. More importantly, the post-breakup."

"Meaning?"

"Life after Tori. As you well-know, her father and I are close friends. We play golf every Saturday morning and attend a lot of the same functions. I don't want you and Tori's breakup to affect *my* relationships." Weston stretched his neck from side to side, like he was ill at ease with this new circumstance. "There's not going to be any drama, is there?" Before Quinn could answer, he added, "Did you part amicably?"

Quinn almost said, "About as amicable as two trapped badgers", since his dad seemed more concerned about fallout instead of feelings. He bit back the smart remark because he didn't want the old man to have a coronary.

What was he thinking by making himself available for interrogation? His parents deserved answers but he was in no mood to provide them. "There won't be any drama, at least from me."

Weston looked deep in thought while he drummed his thumbs on the arms of the chair. "Tori has exquisite taste and a powerful personality. When you proposed, your mother and I were ecstatic because she seemed a perfect fit for our family. Not everyone is cut out to be a Randel, you know."

"She wasn't a perfect fit. Not even close," Quinn replied flatly.

"Perhaps not." Creases grooved his father's forehead and Quinn could feel a flux in the discussion. Weston pulled his iPhone from his suit coat, checked his messages and finally landed on the real reason he was there. "I had a great time at Ty and Maggie's wedding. Your mother and I were able to visit with some old friends. We kept a close eye on you as well. Well, I did. Your mom was too busy talking about blue bonnets and her art class. I have to say, I saw something more disturbing than you and Tori having the occasional heated exchange."

Nothing escaped his father. "Like?"

"Really, Quinn?" The question was loaded with accusation and condescension.

Quinn folded his hands on the desk, waiting for his father to go off on the same uppity tangent as Tori about giving excessive attention to a barmaid.

"You've forgotten that you're a Randel." A vein visibly pulsed in Weston's neck.

"I haven't forgotten," Quinn replied with deceptive calmness.

"I beg to differ."

"Save me the pretentious malarkey that Randels are special. We put our pants on just like everyone else. The only thing that sets us apart is that we put on Armani." Quinn's temper burned through him like someone tossed a careless match onto a parched lawn. "Tell me, Dad, what good is all that money if we're limited to who we should associate with?"

Weston huffed with annoyance. "Where is this coming from?" His eyes thinned. "Does this have anything to do with Ty and Maggie?"

"Does *what* have to do with Ty and Maggie?" Quinn felt his blood pressure rise even higher.

"Ty strayed from the prominent community and found Maggie." Weston moved around in his chair like the leather was slippery. "It happens. Most of the time those kinds of relationships don't work out. In Ty and Maggie's case, I hope it does. She's a nice girl."

Quinn was a hair away from calling his dad a snob. He loved his father despite his wealthy-old-school philosophy where you only dated and married someone from the same background. "This has nothing to do with them. I paid attention to Kylee Steele because she has a killer smile."

"Riiight." Weston worked himself out of the chair and to the wet bar again. He splashed more brandy into his glass. "I made some inquiries about the young woman."

"You did what?" In a heartbeat Quinn was out of his chair, inches from his dad with his arms crossed and anger coming out his ears.

"You're my only child. It's my job to protect you and mom."

Quinn started to tell his father that he didn't need his protection, but the reminder that he was an only child rendered him incapable of standing his ground. He eased back a step. There wasn't a day that went by that he didn't think about being any only child. In fact, each day started with him hugging a picture of his brother Jamie; his sweet, curly haired blue-eyed little brother. A lump formed in Quinn's throat and tears burned behind his eyes at the memory of losing him to a congenital heart defect shortly after his third birthday. The trauma had left an imprint on Quinn's soul.

It was hard to be angry with his dad for butting into his business when the hurt of Jamie hung heavy between them. Quinn placed a hand on his father's shoulder. "I don't appreciate you checking up on Kylee but I understand where you're coming from. I also get that you're trying to keep me from doing something stupid. Dad, you of all people, should know that I have to live life on my terms. It's how you live yours. It's how I want to live mine. If I want to date a barmaid, I'm going to."

"She's an unwed mother, Quinn. The father of her child took no responsibility for the mess he made. I also found out that her parents are divorced. Her father walked away from the family years ago and moved to Florida. Her mom hooked up with some guy she met while waiting tables and she now lives in Arkansas. I'm sure Kylee is a sweet person but she comes with a lot of baggage."

Quinn frowned as hard as he could without bursting a blood vessel. "Everyone has baggage but it doesn't define who they are. For the record, Kylee's going to school while holding down a full time job and she's raising her kid on her own. That says a lot about her character. She's bright, beautiful and determined. What more could a guy ask for?" *Wow. Just wow.* His assessment of Kylee made him uncomfortable.

Weston cocked an eyebrow. "Regardless of what I say,

you're going to see her, aren't you?"

Quinn lifted his shoulder in a shrug. "I haven't decided one way or the other. I'm not even sure she'd consider going out with me."

"If she's smart, she'll stay away from you."

* * *

Kylee wet the rims of two margarita glasses, dipped them in salt and filled them with the tasty slush from the margarita machine. She carried the drinks to the booth where two women were getting an early start on a fiftieth birthday celebration. "Here you go, ladies. These are on the house. Happy birthday." If she wasn't working, she wouldn't mind joining them. She needed a little alcohol to take the edge off what had been a hectic week, and it was only Thursday.

She wandered back behind the bar and glanced at the clock shaped like a giant bottle of beer. She still had four and half hours before she could go home and put her feet up. There would be a textbook in her lap when she got there but at least she wouldn't be moving.

Sam came from the kitchen. "I'm off to do the banking." He glanced at the clock too. "You're on your own for about an hour. Will you be okay?"

"I'll be fine. Do you mind if I make a fresh batch of margaritas?" She gestured to the margarita machine that was almost empty and then nodded toward the women who had downed half of their drinks in just a few sips.

"Have at it, chick." Sam gave her a half-hug on his way to the door. "I struck gold when I hired you, Kylee, and I'm going to miss you when you get your degree and leave me."

"Thanks, Sam, but don't worry, I'll be around to bug you for awhile." Probably until the year 2025 at the rate she was going. Two classes a semester wasn't enough to whittle away at the required curriculum. She considered taking out a bigger student loan so she could work less hours and take more classes, but the debt she'd already accumulated was staggering.

"Atta girl." Sam waved goodbye.

Kylee gathered the necessary items to make more slush: a five gallon bucket, margarita mix, tequila and triple sec. She ran down her cheat sheet to see how much water she needed to add.

Filling the bucket with water to the designated line, she added the other ingredients and stirred. She tried to lift the bucket. "Holy mackerel." A five gallon bucket filled with liquid had to weigh a good forty to fifty pounds. At a hundred and twenty pounds, she was in fairly good shape. She hiked, rode bike and went for walks on the Katy Trail that followed the path of the old Missouri-Kansas-Texas railroad. All that exercise didn't equal upper body strength. Essentially, she was five feet-five inches of wimp.

Asking the birthday girls to help wasn't going to happen either, for liability reasons.

Kylee retrieved a three-step ladder from the kitchen and fit it as close to the margarita machine as she could. She took a deep breath, bent her knees and hoisted the bucket as high as her thighs. Another deep breath and she made it up the first step without straining anything. Second step, she was huffing and puffing like a three-pack-a-day smoker. Third step, every muscle in her body was stretched to the max. Now if she could raise the bucket high enough to pour the contents into the machine, she'd be all set.

You can do this! One. Two.

Before she got to three, a familiar voice rich with masculinity made her jerk. The bucket wobbled overhead and the ladder wobbled below and a green catastrophe was in motion.

"Kylee," Quinn shouted, "be careful."

Kylee leaned too far forward in an attempt to save the five-gallon bucket from falling. In doing so, the ladder cut out. Margarita mix cascaded through the air and the bucket knocked over two bottles of Jack Daniels and tipped over a few other bottles of liquor before clunking to the floor with a loud thud. Kylee would've suffered the same fate had Quinn not been there to catch her.

Mortified, she hid her face in his chest. She needed a moment to collect herself from the panic of falling but also from the panic of being in the arms of the man she couldn't stop thinking about for the last five days. Instead of calming down, her pulse pounded harder and her senses came alive. She was suddenly aware of the firm muscles where her forehead rested and she felt the soft matting of chest hair beneath the cotton of his shirt. A combination of smells met her nose; fragrant dryer sheets, an earthy men's cologne and the clean scent of deodorant.

"Are you okay?" He asked.

Kylee lifted her head and blinked up at him. "A little embarrassed but in one piece, thanks to you." She struggled from his grasp, grabbed a bar towel and blotted the splotches of slush from the front of her shirt.

"Now I can tell the guys you fell for me." Laughter shook Quinn's solid frame.

"I didn't…" Kylee stopped. There was no need to offer a rebuttal since he was joking. Hopefully. "Technically, you're right." She placed a hand on his forearm. "Thank you for saving me from a concussion. I'm sure my head would've hit the edge of the bar." Why the heck was she touching him? She casually removed her hand from his arm, but there was nothing casual about the mess going on inside of her. She was happy to see him. She was afraid to be near him. She wanted him. She didn't want to want him. Kylee stifled a whimper that was part joy, part distress.

"My pleasure."

The sexy undertones in Quinn's voice warmed her in an instant. She turned away to hide the blush that covered her face and neck. "Gin and tonic, right?"

"You remembered."

Again, there were deep underlying notes of seduction in his tone.

"I did." Kylee put her hand to her stomach like she stop the excitement from reaching certain body parts. She was mystified that just a few words between them had turned her on. She could deny it, but the truth was that his nearness brought out her hidden hussy.

There was a curious gleam in his eyes that had her shifting from one foot to the other. Thank goodness the birthday gals signaled Kylee from their booth.

"I'll help myself to a cup of coffee, if you don't mind," Quinn said.

"Sure. Yes." Kylee needed space to get her bearings, even if it was as minimal as fifty feet. Any and all interruptions would be welcome. And if she had to ply the women with additional free booze to keep them there, she would. "You ladies ready for a refill?"

One gal grinned from ear to ear. "You okay, hon'?"

"I'm fine. I had a klutzy moment, but I didn't break anything."

The second woman chuckled. "Chantel is just being nosey. We witnessed a whole lot of yummy going on between you and…" She pointed to Quinn who had his back to them.

"His Royal Highness?" Kylee giggled.

"He's royalty?" The woman's eyes widened.

Kylee smirked. "He *thinks* he is."

"Ahhh. One of those." Chantel's brown eyes danced with amusement. "We've been burned by a prince or two, haven't we Gloria?"

"We sure have," Gloria jiggled with a laugh. "Be careful, sweetie. He might seem like he's all that, but at the end of the day he burps and farts like a commoner."

Those wicked sense of humors were exactly what Kylee needed to lighten up. "I love you, ladies."

Chantel patted Kylee's upper arm. "Hate to leave ya while his princeliness is here, but we're doing a pub crawl by way of the bus. If we're going to make the next one, we have to get moving." She slid from the booth. "Be on your guard, doll. That prince has too much going for him. Yowza! He has a sweet body."

Gloria also stood to leave. "Is princeliness even a word?" She shoved a twenty dollar bill in Kylee's hand.

Before Kylee could thank them, they were out the door and on their way to the bus stop down the street.

Princeliness. Kylee chuckled her way to the cash register. Their drinks had been on the house. Since she'd wasted more than twenty dollars worth of slush ingredients by spilling them all over the place, she couldn't in good conscience consider the twenty a tip.

Grabbing a fistful of towels, she went at the mess with a vengeance.

Quinn shadowed over her with another handful of towels and dropped to his knees.

Placing a saturated towel in the bucket, Kylee slanted him a smile. "You really don't have to help."

"I want to help. And I want *your* help. This weekend. I know Sam's given you the details and that you've graciously accepted my request, but I wanted to come by to...," he paused, "...say thanks."

You didn't come by to say thanks. You came by to continue turning me into a nervous wreck. "No problem," she said, like it was no big deal. "Happy to help." She squared herself in front of him. "By the way, thanks for allowing my daughter to come along. I promise she won't be a problem. "

"I'm not a big fan of kids but I know you're a package deal." He drifted closer and Kylee automatically backed up. She didn't know whether to be offended by his admission that he didn't care for kids or give him big points for being honest.

"We are." She modestly cleared her throat. "A package deal." If he was going to be straightforward, so was she. "If Gabs couldn't come, neither could I." She needed for him to know that her daughter was her first concern and always would be.

Quinn's blue-grey eyes sparkled with something indefinable. "Good to know." He dropped a slush-soaked towel in the bucket.

Kylee moved liquor bottles out of the way so she could clean the gunk that had splashed behind them. She reached for a decorative bottle of Jim Beam that had tipped on its side and in the process the fine hairs on her arm brushed the fine hairs on Quinn's. Her eyes flew to his as electricity crackled through her body setting small fires along the way.

Oh God. She was in trouble. Can't-think-straight, lust-driven trouble.

She fought to breathe.

In the span of her next heartbeat, she was wrapped in Quinn's arms and he was staring into her eyes for possibly the longest few seconds on record. He crashed her mouth with a hard, scorching kiss.

Kylee trembled from a combination of shock and delight. She couldn't help herself and returned the kiss with same eagerness as Quinn. The sweet ache of desire that had been simmering since they met turned into a hot cauldron of passion. Her body was on fire. She arched into him. She wanted Quinn. Wanted his kisses. Wanted him to memorize her body with his hands. Wanted him in… *Nooooo!* She couldn't go to bed with him. He was trouble. Angie had made that plain. When he pried her mouth open with his tongue, her resistance crumbled and that emphatic no turned into a solid *yessssss!* Damn the mess this was sure to create. Despite every warning not to, she was going to enjoy all that this millionaire bad boy had to offer.

Quinn dipped his tongue in for a taste and began to push it against hers. He backed it out and thrust it back in. It was the most disturbingly sensuous, erotic thing he could've done. Kylee moaned from pure pleasure. Rather loudly. The sound was nothing compared to the groan that came from Quinn at the jingling of bells when the entrance door opened.

They jumped apart. Or rather, she jumped away. Quinn stayed where he was.

Kylee spared a guilty look toward the door and her windpipe compressed at the sight of Sam standing with his hands on hips, studying the situation. She rushed to explain and stumbled over her words. "I made the…went to pour…it's all over me…I fell."

"You fell?" Sam rushed behind the bar. "Are you okay?"

Kylee giggled nervously. "I'm fine. It was a minor mishap that made a big mess. Quinn's helping me clean up."

Sam lifted an eyebrow. "Looks to me like he's helping himself."

Quinn slapped Sam on the back. "I stopped in to thank Kylee for coming to my aid this weekend and to give her directions."

"You sent me the directions in an email. I forwarded them on to Kylee per your instructions."

Quinn's grin was sheepish. "Oh yeah."

Sam rolled his eyes. "Pathetic, Randel," he mumbled. "By the way, Kylee, you have a flat tire."

"Noooo. Really?" Kylee was still reeling from Quinn's kiss but the news that her tire was flat again was as good as dumping water on what had become a raging bonfire. She tried to get her emotions under control to address the deflated hunk of rubber that had been giving her fits for the past two weeks. Every other day she had to put air in the darn thing. She was surprised she didn't have to put air in all four. The tread was worn off and she needed to replace them. There was also a knock in the engine. Since there was no extra money this month she had to baby those tires and pray that whatever was ailing the engine wouldn't kill the car before she could afford to get it fixed.

Sam put both hands on her shoulders. "I know a guy who will take it off, patch it and put it back on for a modest fee."

"But…" She had difficulty allowing Sam to take care of things. He shouldn't have to deal with the tire.

Sam waved his finger. "Don't argue. I've got this." He retrieved his cell phone from his shirt pocket.

"Thank you," she replied humbly.

"You'd do the same for me." Sam moseyed to the kitchen to make the call.

When she and Quinn were alone again, Kylee couldn't meet his eyes. That deflated hunk of rubber was so much more than a flat tire; it was a brutal reminder that their lives were so different. Quinn was mega-rich. She was mega-poor. The only place they'd have common ground was in bed, but it wasn't enough.

Quinn watched the hot emerald brilliance in Kylee's eyes turn to a murky shade of worry. He rubbed her upper arm and she flinched under his palm. "I'm not sorry that I came here and I'm sure as hell not sorry I kissed you."

Kylee shrugged some distance between them. "There's no doubt that we're attracted to each other, Quinn, but nothing can happen between us." She touched her lips. "Nothing more anyway."

"We'll see." He wouldn't allow a flat tire, and the fact they got caught by Sam, to cool things off between them.

Kylee's voice rose sharply. "No. We won't see. For more

reasons than I can say, you need to back off."

Quinn moved so close he could smell peppermint on her breath. He twirled a strand of blonde hair around his finger. "Listen, Kylee, I know about all the things you have going on. But I still want you…" An emotion he wasn't familiar with clogged his throat. "…to work at my party." Damn. Could he sound any lamer?

"That can't happen now." She began gnawing her thumbnail. "Not because of the kiss. I mean, the kiss figures into my decision, but the trip to the resort is over three hundred miles. I'm not sure my bucket of rust will make it that far."

"Not a problem. I'll send a limo to pick you up."

A flash of interest flashed through Kylee's eyes. "No thanks."

He wasn't letting her back out. They'd signed a verbal contract. "I want you there." Before she could further reject the idea he threw out a second option. "If you won't accept a ride from my limo driver then I'm buying you a car."

Kylee started to laugh but gave him a weird look instead. "You're going to a lot of trouble for someone who's not going to sleep with you."

He tried not to smile.

Chapter Four

"I've officially lost my mind." Kylee slumped into the recliner with a bowl of popcorn.

"Yes you have," Angie teased.

"Seriously, I have. I let him kiss me, Ange', and I liked it. Really, really liked it." Kylee still couldn't believe she'd engaged in a powerful lip lock with the infamous millionaire. "Quinn Randel is possibly the best kisser in East Texas. The sad part of the whole deal is that I know I'm setting myself up for a fall."

"You already fell. Off a ladder."

Kylee tried to keep from laughing by doing an exaggerated eye roll.

"Well ya did."

"Smooth move, Ange'."

"Huh?"

"You're trying to keep me from going spastic. Maybe you should become the psychologist."

"Nah. I'd hit the patient with my clipboard and tell them to straighten their ass up."

Kylee laughed so hard she almost choked on a popcorn kernel. "Save that technique for Charlie."

"Speaking of Charlie," Angie rested her elbows on her thighs and put her face in her hands. There was a trace of something odd in her tone. Kylee noticed it right away. "He's been acting weird. He opens the door for me. Gives up the remote every now and then. He kissed me in the grocery store the other day. For him to engage in any kind of public affection is out of the ordinary. And it's kind of nice."

"Maybe the last time you told him to take a flying leap off the nearest skyscraper he thought you meant it."

"I did mean it. I can't take six months of awesome and six months of wanting to drop-kick him."

"What are you doing different this time around?"

The small space between Angie's eyes creased.

"Charlie's behaving differently so there's a good chance you are too, Ange'."

Angie raised her brows and glanced upward with that I-have-no-idea-what-you're-talking-about look. "Should I lay down, doc?"

Kylee lobbed a piece of popcorn across the room. "You know what I mean. Something has changed."

Angie moved to a prone position. "I'm stretching out because I'm tired, not because I want you to analyze me." She fluffed the decorative pillow and put it under her head. "I think you've hit the nail on the head though. I *have* changed something. Instead of keying on the things that won't work in our relationship, I'm focusing on the things that do."

"You obviously care about Charlie or you wouldn't keep trying to make it work. The halfwit probably isn't aware that your attitude has changed but his subconscious has picked up on it and he's responding accordingly."

"He's not a halfwit."

"Ah! Ha! You took the bait. Instead of agreeing with me like you normally would have, you're defending him. You're getting all soft and gushy around the edges, Ange'. I'm happy for you."

"Me too. For once I feel like we're on the right track."

Without coming right out and saying it, Angie was in love.

Kylee wanted to jump from the recliner to hug her best friend but she'd learned not to make a fuss or risk being straight-armed.

The mind was a funny thing. In Kylee's case, it seemed to leap across everything else to grab onto the good stuff and then it would back up to retrieve everything else. Not a bad thing since the good stuff should come first. Kylee skipped back to the peculiar nuance in Angie's voice. Was it her imagination or was there more than love at play here? She rubbed the tight muscles in her neck. Instinct was powerful but so was fatigue and right now, her brain was as sluggish as the rest of her.

Angie rolled to her side with a mischievous grin. "Let's talk about that kiss."

* * *

Quinn climbed into the Cessna beside Trigg. "Thanks buddy. I appreciate the lift."

"I was surprised when you called since you're not a fan of small planes."

Quinn shrugged. "I wanted to get to the resort early since I'm the host."

Trigg wouldn't let it alone. "You could've driven your 'Vette or had Henry deliver your sorry butt."

"I wanted to fly. Is that all right with you?"

Trigg issued a smirk the size of Dallas. "Testy. Interesting."

"Just fly the plane."

"It's a short flight but you'll have enough time to give me the scoop on Kylee."

Quinn looked straight ahead. "There's no scoop."

"The Quinn Randel I know wouldn't have hired a personal barmaid unless he wanted to, well, you know." Trigg gave Quinn a backhanded smack across the small space of the cockpit. "You were sniffing on her at Ty's wedding and now she's coming to the resort. If that ain't a scoop, I don't know what is."

"She's not going to be my personal barmaid. She's going to bartend for all of us. And I don't sniff." In hindsight, he should've been more discreet with his…sniffing. Everyone picked up on it, except the news media. He found that strange. They were all over his split with Tori but they hadn't said a word about Kylee. Hmm. Ty's suspicion about Tori being the leak within their circle was probably accurate. Tori wouldn't want the world to know that she'd been easily replaced so she didn't expose Kylee to the news rats.

Quinn let his thoughts drift to the night before. He was glad he'd gone to Sam's bar to see Kylee before they met again at the resort. That steamy kiss possibly set the mood for the next few days and he couldn't wait to see where they went from there.

"The day you *stop* sniffing I'll be reading your obituary in the newspaper." Trigg taxied the plane down the short runway and spoke into the headset to the air traffic controller. He pulled the mic away and taunted Quinn a little more. "As soon as this baby's in the air, I want to hear why she's bringing her daughter and friend along. What. Is. Up. With. That? Have you misplaced your marbles?"

"You're a buffoon, Sinclair." He flicked Trigg on the forehead. "I'll give you the 4-1-1 on Kylee when you give me the 4-1-1 on Nancy."

Trigg slanted him a weird look.

"Don't act surprised. I might've been sniffing on Kylee but you were definitely sniffing on Nancy."

Trigg threatened to turn the plane upside down if he didn't shut his pie hole.

Quinn laughed and settled back to enjoy the spectacular view of Texas seen only from the air, and to think about those green eyes and that great body that would arrive via his limousine.

* * *

"Henry Mathews, at your service." The tall, thin limo driver tipped his black chauffer's hat.

"Nice to meet you, Henry."

"Likewise, Miss Steele." He nodded politely to Angie and then to Gabbi. If you ladies are ready, we'll begin our trip." He gestured a gloved hand toward the Rolls Royce limousine parked along the street.

Technically, they were ready. Mentally, not so much. Kylee was still a restless mess from over-thinking everything that happened yesterday. Quinn showed up. He caught her before she fell. Kissed her like they were lovers. Fanned the flames of desire so hot that she could've easily ripped her clothes off to let the heat out. If Sam hadn't returned when he did, who knows what might've happened. Before Quinn left the bar, he helped the mechanic change her tire and came back in to let her know it was finished. He whispered that he couldn't wait until tomorrow. Tomorrow was now today, and she was nervous to the point she was peeing every fifteen minutes. She took a deep breath to fill her lungs and let the air roll back out before she responded to the driver. "We're as ready as we're going to be." Kylee offered a smile but she said "Yikes" to Angie with her eyes.

"Excellent. Please allow me to see you inside the vehicle and then I'll stow your luggage."

"Thank you so much."

"My pleasure."

"Woohoo! Three days of R & R," Angie spouted, doing a happy dance down the sidewalk.

Kylee didn't foresee a lot of R & R. Even when she wasn't

serving alcohol to Quinn and his friends, she'd be tense, wondering if he was going to make a move. She clutched Gabbi's hand and proceeded to the luxury car that would take them three hundred miles from their comfort zone. For three days she'd cater to Quinn's every whim. Well, not *every* whim. Hopefully she'd be strong enough to resist the one whim he wanted the most.

Henry opened the door that gave way to the epitome of sophistication and class.

Kylee stuck her head in the stretch limo and found soft leather seats, plush black carpeting, a fully stocked bar with crystal stemware, soft lighting, a TV complete with DVD player, a privacy divider and tinted windows. "Oh. My. Gosh."

"Move so I can see." Angie pulled the back of Kylee's white bartender blouse.

Kylee eased back to grant Angie access.

Angie muttered a few ohhhh's and ahhhh's. She grinned at Kylee, her eyes shimmered with mischief. "This is a love-mobile."

Kylee heard the driver's muffled snicker.

"Oh look! He thought to bring along a child's safety seat?" Angie raised and lowered her eyebrows. "Quinn might be worth keeping."

"No he's not," Kylee said offhandedly. She realized Henry was within earshot of their remarks and tried to smooth things over. "I mean, he's a keeper. But…" She let her words trail off. No use fibbing. Quinn wasn't a keeper. He had a sweet body like Gloria and Chantel from the bar had suggested, but he had too much princeliness going on. She couldn't handle princeliness. "Let's get this over with." She boosted Gabbi into the limo and fastened her snuggly in the car seat.

"Mommy, look!" Gabbi pointed to the small bar.

"That low-down dirty skunk," Kylee said under her breath. Quinn was up to trickery. Winning over her daughter with gummy bears and juice boxes was a pathetic way to get what he wanted from Kylee. She silently grumbled a few expletives.

Angie was all smiles. Kylee kicked Angie's sandaled foot. "Stop grinning."

"I can't help it. I've never been in a love-mobile."

"Ladies, please help yourself to whatever you like. There's alcohol, sodas, milk and juice. Mr. Randel also had me place a cheese plate and bowl of strawberries and grapes in the refrigerator under the bar. Help yourself to whatever you like. If you need anything at all, feel free to lower the privacy window."

Henry closed the door and Angie squealed. "I want a millionaire."

Kylee rolled her eyes.

"What?"

"You can so be bought, Angie Stonehill."

"Nuh-uh." Angie grabbed a fistful of gummy bears and handed half to Gabbi. "Instead of fighting this, Kylee, let Quinn spoil you for a few days."

Kylee retrieved her tube of lip balm from her pocketbook and ran it across her dry lips. "You emphatically said he was trouble and you reminded me that we have class."

Angie grinned with guilt. "That's when you were trying to nab an engaged man."

"What's nab, Mommy?" Gabbi stuffed more gummy bears in her mouth.

"It's when you take something that doesn't belong to you." Kylee patted Gabbi's thigh. "Angie's trying to nab my sanity."

"Not much there to nab." Angie snorted.

"I'm afraid there'll be considerably less after the weekend."

Angie's amused expression evened out. "It'll be fine. Won't it, Gabbi?" She handed Gabbi more candy.

"As long as the gummy bears keep coming," Kylee mocked and removed the candy dish from the slot that kept it from sliding around. She sat it on the seat next to her, out of Angie's reach.

"I'm not reneging on my opinion of Quinn. I still think he's trouble. You'll just have to be on your guard. If he steps out of line, karate-chop him in the neck."

"That's your advice? Karate-chop his neck?" Kylee searched the little fridge for a bottle of water. "I'd get better advice from a monkey."

Angie laughed. "Don't forget that Gabs and I can create a ruckus anytime you need us to." She put her hand up to give Gabs a high-five.

"Now that's a plan I can live with, but I'm hoping for a quiet weekend."

Angie's eyes glistened with mockery. "Yeah, that's probably not going to happen. With the way Quinn looks at you I'm guessing you'll both make plenty of noise."

Kylee dropped her face in her hands. The limousine hadn't even begun to move and she was contemplating the proper way to deliver a karate chop.

* * *

Quinn paced back and forth in front of the main building that was designed as a Spanish country manor. He pulled his cell phone from the pocket of his cargo shorts and dialed Henry again. "Where are you now?"

"We're about ten miles away, Mr. Randel." Henry didn't sound the least bit annoyed that Quinn had called twice in less than fifteen minutes.

"So you'll be here shortly?"

Henry hesitated. "Possibly."

"Possibly?"

"I'll do my best, sir."

Quinn was sure there was a story there but he didn't press

Henry. Hopefully the pipsqueak with the pigtails didn't get sick in the car. He wiped a bead of sweat from his forehead and strode back inside to cool off. He took a whiff of his underarm and made a face. The hundred degree temperature was bringing out his manly essence. It was time to shower off all that manliness…again.

He loved the heat but unless you were in the pool, it was hard to be outdoors for any length of time. It was weird that the northern states were unusually cool for June and the southern states were so hot the ground was starting to peel. There was no happy medium.

He practically ran down the corridor to his hacienda, swiped his key card in the lock and stepped inside when Ty showed up.

"Come on out to the pool and have a beer."

Quinn tossed his key card on a lamp table. "I'm going to take a shower."

Ty chuckled but there wasn't any real laughter involved. He pointed to one of the two recliners. "Give me a few minutes."

"I don't have time." Quinn pulled off his shirt and tossed it on the bed.

"Yes you do. We need to talk."

"We can talk later."

"I think we should talk now." Again, Ty gestured to the chairs.

Quinn did a low growl. "Why don't you go boss Maggie around and leave me alone."

"You don't know anything about women, do you?"

"I know about women."

"It was rhetorical. Now sit your ass in the chair before I physically put you there."

"You're altering my plans."

"Whatever. Sit."

He was about to get an earful. Good. Best friends were supposed to call you a moron when you needed to hear it. "I'm sitting. Now what?"

Ty remained standing. "Now take a deep breath and pull your head out of your rectum."

Quinn let a sarcastic laugh roll out.

"Don't laugh this off, Quinn. I'm serious."

"I know you are. And you know that laughing is how I deal."

Ty finally sat in the adjacent chair. "I told you to leave Kylee alone. What did you do? The opposite."

"I don't need your blessing or permission for anything. I'm a grown man, remember? I'm capable of making my own…" Before he could finish the thought, Ty finished it for him.

"Blatant errors in judgment?"

"Bite my hairy ass."

"I won't have to. Your actions are going to do the biting, big time. Listen dork-face, Kylee is a genuinely sweet person who…"

It was Quinn's turn to butt in. "…has a lot on her plate?" He stood up in a huff. "I'm so sick of hearing that. I freaking know that Kylee's a mom. That she's going to school. And that she'll break if I mishandle things." He threw his hands up in exasperation. "Stop protecting her like she's made of toothpicks." Quinn headed for the bathroom but stopped abruptly. "Kylee Steele is a beautiful, vibrant, interesting woman that I want to get to know better. I think she agreed to come here this weekend because she wants to get to know me too."

"Keep telling yourself that." Ty met him in the middle of the room. "I think an alien snatched your brain. You're not acting like the Quinn I know. Trigg said you encouraged Kylee to bring her daughter along. Is that true? Or is Trigg full of shit?"

"Get out of my room."

* * *

"You have to pee again?"

Kylee left Angie's question unanswered and scooted from the limo. She ran into the gas station and to the Ladies room. "Are you kidding me?" A notice on the bathroom door read: Door is kept locked. See the cashier for a key. With her thighs tightly clenched she waddled to the front and stood in line behind two other customers.

The teenage cashier was decked out in an over-sized cowboy hat, a denim shirt with the shape of Texas stitched on the pockets and a bolo tie with a large turquoise stone in the center. He was taking care of the first customer at the blinding speed of a snail and sharing his plans to head to San Antonio as soon as his shift was done.

Under her breath, Kylee pleaded with him. "Hurry. Hurry. Hurry." Any second now she was going to sprinkle the black and white flecked floor tile.

She tried to distract the impending disaster by browsing the magazine and newspapers in the rack next to her. One particular headline grabbed her attention: *A Week Without Tori – How is Quinn Faring?* "Oh Lord," she mumbled sarcastically. At the same time her ability to hold on crumbled. "Key. Restroom," came out scratchy and loud. Everyone turned around simultaneously. "Please," she added.

The cashier's unhurried smile was testing her ability to be polite. He held out a wooden ruler with a key dangling from the end. She snatched it with haste and over her shoulder offered thanks.

Trying to unlock a door without peeing seemed a monumental task. Kylee fumbled and cursed until she got the key in the lock. To her dismay, the blasted thing wouldn't open.

A grey-haired woman holding hands with a small child arrived to use the restroom too. "Darn thing is tricky. Put your weight against the door and turn the key."

The little girls' eyes were wide with alarm. "Grandma, I have to go really bad." She bounced up and down holding her belly.

Kylee gave the door a hundred and twenty pound push, turned the key and voila! The door opened. She motioned for the woman and child to go in ahead of her.

"Are you sure?"

Kylee tried to smile. "I'm sure."

While she waited, she scolded herself for letting her overactive imagination turn her into a peeing machine. She recognized the urgency to go for what it was – panic. The level of anxiety she'd been dealing with all week was known to trigger a fight or flight response. Three pit stops in the last hour was definitely a flight response. From out of the blue, it dawned on her that she just might make a good psychologist after all because she was experiencing the many stages of fear and indecision: fear of giving her heart to someone who was going to snap it in half, fear of missing out by not giving it to him, fear that once she gave into all the desire flooding her body that she'd never be the same, and her most pressing fear – if she didn't get in the restroom soon she'd need a mop and change of clothes.

"Whew! That was a close one," the woman said, stepping from the restroom with the child in her arms. "Thank you, dear."

Kylee nodded and brushed past them, just in the nick of time.

After sweet relief, Kylee worked her way back to the limo taking a deep breath with each step. She looked around at the dramatic, craggy landscape. It was beautiful and serene and in the middle of nowhere. Before she made a beeline into the gas station, Henry announced that they would soon arrive at the resort, which meant there'd be no more bathroom stops and no more opportunities to pull herself together before she came face to face with Quinn. Miles from home with Gabbi and Angie, there'd be no flight. Just fight.

Henry met her before she reached the limousine. "Feeling better, miss?"

"Much better. Thank you." She was embarrassed that Henry had to make repeated stops.

"You're welcome." He had a strange look on his face and leaned toward her with a whisper. "I understand why you're nervous, miss."

The comment took her by surprise. "You do?"

Henry kept his voice low like he was sharing a secret with a good friend. "When I met my wife, I had to, well you know…" He raised his eyebrows and the bill of his hat moved up to reveal concern in his brown eyes. "…find a restroom often too." A smile played at the corners of his mouth. "I was a taxi driver in New York City and Rebecca was there on business. The moment I laid eyes on that plus-size gal I was hooked. She had the sweetest disposition and she nailed the art of conversation. Long story short, Rebecca made opportunities for our paths to cross. I was a rather shy guy and she made me a nervous wreck. At the same time, I was head over heels." He flashed his wedding ring. "We've been married for ten years now and have two lovely daughters. *And* we have quite a bit of money, thanks to her grandfather." His smile grew bigger. "You're probably wondering where I'm going with this and why I'm a chauffeur." At her nod, he explained. "I'll address it in two parts, if I may. First, Rebecca is from money. It was a little intimidating in the beginning but I came to realize that's not who she is, and I didn't let my sudden change in finances change the person I am. I love to drive. I just don't drive taxis any more. Rebecca's grandfather is good friends with the Randels and they offered me a job. Secondly, Mr. Randel has retained the wait staff at the resort but not the bar service. He's brought you on for that. Essentially, he's doing what Rebecca did – he's making an opportunity for your paths to cross again. What you do about it is up to you. I took a risk with Rebecca and I've not regretted it for a second."

Was she that obvious with her feelings that even the limo driver picked up on them? "You truly are a kind man." She stood on her tiptoes to deliver a hug. "Rebecca's a very lucky woman." Planting her heels once again firmly on the ground, she braved honesty and hoped that Henry wasn't a plant for Quinn. "There's definitely something going on between Quinn and I, I'm just not sure what it is. Actually, I'm afraid to entertain what it might be."

"Love is worth the gamble, miss."

Love? Kylee was jarred by the word. She and Quinn had flirted and kissed. In no way did that bring them close to love. She smiled warmly at Henry. He was either a hopeless romantic, or a nut job. "Who are you? Cupid in disguise?"

He tipped his hat. "Just a limo driver, miss."

"You're so much more than that."

Henry opened the door and Kylee hesitated. "Thank you for making all the pit stops and for your words of wisdom." She climbed into the luxury car and the interrogation began.

"What was that all about?"

"Opportunities and remaining true to who you are."

"Huh?"

"Tell you later." Kylee fastened the seat belt around her and checked on Gabbi who was still deep in a nap.

Angie motioned to the privacy divider. "He can't hear you, so tell me now."

Kylee returned to their earlier conversation. "Trouble is on the horizon and it's too late to turn around."

* * *

Quinn returned to the lobby in time to catch the arrival of the limousine. His heart rate spiked and he hurried outside to grab the handle of the car door before Henry had a chance. "I've got it." The second the door was open, he searched for Kylee. "It's about time you showed up." The remark came out wrong. He sounded irked instead of excited but he didn't try to fix it.

Kylee's eyes glistened with hurt before she looked away and unlatched her seat belt. "I'm to blame," she said, loosening the restraints that had held her sleeping daughter firmly in place. "I didn't mean to delay your party."

"You didn't delay anything. Ty and Maggie are soaking up some sun by the pool. Trigg is bothering the help. A few others are running behind." Instinctively, he looked at his watch. "They should be here in about an hour." He extended his hand to help her from the car. The second flesh met flesh their eyes crashed into each other with such force that he was suddenly nervous, and he was never nervous. "Why are you wearing your uniform?"

"It's appropriate attire for the job."

"You don't have to be appropriate this weekend." *Lame.* Something about those green eyes made weird things come out of his mouth.

Kylee pulled the fabric of her shirt forward to reveal the company logo. "You hired Sam's bartender service so I should probably play the part."

"If you two are done gushing all over each other, I'd like to get out of the car," Angie prompted.

Quinn grinned like the cocky bastard that he was. "Are we done gushing?"

Kylee didn't reply. She bit down on her plump bottom lip and stared at him with those amazing green eyes. God he wanted to take her in his arms and kiss that sweet inviting mouth. He wanted to nuzzle her neck and breathe deeply against her skin while his hands memorized her curves.

"I should probably get Gabbi out of the car."

"Right." Quinn extended a hand to Angie. She sliced him with a threatening look and he backed off. It was no secret that he and Angie didn't warm up to each other at the bar and he didn't expect anything different on his turf. "Angie," he said in greeting.

"Quinn." A distinct icy coolness frosted her tone.

Sweet. Not.

Kylee wandered around the car and gathered her sleeping child in her arms.

Quinn rushed to help. "Here, let me."

Her silky blonde brows furrowed slightly. "Are you sure?"

"It's not a problem. I can carry her to your room." He understood why Kylee was hedging. Yesterday, he'd professed that he wasn't fond of kids. He could've worded it better. He felt like he should set the record straight that he wasn't anti-kids but it wasn't the best time. Kylee was clearly on her guard and Angie was giving him mean eyes.

The little girl rested her head so naturally against Quinn that he almost handed her back to Kylee. Instead, he led them inside to the front desk to retrieve their room keys.

"Hacienda number ten," the manager said.

"Your room is across from mine." Quinn tried not to grin when Kylee's eyes widened.

Angie didn't mince words. "How convenient."

"Angie," Kylee warned quietly, "be nice."

"I am being nice." Angie put her teeth together in a fake grin. "See. This is me being nice."

"All righty then," Quinn quipped with matching sarcasm. The glaring reality was that he wouldn't make any progress with Kylee unless he won over Angie too, and he didn't see that happening anytime soon.

The sight of Gabbi nestled against Quinn was

heartwarming. At the same time, guilt tugged at Kylee for Gabs not having an active father in her life. She didn't even have a strong male role model. A wayward and unexpected sound of regret came out on its own.

Quinn turned around. "Everything okay?"

Before Kylee could fib, Angie chimed in. "She probably has to pee."

Kylee couldn't stifle a chuckle. She and Gabs might not have a guy in their life but they had Angie. "I don't have to pee."

Quinn looked from Kylee to Angie and back, trying to figure out if they were misbehaving behind him.

Angie elbowed Kylee. "Let's check out our room. Onward my good man."

Kylee jiggled with more laughter. Angie was over the top. Thank God.

Quinn blinked with an unreadable expression and rebalanced Gabbi in his arms. He headed down a side corridor until he came to the end. "Here we are."

Kylee opened the door to the hacienda and discovered accommodations so luxurious that she was rendered speechless. Two king-size four-post beds with plush cream-colored comforters were accented with a dozen decorative pillows in different shades of brown. At the end of each bed lay an Aztec print fleece throw. The rustic luxury continued with a wooden cathedral ceiling arched above them and a stone fireplace for added charm. She peeked into the bathroom. "There's a bathtub big enough for six." As soon as the comment was out of her mouth, she remembered the bit about an orgy. She couldn't look at Angie or risk bursting out laughing.

"And the fun doesn't stop there," Angie teased. "We have a bidet." She wiggled her butt.

Kylee lifted her eyebrows to Quinn. "We don't get out much."

Quinn laid Gabbi gently on the first bed.

Kylee continued to inspect their accommodations. There was a designated sitting area with a sofa, two recliners, full screen TV with a DVD player and a small bar with a wood-grain refrigerator underneath. French doors opened to a patio complete with a private pool, a hot tub and a spectacular view of desert willows, magnolia and lacey oak trees. In the distance, there was a grape arbor and gazebo. "This is incredible!"

"A slice of paradise in the foothills," Quinn said.

"I promised Gabbi and Angie they could swim, but I didn't know how I was going to make it happen." Kylee folded her hands and rested them just below her mouth. "They'll be able to swim to their hearts' content." Without thinking she touched Quinn's arm. Her eyes widened at the realization that she'd initiated personal contact again. She tried to appear unaffected but inside her blood was pumping hard through her veins. "Thank you for allowing all three of us to have this experience. We've needed a vacation for awhile." She rushed to correct her comment. "I'll be working but it will feel like a vacation. No books or tests to contend with for a few days."

"I promise not to be too tough on you. You can sleep in, eat as much as you want, indulge in a little alcohol and have some one-on-one time with Gabbi."

Kylee was caught up in the moment and gave him a half-hug.

"Get a room," Angie said, reminding them she was there. "Oh wait, you have a room." She pointed to the door. "Across the hall."

Quinn emitted a small laugh but the merriment didn't reach his eyes. "Okay, mother."

Angie smirked.

Quinn cleared his throat. "You'll find me at the main pool just off the lobby. That's where we'll be spending most of the weekend."

"Do you mind if I hang around here until Gabbi wakes up? I'd like to acquaint her with her surroundings. She should be awake soon."

"Sounds like a plan." Quinn leaned into her with his shoulder and Kylee's muscles turned to spaghetti. She clutched the end of the bed for support.

He moved toward the door and turned around. "Shuck the uniform."

The second he was gone, Kylee wandered through the French doors and motioned for Angie to join her on the patio. "Can you believe this place?"

Angie plopped down in a padded chaise lounge. "I'm never leaving." She ran her hands back and forth over the arms of the chair.

Kylee sucked in a breath of fresh air, relishing the serenity of the wide open spaces. "Maybe we should inquire about working here full time."

"Or maybe His Highness will fall madly in love with you this weekend and he'll buy you the resort for a wedding present."

"Or maybe you've been taking drugs behind my back."

They shared a laugh.

"I noticed that Quinn didn't hesitate to help you with Gabbi," Angie said from out of the blue.

Kylee occupied the vacant chaise next to Angie. "Just when I think I have him figured out he does something that changes my opinion."

"You've got to give the guy credit. He knows how to woo a woman."

"He's not wooing me."

"Ohhhh, he's wooing you. He's just more subtle than most guys."

Kylee looked around. "You call this subtle?" She didn't wait for a response. "I'm going to check on Gabbi." She quietly closed the double doors but the click was enough to rouse her daughter. "Hey, Gabs."

Gabbi yawned and looked around. "Where are we, Mom?"

Kylee scooted onto the bed and pulled Gabbi onto her lap. "Remember when I said we were going to a place with a pool? Well, we're here. This is our room. We have our own pool. How cool is that?"

Gabbi's eyes grew wide. "Do we have a horse?"

"I saw some horses on the way here." She'd checked the place out online and found that they gave carriage rides but she wouldn't mention that in case it wasn't part of the resort package that Quinn so generously paid for.

It was a good thing Gabbi had the attention span of a gnat and changed the subject. "Do they have food?"

Kylee glanced at her watch. It was past lunchtime. "Let's get Angie and we'll go find something to eat."

* * *

Dressed in swim shorts, a Metallica t-shirt and sunglasses, Quinn followed the smell of chlorine to the pool that was protected by a privacy fence and palm trees of assorted sizes. There were padded lounge chairs, several round tables with sun umbrellas and just beyond the south side of the pool, a fireplace. Quinn did a double-take on the fireplace. It seemed like an odd thing to have outside let alone near a pool. But hey, the resort was all about excellence in atmosphere and comfort.

"It's about time you found your way here." Trigg sighed and nodded to where Ty and Maggie were cuddled up in one chaise lounge. "The lovebirds are having their own party."

Quinn folded his sunglasses and laid them on the table, stepped out of his flip-flops and pulled off his shirt. He pointed to the pool and whispered, "Cannonball."

Trigg's ho-hum mood took a visible leap to mischief. His

brown eyes sparkled with complicity and he couldn't seem to shed his t-shirt fast enough. He held up one finger. Then two. On three, he and Quinn bombed the pool near Ty and Maggie. Water cascaded over the cuddled-up duo like a hundred buckets of water were dumped on them at once. Trigg laughed like they'd pulled the prank of the century and did a dramatic high-five with Quinn.

Ty jumped from the chair ready to kick some butt but he handed Maggie a towel and kissed the tip of her nose before took off after the hooligans. "Game on, boys."

Quinn swam one way, Trigg the other. Ty went after Quinn first. He caught him with little effort and it became a wrestling, splashing, laughing show that ended with Quinn getting dunked several times. Trigg signaled from behind Ty to tag-team him. Quinn lunged forward and Trigg climbed on his back. Arms and legs thrashed and heads bobbed until it was time for air.

Quinn shot to the surface first, followed by Ty and then Trigg.

Ty wiped water from his face and pumped his fist in the air. "I'm claiming victory. Two against one and I'm still breathing." He chopped the waves like a whacked-out water ninja, sending water toward Quinn and Trigg. "Don't be splashing my woman."

"Married a week and you're already…" In a short amount of time, Maggie had won Quinn over with her big blue eyes and warm personality so he clearly understood why Ty had easily turned into a love-sick fool.

Ty egged him on. "I'm already what?"

"Whipped." Quinn raised and lowered his eyebrows at Maggie.

"Damn straight he's whipped." Trigg gave Ty a small push.

Ty put his hands on his hips and puffed out his chest. "Proudly whipped. So are the two of you."

"Yeah right." Quinn knuckle-bumped Trigg. "How is it possible for us to be whipped when we're not actively involved with anyone?"

"It needs no explaining." Ty beamed a smirk toward the opposite end of the pool.

Quinn turned to find Kylee trying to sneak by without drawing attention. He didn't want to smile with Ty and Trigg there, but he couldn't help himself. Kylee had replaced her uniform with a soft blue V-neck shirt, a pair of white Capri pants and flip flops. Gabbi was holding her hand, and Angie was close behind. "She's my employee."

"Yet you want to sleep with her."

Duh. Of course he wanted to sleep with Kylee. Did that make him whipped? No. It just meant she had all the right stuff and he wanted it. "Go play in traffic," Quinn said, swimming to the edge of the pool. Before he could pull himself out, Tori bustled in with her usual everyone-pay-attention-to-me manner. The second she spotted Kylee the theatrics intensified. "Well, well. What have we here?" Tori lowered her sunglasses to look over the rims. Her forehead creased while she assessed things. The wrinkles deepened when she noticed Gabbi.

Quinn was out of the pool in a heartbeat, with Ty and Trigg on his heels. He heard those two still refuting the claim that they were whipped.

"You couldn't keep your eyes off of Nancy Reeger at the wedding," Ty said. "By the way, Quinn invited her to join us."

"I wasn't hawk-eyeing Nancy Reeger," Trigg scoffed. "She's not my type. Did you really invite her, Quinn?"

Quinn tuned them out to focus on what was unfolding between Tori and Kylee.

Ty slapped him on the back. "Beer?"

"How about you knock me back in the pool and hold me under water until the bubbles stop."

"That was Plan B. I hope you have a Plan A."

Tori's backless sandals slapped against her heels as she stomped her way to Quinn. "You've known her a week and you invited her to the shindig for Ty?" Her nostrils flared with anger. "And you allowed her to bring a kid along?"

"Nice to see you too, Tori," Quinn bit in reply. "Not that I have to justify my actions, but I hired Kylee as our barmaid for the weekend."

Tori scrunched her face with vivid disgust. Her narrowed eyes zipped from Quinn to Ty to Trigg before she settled them back on Quinn with an even tighter squint. "What's gotten into you guys? Ty got married at the speed of light." She rapidly shook her head like she was trying to clear the insanity. "And you're trying to do the same thing. I think you both need shock therapy."

A soft chuckle from Maggie made them look in her direction. She grinned from ear to ear and lifted her shoulders in a shrug.

"Listen, Tori, this weekend is supposed to be a celebration. So correct your attitude," Quinn said authoritatively. He fell short of saying, "Or you can leave right now." His gaze swept past her. "Where's Jake?"

Tori pushed her sunglasses up with her index finger. "How would I know?"

"I thought you'd make the three hour drive together."

"You thought wrong," she said testily.

He'd hit a nerve. Maybe several. The spark he saw between Jake and Tori must've suffered a cruel but expected death. "He is coming, isn't he?"

"Again, how would I know?"

Quinn lowered his voice so only Tori could hear. "Sorry, Tor'." He remembered that she hated to appear vulnerable, yet he'd heard a slight whimper in her voice that indicated she was in distress.

Tori pulled her head back. In turn her chin lifted. The

pretense that everything was peachy took over. "He's too reserved for my taste."

"He's always been quiet. Did you think because you were suddenly in his space that he'd open up?"

Tori did a series of heavy blinks. "I'm going to change into my swimsuit. I hope you have plenty of wine on hand."

"You're covered."

Without another word, Tori spun on her heel and headed inside.

Quinn trekked the last few feet to Kylee. "Sorry about that."

Kylee lowered her head slightly. "I didn't mean to cause a ruckus. It's just that I needed to get Gabbi some lunch."

"You didn't cause a ruckus." He smiled at Gabbi. "Hi. I'm Quinn." He wanted to crouch so he was eye to eye with Gabbi but he didn't want to scare her.

"Gabbi, this is the gentleman that invited us here. Quinn Randel, Gabbi Rose Steele."

Quinn took note that Gabbi's last name was the same as Kylee's. Not that it mattered but he wondered why. For the first time since he met Kylee it sank in that there had been – and maybe there still was – another guy in her life. It immediately bothered him. His dad had pointed it out when they discussed Kylee in his office, but it didn't hit home until now. "Nice to meet you, Gabbi."

"Nice to meet you too, sir."

Gabbi couldn't be more than three or four, but she was well-mannered. "Umm…" He had no idea what to say to a wee person. "They have chicken tenders in the restaurant, if you're interested."

Gabbi laid a hand on her belly. "My stomach is growling. I should probably put some chicken in there."

Quinn couldn't contain his laugh. "Good idea."

"Thanks, Quinn," Kylee said softly.

Gabbi mimicked her mom. "Thanks, Quinn."

Kylee fidgeted in place. "I'll be back in a little bit."

"There's no hurry. Take your time."

A range of emotions played across Kylee's expression and Quinn wondered if she was feeling the same things working through him – everything from the urge to have Henry drive him back to Dallas before things fell apart, to a rush of anticipation for good things to come.

Kylee tried to appear relaxed even though her pulse was going haywire. It was the first time she'd seen Quinn without a shirt. His simple act of removing one article of clothing took her fascination to a whole new level. He had a thin matting of blond hair that enhanced his fabulous pecs. To make him even more delicious his swim trunks hung low on his hips, showing off a tight stomach and teasing her with a hint of more blond silk that dipped lower. She had to peel her eyes away or risk drooling down the front of her shirt. She settled her attention on Maggie. Maggie was safe. "If you'd like something from the restaurant I'd be happy to bring it back."

Maggie's smile was warm and friendly. "I'm good. Thanks anyway."

Ty held up a bottle of beer. "I have all I need – my woman and beer. It doesn't get any better."

The way Ty and Maggie looked at each other it was clear they were in love. "If you decide you want something later on, I'll be happy to get it for you." She smiled at Quinn without meeting his dreamy eyes. She also steered clear of looking at his chest again. If he caught on that she liked it so much, he'd probably go shirtless all weekend. "Come on, Gabs, time for chicken tenders."

Angie muffled that this had all the makings of a reality show. Kylee was so going to throttle her when she got a chance. Nervous laughter collected in her chest but she didn't let it loose until they were in the lobby. When she finished laughing she swatted Angie on the arm. "You're having too much fun with this whole awkward situation."

Angie ramped up the teasing. "It's not a situation. It's an opportunity."

"I can't wait until you have your own *opportunity* to handle."

Something weird raced across Angie's face. It almost looked like guilt.

"Ange', you're holding out on me. What's going on?"

"Nothing." Angie repeated it again. "Nothing."

"Two nothings. Something is up and you better spill your guts."

"Something is up?" Gabbi asked.

Kylee laughed. "Everything's fine, Gabbi. I'm just teasing Ange'." That seemed to satisfy her daughter. Kylee was beyond curious but for now she'd let it go.

Angie tugged on Gabbi's pigtail. "Everything is peachy."

Everything *was* peachy. For the moment anyway. She'd survived a scathing encounter with Tori and a disturbing yet blissful one with Quinn.

Darn. She had to pee again.

Fight or flight?

Definitely fight.

Chapter Five

Quinn berated himself for being a total dunce. He should've left Tori off the guest list. Although, not inviting her wasn't an option since she was part of his select group of friends. He sighed. All he wanted was a fun weekend with plenty of alcohol, some good food and if he was lucky, maybe some lovin'. At the moment, all he could imagine was three days of snippy remarks and Tori grabbing Kylee by the hair. He cussed his way to the stainless steel cooler that was parked under the shade of a gazebo-type bar. Instead of taking a beer he went for a bottle of Jack Daniels, uncapped it and downed a big swig.

"Nerve medicine?"

Without turning around, he answered the voice of a late arrival. "You might call it that."

"Sounds like you might need more than a bottle of Jack."

Quinn turned with a grimace. "Let me guess, Trigg's been texting you a minute by minute accounting of what's been going on."

Jake couldn't pull off a poker face if he tried, which made him easy pickings in a card game and the go-to guy if you wanted the truth. "Yep."

"You clowns are getting on my last nerve."

"Nah. I'd say your ex is to blame."

"Damn straight she is." Quinn took another swig of whiskey. "Speaking of Tori, how are things going between you two? Are you hooking up?" Jake twisted his mouth to the side like he was trying to compose a suitable answer. Quinn rushed to smooth things out. "It's okay if you are."

Lines creased Jake's forehead. "We're not hooking up."

"The way you were falling all over each other at Ty's wedding, everyone thought you were an item."

Jake seldom cussed but he dropped the f-bomb with no hesitation. "I'm sorry about that, man. It's just that she was distraught and you know how I am when it comes to women."

"A pushover?"

Jake winced. "Tears work every time."

"They don't work on me. I'm immune to the suckers."

"Lucky you."

"It's not necessarily a good trait, but it is what it is. That's why you're better for Tori than me."

Jake made a snort of derision. "I don't have the strength to deal with Tori Caye."

Quinn put his teeth together and sifted air through his teeth. "No one does."

Ty wandered into the conversation. "You might be missing out, my friend."

"Y'all are so freaking funny." Jake swiped the bottle of Jack Daniels and took a healthy guzzle.

Quinn tried not to smile. Jake almost never imbibed in anything stronger than beer. In less than five minutes he dropped the f-bomb and tossed back a mouthful of Jack. Interesting.

Ty was in heckle-mode. "Yowza!" He took Jake by the shoulders and turned him to face the pool.

Tori had returned and had just dropped her sarong to reveal a bright yellow bikini that left nothing to the imagination.

Ty pushed Jake forward. "All yours."

Again, the f-bomb slid effortlessly from Jake.

Quinn looked at Ty with a conspiratorial grin. Completely in synch, they grabbed Jake and tossed him in the pool.

From his chaise lounge, Trigg hollered, "Yee Haw! Now it's a party."

Jake swam to the bottom of the pool to retrieve his sunglasses and then worked his way to the shallow end. Still in his shoes, shirt and sandals, he stood soggy and scowling. He sloshed over to a table stacked with thirsty monogrammed resort towels. He blotted his face and the back of his neck and then removed his shirt to wring it out. "I'm headed in to change into my trunks." He pointed to each guy, one by one. "Be warned. When I get back, you're going in the pool." A cacophony of cackles and scoffs made him laugh too.

The sound of the lobby doors opening and closing made Quinn sit up a little straighter. Kylee, Gabbi and Angie had returned. Gabbi gave him a smile and a thumbs-up. A weird feeling invaded his chest and he instinctively frowned. Gabbi flinched and leaned against her mom.

Quinn looked away and told himself it didn't matter. But dammit, it did. He wasn't an ogre who spooked little kids. In record time he was out of his chair. "How were the chicken tenders?"

It was a good thing kids were resilient and forgiving. Gabbi smiled up at him and another strange emotion took a hold. He was careful not to make a face this time. For lack of something better to say he told Gabbi that he liked his chicken tenders with honey mustard.

Gabbi wrinkled her nose. "Euw! Mustard!"

Angie latched onto Gabbi's hand and gave it a tug. "Let's get our suits on, Gabs. It's too hot out here. We need to cool off. We'll swim for awhile, eat Cheetos and pretend we own the place."

Excitement spilled over Gabbi. "Sweet."

Quinn shook his head in amazement. "Are you sure you're only three?"

Gabbi gave him an odd look like she didn't understand the question, but Kylee's face was filled with pride. "She'll be four on July thirtieth."

"Mom's going to make me a Little Mermaid cake, aren't you, Mom?"

"I'm going to *try* to make you a mermaid cake, Gabs. We'll see how it turns out."

Gabbi smiled up at Quinn. "You should come to my birthday party."

Quinn fought another urge to scowl. "We'll see. I might be out of town." Or out of my mind if I agree to attend a little kid's birthday party.

A long, awkward moment lapsed and Kylee came to the rescue. "You better get out of the sun, sweetheart, before you get sunburned." She instructed Angie to be generous with the sunscreen and to go lightly on the Cheetos. When her daughter and weekend nanny were well away, she cracked a smile.

"What can I get you to drink, Kylee?"

Kylee's laugh was hearty. "I should be asking you that question instead of the other way around." She rubbed her hands together. "Are you in the mood for a gin and tonic?"

I'm in the mood for you. Quinn wanted to ditch the party and take Kylee to his room. "I started with beer but made the mistake of switching to whiskey. I better add a little cola to it or my lights will go before dinner."

Kylee brushed past him. "Jack and Coke, it is."

Quinn watched the seductive sway of her hips as she walked to the gazebo. Damn. Those green eyes and that sweet body were already playing with his head. By Sunday night, he was either going to be blissfully content or so messed up he couldn't think straight.

Kylee delivered Quinn's drink. Before the millionaire

Adonis could strike up a conversation she returned to the gazebo. She took a few refreshing sips of Perrier and looked around. Brick. Marble. Palm trees. A pool with a waterfall on one end and a fireplace on the other. A ten person hot tub off to the side. This place was an extravagance known only to those who wore Gucci and Armani. Yet she was there, dressed in clothes from a clearance rack. Compared to Quinn and his friends, she was a scraggly piece of coal in a world of diamonds.

"More wine!" Tori's shout made the hair bristle on Kylee's arms.

Suck it up, Steele. Kylee hurried over with a bottle of Chardonnay and refilled the large goblet that could've easily doubled as a candy dish. "Here you go."

"I'd also like a Rueben, light on the sauerkraut. Make it snappy, I'm starving."

Kylee didn't bat an eyelash. "Yes, ma'am." She'd let Tori boss her around if it meant an escape from the hot sun for a few minutes. The air was so heavy it hung around her like a wool cloak. She wiped away a bead of sweat and sunscreen that was set to trickle into her eyes. Eager for the relief of air conditioning, she started for the restaurant.

"Stop," Tori commanded.

"Yes?"

"I changed my mind. Instead of a Rueben I'd like a Cobb salad with light vinaigrette dressing."

"Would you like the dressing on the side?"

Tori pulled down her sunglasses and looked over the rims like she'd done earlier. "If I wanted it on the side I would've said I wanted it on the side. Have them drizzle it. If they put too much on they will have to make me a new one."

Kylee was close to telling Tori where she could put the vinaigrette…and the Cobb salad…but she had ten thousand reasons why she couldn't. "Got it." She rushed off before Tori could change her mind again. When she passed Trigg, he offered a great idea. "If Tori gripes about her salad, I'll eat it. I'm not a picky shrew like she is." He said it loud enough to draw a scowl from Tori.

Quinn broke out of his conversation with Ty to tell Tori to stop being a pain.

Kylee was glad that Quinn had heard so when she put Tori in a sleeper-hold he would understand.

The second she was through the automatic doors, she undid a few buttons on her shirt to let the heat out and the cool in.

"Undo a couple more."

Quinn's rich, silky voice made her jump.

Kylee offered a shy smile. "Not a good idea."

"It's a great idea. But I have a better one. Why don't you slip into your swimsuit and join us in the pool."

"Again, not a good idea."

Quinn centered himself in front of her. "On second thought, you're right."

Kylee didn't know how to handle him in her personal space or what his comment meant. She tried to step around him.

"Hold on." He touched her arm. "You can't let me say something like that without me giving a reason."

"I'm not sure I want to hear the reason."

Quinn snaked an arm around her waist and drew her close. "Yes you do. Everything about you has said yes from the moment we met. You're still saying it with your eyes." He ran his thumb over her lips and an involuntary tremble coursed through Kylee. "You're saying it with your smile too." He pulled her tighter so the only things separating them were clothes. "The reason it's probably not a good idea for you to strut around in your bathing suit is because…" He paused. "How should I put it?" His right eyebrow rose with too much confidence. "Everyone will be aware of your effect on me." He shook with a small laugh. "I'll have to stay in the pool until it gets dark."

Kylee laughed nervously at that visual. "While we're being honest…" She pushed away and straight-armed him so she could lift the fabric of her shirt away from her skin. "I'm really sweaty and one whiff of me will cure any effect I may or may not have on you."

Quinn used his hand to kink her arm so he could get close again. Then he buried his face in her neck and breathed deeply.

"I meant to say, please, take a whiff," she teased.

"You smell like flowers."

Kylee gave him a firm look, even though her knees were jelly. "Maybe I have been saying yes with my eyes…"

Quinn cut her off. "But?"

"But…" She laid a hand across her heart. "I don't think we should get involved."

"We're already involved."

Kylee was set to argue but she remembered his thorough ravishment of her mouth yesterday in the bar. Agreeing to bartend at this private function only served to deepen the involvement; or it would before the weekend was through. "We should stop before…" She was having difficulty finishing her thoughts. She tried again. "I don't want to get hurt, Quinn."

Quinn circled her with his arms again which stole any possibility of escape. "I'm not out to hurt you, Kylee." He stared deep into her eyes. "I want to be with you." He freed a hand to run his thumb along her jaw line. "I don't know how you interpret that, but it's the truth. I want you. And the only way you'll get hurt is if you think long-term about us." He brushed his lips across hers. "I'll be honest with you. I can't promise anything beyond this weekend."

The intimate contact of their lips distracted everything but him. His candor, however, made the truth sink in, one word at a time. He wanted sex with no follow-up. She shouldn't be surprised and there shouldn't be tears burning behind her eyes. "Thanks for the reality check."

"I've made you mad."

"No you didn't. You laid out all the cards."

"Kylee," he said softly, "I'm just as messed up about all of this as you are."

"I doubt it," she said spontaneously.

"I sound like a callous lecher but I'm not. I'm being straightforward with you. In no way am I marriage material. I don't want a family. Sleeping with you, no matter how incredible, won't change how I feel." He held her eyes with a solid look. "For the record, I don't deserve my reputation. Some of what they say is true, but not the part about sleeping with a lot of women. That's completely false. In fact, I've had a long, dry spell."

Kylee was a jumble of emotions. She was torn between thanking him for being sincere and wanting to lose the club sandwich she'd had minutes earlier. "What about Tori?"

"We haven't been intimate for a long time." He put his hand up like he was swearing the whole truth and nothing but the truth. "Long story short, we didn't click in bed." He snickered but there wasn't a trace of amusement in his eyes. "She said she doesn't like sex."

Kylee couldn't imagine anyone not liking sex. It was one of the best things that two people could share. Not that she had tons of experience. "Seriously?"

"Maybe I'm a lousy lover."

"I'm sure you're fine." A dozen thoughts raced through her mind. The dominant thought was that all the fire and attraction mounting between them was nothing more than pent up sexual frustration. Quinn hadn't had sex for awhile and she was easy prey.

Quinn smirked. "Fine? Ouch."

"What?"

"You're sure I'm *fine*?"

"Fine is a good thing." Kylee left Quinn standing with his mouth open.

* * *

"You have to eat, Quinn." Maggie's blue eyes sparkled with laughter but there was an edge of bossiness in her voice. "I'm told they have a t-bone steak with your name on it."

"Not hungry."

"Whatever," Maggie said, putting both index fingers in the air. "Your turn, Ty." She motioned for him to pry Quinn from the chaise.

"Come on, buddy." Ty took an arm and Maggie took the other. "Too much Jack D. and no food, equals throwing up. I'm not up for that. Are you up for that, Maggie?"

"Nope."

Quinn staggered to a stand. "What choice do I have? It's two against one." He wobbled sideways and Ty straightened him. "Kylee, honey," Quinn slurred. "Let's eat."

Kylee stopped gathering empty beer bottles. "I'm going to have dinner with Gabbi and Angie, Quinn. I'll catch up with you guys later, if that's okay."

"It's okay. Your daughter is probably missing you. She's so cute, Kylee."

Ty took charge. He waved to Kylee and put an arm around Quinn to steer him toward the restaurant.

"I like her, Ty," Quinn admitted freely.

"I know you do. She's still off limits."

"No she's not. I told her…" Quinn's mind hit a blank. "I told her…" Shit. He couldn't remember where he was going with his thought.

"You're going to have a massive headache in the morning, mister," Maggie warned.

"Probably." He leaned against Maggie and the thought he struggled with came out loud and clear. "I told Kylee that I can't promise anything beyond this weekend. She understands."

"Uh-huh, sure she does," Maggie replied. "Keep telling yourself that, handsome."

* * *

Kylee found Gabbi and Angie sitting together in an oversize padded rocker on the patio, eating pizza with half cheese, half pepperoni. "There's my sweet girl."

Gabbi's eyes lit up. "Mommy."

She pulled Gabbi into her arms and sat on the end of a chaise. "I hope you and Angie weren't too bored."

"We weren't bored. Were we, Angie?"

"Who could be bored with a pool right outside your bedroom? We swam for almost an hour, took a walk to check out the flower gardens and to look for butterflies, and we ate a half bag of Cheetos before we decided to order pizza."

A twinge of guilt for not being part of the fun made Kylee bury her face in Gabbi's hair. "I love you so much."

"Love you too, Mom. Angie also let me play Candy Crush on her iPad. It's a hard game."

Angie took another slice of pizza. Between bites she garbled that Gabbi did good and was already up to level six. She winked at Kylee.

"Thanks, Ange'." Kylee pinned her friend with a questioning look and said under her breath, "I want to hear your secret."

Angie took a sip of soda and grinned over the edge of the glass.

"Mom, they *do* have horses. I haven't seen any but I know they have them. Can we go for a ride tomorrow? Please?"

Angie held out a brochure. "Gabbi found this in the desk.

They offer carriage rides."

Kylee tweaked Gabbi's chin with her thumb. "I'll check into it."

Gabbi hugged her tight. "I really, really want to go for a ride."

"I know, baby."

After satisfying her hunger with two slices of pizza and a bottle of water, Kylee and Gabbi took a shower. It was good to wash away the sunscreen and salt from sweating under the intense heat.

Dressed in a Little Mermaid nightgown, Gabbi scooted onto the bed and patted the space beside her. "Can you read to me?"

Kylee glanced at the clock on the nightstand. "I have time for one book." From a tote bag filled with books and toys, she retrieved Gabbi's favorite, *Love You Forever* by Robert Munsch. By the time she got to the end of the story, Gabbi's eyes had drooped closed. "Love you forever, punkin," she whispered softly and carefully slid from the bed and into the bathroom. She brushed her teeth, fished a tube of cotton candy gloss from her pocketbook and ran it over her lips.

"Primping are we?" Angie asked.

"Just freshening up."

"You're primping."

Kylee pressed her lips together to distribute the gloss evenly. "Care to tell me what that look meant earlier?"

Angie lifted her wrist to reveal her watch. "Holy cow! You really should get moving. It's eight o'clock."

"Dodge me now, but we're talking later."

Angie put her teeth together in a toothy grin.

"Ange', if you know something you better speak up."

"It's nothing about Quinn."

Kylee studied her friend. "Good to know. Wait up for me. Okay?"

Angie did a spectacular yawn. "I'll try."

"Over-actor."

"Yep," Angie chortled. "Now get moving and have fun."

"Fun? Quinn is already three sheets to the wind. The others aren't far behind. Before the night is over I may have to switch from barmaid to lifeguard."

Angie fanned her hands out. "I can see the headline now. *Kylee Steele dives in to save millionaire Quinn Randel. Who will save Kylee from Quinn?*"

"Ha. Ha. You're a laugh a minute."

Angie plopped on the empty bed and grabbed the TV remote from the nightstand. "I'm just saying."

Kylee wrinkled her nose, fluffed her hair and headed outside. On the way to the pool, she passed Tori. To be polite she asked, "How was dinner?" She braced for sarcasm.

"The ivory salmon with carrots and ginger was to die for." Tori swayed but caught herself before she slammed into anything. "The sommelier kept the cabernet flowing."

"It sounds lovely."

"It ought to be lovely at ninety-five dollars a plate and thirty-five dollars for each glass of wine."

Kylee couldn't fathom how anyone could spend that much money on a meal or glass of wine. She tried not to openly react but she couldn't hold in a gasp.

Tori arched a meticulously plucked eyebrow. "You think that's exorbitant?" The laugh that followed was devious. "Guess how much it costs per night to stay here?"

Kylee shook her head. "I don't want to know."

Tori's eyes flashed with a whole lot of uppity. "Four figures, that's how much."

Kylee had a strong feeling that she'd never fit into Quinn's world and now she was sure. Quinn was upper-class. She was lower-class. Plus, they were wired differently. While Quinn thought nothing of throwing around a vulgar amount of money to impress people or to get what he wanted, she thought about all the good he could do with that kind of money. Even though opposites were known to attract, they were too far apart in every direction. That was the point Tori was trying to wedge into her brain. "I should get to the pool to do my job."

Tori sneered like she could care less what Kylee did and headed toward her hacienda.

By the time Kylee got poolside only Ty, Maggie and Quinn remained. Quinn was stretched out in a lounge chair and Ty and Maggie were sitting at one of the tables in hushed conversation.

"Ahhh, there you are." Quinn ran a hand through his wet hair. "I wondered if you were coming back."

Kylee could tell he was intoxicated by the slow, calculated way he was talking. She sat on a bar stool in the gazebo. "I had to get Gabs to bed."

"Good girl." Quinn closed his eyes.

She wasn't sure if he passed out or not.

"Do you mind if I put on some music?"

Still with his eyes closed, he said, "Have at it."

Kylee searched the CD's stacked near the CD-player. As soon as she discovered Gary Allan's Greatest Hits, she popped it in the player. First up, *Smoke Rings in the Dark*. It was an older song but it was her all-time favorite. Gary's sexy voice got her through many a lonely night.

When the music began she swiveled away from Quinn, closed her eyes too and started to move to the music. She flinched when warm arms circled her from behind.

Quinn whispered, "Dance with me." The smell of whiskey was heavy on his breath. He loosened his arms, but didn't remove them completely and turned her around to face him.

Kylee looked for Ty and Maggie. They were nowhere to be seen. Darn newlyweds.

The setting was perfect. The sun was on its way down and

the moon was on its way up. The air was still hot but now it was accompanied by a breeze.

Quinn hit the replay button on the CD-player. "Come on, beautiful, let me hold you."

Kylee trembled but moved into his arms. Right away he claimed her mouth with a hot kiss. His hands roamed freely over her body, cupping her breasts and gliding down her back to caress her bottom. She moaned softly.

Quinn left her mouth to nibble her ear. He whispered, "I've wanted you for what seems like forever."

Kylee was incapable of fighting the pleasure. It felt good to be touched and kissed.

Quinn seared a path down her neck with his lips and didn't stop until he reached her cleavage. He dipped his tongue between her breasts and then raised his head to connect their eyes. "You're delicious, Kylee. I knew you would be." He began unbuttoning her shirt. When her chest was completely exposed, she arched her back to push her breasts forward. She felt wanton and wild. Her subconscious tried to intervene and she shut it down. She didn't want a niggling reminder of all that could go wrong by surrendering to Quinn. She wanted him. Quinn slid her shirt from her shoulders and down her arms. He toyed with the hooks of her bra until they opened and carefully removed it. Instead of letting the bra drop beside them, he tossed it over his shoulder. Kylee experienced a moment of indecision and covered her breasts with her hands.

"Let yourself go, Kylee. I promise to take good care of you."

She dropped her hands.

Bathed in moonlight, with *Smoke Rings in the Dark* playing a third time, Quinn descended to her nipples, lathering them with his tongue, occasionally pulling them with his lips. Kylee thought she would die from an overload of pleasure.

"Ohhhh nooo," Quinn said, leaning into her like he was

trying to keep his balance. "Why did I drink so much?"

His inability to stay upright killed the moment. Kylee guided him down against the wall of the bar so he wouldn't fall. She rushed to her bra and shirt and slipped them back on before anyone wandered outside. She covered her face with her hands and looked through her fingers. If Quinn hadn't indulged in too much alcohol to the point of passing out they'd probably be in the gazebo, naked and in the throes of passion. What was it about this man that made her lose her inhibitions so easily?

In the shadows of the gazebo, Quinn fell sideways. Kylee caught him before his head hit the black and white tiles of the floor.

"Quinn? Kylee?"

Kylee jerked when she recognized Trigg's voice. "Over here." She checked her shirt to make sure it was buttoned all the way. "Quinn is out like a light. Any chance you could help me get him to his room?"

"I knew all that whiskey was going to bite him in the ass. Oops. Sorry. I forget myself sometimes."

Kylee hid her grin when she realized Trigg was still in his swim trunks but instead of flip flops he was wearing cowboy boots. "No worries."

Trigg was a burly guy who had little difficulty pulling Quinn up and sliding a shoulder under him for easy hauling. "Lead the way."

Through the semi-darkness, they made their way down the narrow path lined with pygmy date palms and sneaked Quinn through the corridors to his hacienda. Kylee fished in the pocket of his shorts until she found his keycard to gain them entrance.

When they were inside, Trigg dropped Quinn onto the bed. "There ya go, pretty lady. I'm headed back to the pool for a beer. Then I'm going to watch Pawn Stars until I fall asleep.

Partying bunch, ain't we?"

Given Quinn's condition, the answer was a solid yes but Kylee chose to keep her opinion neutral with a shrug.

"It's barely nine o'clock and we're done for the night." Trigg chuckled. "Too much sun and starting at two in the afternoon will do that to ya. Hopefully tomorrow will be a different story. We'll start at noon." His whole body shook with another laugh. "Just kidding. See ya at breakfast."

"Thanks, Trigg."

"Happy to help." He waved and made a quiet exit.

Kylee laid Quinn's key card on the nightstand and tiptoed to the door. A rustling behind her made her glance over her shoulder. Quinn had rolled to his side and was close to falling off the bed. Crap. She tiptoed back and stood with her arms crossed. Roll him toward the center of the bed? Or leave well enough alone? While she deliberated the risk of touching him again, her thoughts swept back to what had taken place before he passed out. Would Quinn remember that he'd scorched her mouth with a kiss so hot her lips should be blistered? Kylee blew out a breath. His hands and her hands had been everywhere and the sounds they'd made should've alerted every coyote within a ten mile radius, or at least made the resort manager grab his gun.

If Quinn hadn't passed out there was a good chance they would've made love right there, under the blessing of stars and a half moon. Kylee asked the same question she'd been asking herself since she met Quinn – *What the heck am I doing?* Losing her mind by agreeing to bartend at the resort was one thing; giving Quinn free reign over her body was quite another. Allowing it to happen in the open for anyone to stumble upon was just plain reckless. When it came to Quinn Randel though, her brain seemed to stop functioning altogether. He made her forget that most men were a giant pain in the neck. He also made her forget that even protected intimacy could result in nine months of maternity clothes and a lifetime of caring for another beautiful miracle. When this glamorous weekend was over, she would return to her real life; the one that included ramen noodles and hot dogs, the one where she had to budget every cent, the one with no free time to deal with morning sickness and OB/GYN appointments. Trigg had said he hoped tomorrow would be different, for her it would be. She'd make sure of it.

A gurgling sound made her wince and spring into action. She knew that sound only too well. In a flash she was in the bathroom, pulling plush towels from a shelf above the toilet. By the time she returned Quinn had thrown up. Thankfully the mess was contained to the comforter. His eyes fluttered opened and closed like he was coming to life and trying to figure out what was happening.

"Don't move, Quinn." She ran to the bathroom again for a dampened wash cloth.

Climbing onto the unsoiled part of the bed, she gently cleaned his face and neck. His shirt had taken the brunt of the mess.

The sound of a crying child permeated the heavy oak door. It took a second to register that it was Gabbi. Kylee was on the move again. She swung open the door and gathered her daughter in her arms. "What's wrong?"

Angie waved a hand in front of her nose. "I might ask you the same thing." She leaned past Kylee to look inside the room. "Euw!" She cringed. "Sucks to be you."

Gabbi's cries intensified. "You forgot to bring my Little Mermaid DVD. You said you'd bring it."

Crap. Double crap. Her mind had been a thousand different places when they'd packed. She thought she'd set the DVD out so she wouldn't forget it to put it in the tote bag.

Miles from home. No Ariel. No Prince Eric. And a host drenched in barf. Her nutty life just moved up a few notches on the crazy scale.

Kylee guided Gabbi's head down onto her shoulder and gave Angie a quizzical look.

"I was playing casino slots on my iPad and she bolted upright looking for you. I tried to smooth things over but you know how she can be sometimes. Nothing I said was of any comfort."

Kylee cuddled Gabbi closer. "It's okay, baby." Gabbi needed her. So did Quinn. No-brainer. Gabs took preference. Besides, Quinn had been a bonehead by drinking too much. He'd made his bed. Now he had to lay in it. Literally.

She motioned to Angie that they were leaving.

"Urghhh." Quinn's eyes were closed and he was making sounds like he was in misery. His hands were on his stomach like round two of spewing was about to begin.

She had to get Gabbi out of there fast. It was bad enough that her daughter had seen and smelled the mess Quinn already made. Allowing her to witness him getting sick again would be irresponsible. They were almost to the door and Quinn let out another wretched sound.

Gabbi rose up from Kylee's shoulder and ran the back of her hand across her eyes. "What's wrong with Mr. Randel?"

Think long. Think wrong. They should've already been out of there. Kylee tried to turn Gabbi so she couldn't see Quinn. Wasted effort. Gabbi twisted in her arms so she could see him. Kylee quietly sighed. "His belly is being cranky."

Gabbi eased down and walked to Quinn. She took his large hand and patted the top. "Don't worry. We're here to help."

Kylee looked at Angie with big eyes while shame coursed through her. She was a bad mom. "Oh God, Ange'," she whispered.

"Relax. You know all that compassion you extend to other people? Well, your mini-me paid attention." Kylee winced and

Angie continued. "You won't scar the child by letting her fuss over His Royal Highness."

"I don't know. If he hurls, she won't be able to un-see that."

"Oh for God's sake, she'll see worse things when she goes to kindergarten."

Kylee made a face.

"You take Gabs to our room. I'll clean up after the dog," Angie spouted.

Nerves and Angie's theatrics made Kylee laugh. "No. You were hired to be a nanny not a sick room mom. I'll take care of Quinn but you and Gabbi can lend a hand." Kylee knelt in front of her daughter. "You and Ange' find the night manager. Ask him for a clean comforter and a stack of fresh towels. Will you do that?"

Gabbi hugged her mom. "I hope Mr. Randel will be okay. Ange' says he's a cool dude."

Kylee swung her head to Angie. "Cool dude, huh?"

Angie jiggled with a laugh. "Let's go before you also tell your mom that I think Quinn is faking it."

Quinn expelled another moan like he'd heard the comment. Angie swept Gabbi in her arms and they were out the door in two seconds flat.

After they left, a framed picture on the nightstand grabbed Kylee's attention. It was a photo of a little boy with blond hair and blue eyes and a Tonka truck. "You brought along a childhood picture of yourself?" Who does that? Her eyes dropped to His Royal Highness. "You seemed so normal."

Chapter Six

"Another Jack and Coke said no one ever after drinking too many of them the night before." Quinn carefully bent down and guided himself into the chair across from Trigg and Jake.

Trigg slanted a smirk at Jake but spoke to Quinn. "You look like hell."

Quinn winced at the truth. He felt like hell and looked the part in his ratty t-shirt and wrinkled cargo shorts. "At least I have a reason. What's your excuse?"

Jake forked a section of pancake in his mouth. "He's got ya there, Trigg."

The teasing banter was interrupted by an enthusiastic waiter with a menu and pitcher of ice water. "Good morning, sir."

Quinn left his sunglasses on and cleared his scratchy throat. "Good morning."

The waiter filled his water glass. "Coffee?"

"Please." Quinn turned his coffee cup upright. "I think I'm going to need a pot just for me."

A knowing grin slowly made its way across the waiter's face. "Yes, sir."

Trigg waited until the waiter left before he elbowed Jake. "I wonder how much he remembers."

Quinn didn't need a recap of his behavior from the night before. "Don't go there." He rubbed his stiff neck and stretched his back to try to loosen a kink. He took a sip of water. The coolness felt good against his parched mouth and he drained the rest of the glass with one long guzzle.

"A little birdie overhead Kylee's friend tell the manager that Quinn puked all over his bed." Trigg leaned back in his chair like he thought Quinn would come across the table after him.

Quinn removed his sunglasses and laid a bead of warning on both guys. "Do you mind? I'm about to have breakfast." Trigg started to say something else but Quinn shut him down. "Close your yapper before I close it for you."

Trigg laughed in the face of danger. "I'm bigger than you."

"I'm smarter and faster. Aaaaand, if you don't pipe down I'll tell the world about the special affection you have for Nancy Reeger."

Animation twinkled in Trigg's eyes. "I'm not sweet on anybody."

Quinn lowered his head. "Shh. Here she comes."

Trigg's head snapped around to the entrance. "You bastard."

Quinn and Jake knuckle-bumped. "Did you see how red he turned when I said her name?"

Jake shook his head no but said, "Yes." He pointed his fork at Trigg. "She'll be here this afternoon. You might want to shave."

"You might want to eat your pancakes before I push your face in them," Trigg threatened.

Coffee arrived and Quinn thrust his cup out like he had to have some right now.

The waiter filled the cup and waited for Quinn to take a few sips before he asked if he was ready to order.

"I'm starving for a full breakfast but I think I'd better stick with toast."

Jake piped up with more information than Quinn wanted to hear. "Toast alone won't revive you. You're also going to need two scrambled eggs and a banana."

Quinn's queasy stomach roiled with discontent and he puffed out his cheeks. "Probably not."

"Eggs contain cysteine that helps break down hangover toxins and the bananas will restore your electrolytes and potassium."

Trigg feigned surprise. "Well I'll be damned, you *are* brighter than a burned out light bulb."

"I know a few things *and* I can tie my own shoes."

"I'll give the eggs and banana a try. I also need a favor." Quinn motioned for the waiter to crouch so he could whisper something in his ear.

"I'll get right on it, sir."

Trigg's eyebrows shot up. "What was that all about?"

"Nothing that concerns you."

A giggle floated across the room.

Trigg kicked Quinn under the table. "Your day is about to get better."

Quinn narrowed his eyes to a squint. "Shut your pie hole, Sinclair."

Kylee spotted him right off the bat. She gave him a small, impersonal wave.

Hmm.

Angie lifted her head in acknowledgment. Gabbi, on the other hand, was bursting with energy and dashed across the room. Quinn had to put his hand out to catch her so she wouldn't hit the table. She blinked at him with concern. "I was so worried, Mr. Randel."

Every time Gabbi spoke to him something foreign welled up in Quinn's chest. At the moment, the odd feeling pooled with an immense amount of embarrassment and regret for his less-than-stellar behavior. He hated that Gabbi had seen him like that. He hated that Kylee had too. Even worse, he was mortified that Kylee had taken care of him. Talk about an attraction killer. He smiled at the little person who was the mirror-image of her mom. "Don't worry, Gabbi. I'm fine." He started to explain what happened but he caught himself. She was three years old and didn't need those kinds of details. Kylee and Angie caught up to Gabbi. "Today will be better. I promise," Quinn said.

Gabbi leaned against his arm and used her eyes the same way her mom did – with expertise. She batted her lashes and poured on the charm. "They have horses, Mr. Randel."

Angie chipped in her two cents. "Nothing gets by this one. She found the brochure for carriage rides."

"Would you like to go on a carriage ride, Gabbi?" Quinn sought Kylee's after-the-fact approval, which she didn't give right away because she was too busy studying him with a vague expression. Was she angry? Disgusted? Who wouldn't be? He wondered if those emotions were solely for him, or if she was dealing with some of her own. Thanks to the lingering effects of Jack Daniels, his mind was fuzzy on a few things except when it came to Kylee. He remembered storming her mouth and she'd done the same to his. He'd touched her sweet spots and the sounds she'd made in response were forever etched in his mind.

Gabbi tugged on Kylee's arm. "Can I, Mom?" She didn't give her mom space to answer. "You have to say yes. You know how much it would mean to me."

Quinn cracked up laughing at the brilliant pint-size drama queen.

Jake made a slurping noise with his coffee. "I'm in. You in, Trigg?"

"I'm in," Trigg quipped.

Those two knuckleheads were pains in the butt most of

the time, but they were also great friends who were trying to help him smooth out the morning-after with their humor.

Kylee sighed. "I guess we're going on a carriage ride."

Quinn was happy she gave in but it dawned on him that Kylee and her daughter were a lethal blend of awesome. He'd have to be careful or he'd fall prey to the whole marriage and kids bit before he knew what hit him. "How about after lunch?"

Kylee shifted from foot to foot and averted her eyes. "Sure." She wanted to strangle Quinn and kiss him and run away while she still had a thread of sanity to cling to.

The sound of metal clanging drew everyone's attention. Tori almost mowed over a bus boy carrying a tub of silverware. She frowned like he was to blame for the near-miss.

"Sweet," Quinn said snidely.

Tori was dressed in a gauzy white dress with a stylishly wide belt, Roman-style low-wedge sandals and sterling silver hoop earrings. She looked as classy as ever. Unless you counted the frown. She twirled a pair of chunky sunglasses in her hand. "Good morning." She didn't wait for a return greeting and turned her attention to Jake. "How'd you sleep?"

"Like a log." He crinkled his forehead. "Weird. Logs don't sleep."

Kylee took a second to assess her own choice of clothes. Khaki Capri pants, navy blue tankini and an airy polyester sleeveless shirt with a bright red and navy paisley pattern. She wasn't chic by any stretch of the imagination but she was content with how she looked.

"We're having pancakes, Tori. Want to join us?" Trigg stabbed a portion of pancake from Jake's plate instead of his own and held out the fork.

"No thanks. I had fruit and coffee brought to my room. Now I'm off to shop. Quinn, can I borrow Henry to drive me to Houston?"

Quinn shook the crystal drinking glass so the ice cubes made a clunking noise. "Houston is an hour away."

"What's your point?" Tori gave him a pinched look.

"You can borrow Henry, but only because he has an errand to run for me."

Tori didn't bother to thank Quinn. Again, she riveted her attention to Jake and laid on the sugar. "Would you like to come along? We could drink wine and talk." She swept her long lashes across her eyes.

There was no hesitation on Jake's part. "Sorry. I'm going for a carriage ride."

"A carriage ride? Whose idea was that?"

"Gabbi's," Jake and Trigg said at the same time.

Tori's gaze zipped to Gabbi. "How sweet." She swung her penetrating amber barbs to Kylee. "Carriage rides are pricey. You do know that Quinn is shelling out a ton of cash for you to stay at the resort, right?"

Instant anger heated Kylee's cheeks and she instinctively tucked Gabbi behind her to protect her from the wicked witch of East Texas. "You do know how much money it will cost Quinn to give you a pampered ride to Houston, right?"

Tori's mouth gaped open.

Trigg coughed the word "Zing" into his hand.

Kylee straightened her posture. "I'm not a wimp or a pushover. Never have been. Never will be. Shove me to the edge of a cliff and you'll be the one going over, not me."

Quinn flew out of his chair and stepped between Kylee and the platinum-haired troublemaker like he needed to diffuse a girl-on-girl smack-down. "Tori, one of these days your mouth is going to get you into something you can't get out of. I can't speak for the rest of the group, but I've had it up to here." He gestured to his neck. "I won't stand for you talking down to Kylee or to anyone else. I'm drawing a line in the sand. Cross it and see what happens."

Happiness, gratitude and that hard to define feeling when someone does something nice for you and you're not sure how to thank them properly – all pulsed through Kylee. She wanted to thank Quinn or at least give him a hug but decided it would be best to do nothing.

"Understood," Tori said with uncharacteristic nonchalance. "Old habits are hard to break." She moved away from the conversation to home in on Jake again. "Can I get you to change your mind about Houston?"

Jake sputtered in his coffee. "Thanks for the offer but I'm here for the whole resort experience."

"Sure you are," Tori said dryly. She drew her chin to her shoulder and did a slow, mocking blink.

Watching the fragrance heiress *not* get her way every stinking time was a wicked kind of enjoyment. The urge to smile was huge but if Tori saw the corners of Kylee's mouth tip up it would be the same as pulling the pin on a grenade.

Trigg stirred the pot. "Jake would rather let me beat him in a game of golf than shop. He promised to play nine holes."

"You get to beat me in golf. I get to beat you with a club. Sounds fair."

Kylee was developing a fondness for Quinn's quirky friends. She zeroed in on Quinn's ex to gauge her reaction. Instead of being miffed, Tori looked like a wounded bird from Jake's rejection. Heiress or not, starting the day with a hundred percent disapproval rating and getting snubbed by the guy she had her sights set on, had to hurt. "When you get back, Tori, let's have a margarita."

Tori didn't easily accept the olive branch. "Whatever." The stiff response was accompanied by a sharp turn and hasty exit.

Kylee had a feeling the snooty blonde was fighting tears but she was too proud to allow anyone to see.

Jake continued shoving pancakes in his mouth but he avoided meeting anyone's eyes.

Kylee looked at Quinn and found him boring a hole through her.

"It was nice of you to cut her some slack," he said.

Excitement lurched from its hiding place to warm Kylee with a blush. "I think beneath that abrasive exterior is someone who just wants to be a regular person."

Trigg bumped in with his take on things. "Not."

Kylee felt the need to explain. "I see Tori as a woman with a lot on her shoulders."

It was Jake's turn to scoff.

"Think about it. She's an heiress. Right away that raises people's expectations. She has to dress a certain way, mingle with select people and always be on her guard. That has to be mentally exhausting. Plus, she recently called off her engagement to the guy she went with for a few years."

"I forgot. You're going to be a head doctor. You can see through people," Trigg jested.

"I'm going to be a psychologist." Kylee wrinkled her nose in amusement. "I won't have the ability to see through people. That requires an X-ray machine." Trigg Sinclair was a big guy with a huge personality to match. He was classic Texan; tall, dark and handsome with meat on his bones and prickly chin stubble. A dashing cowboy. In their short acquaintance, Kylee determined he loved to mock and be mocked. Contrary to the conversation she'd overhead at Ty and Maggie's wedding where Quinn and Jake told him to stop bellyaching, Trigg seemed to be a laid-back man who let things easily roll off. He was fun, jovial and best of all, he hadn't mentioned – at least publicly – that he'd found her and Quinn in a disturbing state of affairs last night. Kudos to him for not making it an issue.

Quinn raised and lowered his eyebrows. "You fit it into this crazy group just fine, Kylee."

"Thanks. I think." She smiled but questioned if there was a deeper meaning behind the remark. *Gah!* She had to stop over-thinking everything that came out of Quinn's mouth. Sometimes a comment was just a comment.

Gabbi peeked around Kylee's thigh. "A cinnamon roll is calling my name."

A vibrant round of chuckles made Gabbi laugh too, although Kylee was certain her daughter had no idea why she was laughing.

"Miss Gabbi, you're too articulate to be three," Quinn said.

"She's around adults a lot and soaks up everything she hears." Kylee winked. "We have to watch what we say." She hoisted Gabbi up, anchored her high on her thigh and started for the table that held her sunglasses and key card. "Time to feed the munchkin."

"We have room at our table."

Jake and Trigg jumped up and pushed two tables together.

Angie whispered in Kylee's ear, "Barmaid my ass."

Yeah. She and Quinn kind of blew by the boundaries of employer-employee starting with the kiss at the bar. Last night's kissing and caressing didn't keep things professional either. She'd fallen asleep thinking about her *boss* and what an amazing kisser he was. She woke up with those same thoughts. Of course, Ange' reminded her at least ten times before they made it to the restaurant that Quinn was super hot but he drank too much and it was probably not a good idea to get too entrenched in him. Too late. She was already up to her eyeballs in lust with him. His overindulgence in alcohol, however, was one more reason to cut and run while she still could. But the way he kissed… Her eyes flew to his mouth. Cinnamon rolls were calling Gabbi. Quinn's lips were calling Kylee.

* * *

Quinn was still sluggish and had been trying to recharge

his batteries with a quick nap before the carriage ride but people kept bugging him. Sam Bright called to ask how the party was going and to ask if he needed anything. He knew the real reason for the call. Sam was still trying to protect Kylee. He couldn't fault him for that. In fact, he had a strange desire to protect her too. He rolled into his pillow and muffled a groan. This wasn't how he imagined the weekend going. He'd pictured spending time with the green-eyed beauty and if he was lucky they'd do a dance between the sheets. So far all he managed to do was kiss her, feel her up, make nice with her kid and hurl.

His father had also called. Twice. Someone blabbed that he'd taken Kylee and her daughter along to the resort. Quinn would eventually find out who narked and when he did, he'd wring their neck. His dad went into the same long-winded sermon he gave Quinn in his office a few days earlier – that it wasn't wise to draw Kylee into the fold. Of course, anything his dad said made him want to do the opposite. The phone call ended with Quinn telling his dad to butt out.

Quinn rolled to his back again. He breathed deep, held it for a few seconds and blew the air back out. He repeated the process a few times, hoping it would relax him so he could doze off. He was almost there. He could feel the tightness in his muscles release and his eyes finally stayed closed.

A loud knock on the door blew the chance of nap to smithereens.

"Open up, egghead." Ty persisted with knocking until Quinn threw his legs over the side of the bed and traipsed to the door to let him in.

Quinn yawned. "Thanks a lot."

"For what?"

"I was trying to sleep."

Ty pushed open the black-out curtains to expose sunshine. "You can sleep tonight." He helped himself to a bottle of water from the 'fridge and plopped down in a recliner. "I hear we're going for carriage rides in a little bit. Maggie's ecstatic. She said to give you a hug." Ty made a face. "That ain't happening."

Quinn finally cracked a smile. "Wise choice." He dropped into the adjacent chair.

Ty messed with the label on his bottle of water. "Going for a carriage ride is so not you."

"It wasn't part of the plan." How did that poem go by Robert Burns? Something about the 'The best-laid plans of mice and men…'

He needed a new plan.

Chapter Seven

Three hundred acres of vineyards, flowers and desert willow trees was too much for any guy to deal with. Had Kylee's thigh not brushed against his numerous times Quinn would've ended the ride after the first fifteen minutes. Every time they touched their eyes met. Kylee would blush and Quinn would scoot closer. After an hour and a half of wanting to rip her clothes off, he either had to move to the opposite seat or act on the impulse to kiss her right there, in front of her daughter and Angie.

The carriage driver brought the horses to a halt. "That's it, Mr. Randel. We have permission to travel on the roadways if you'd like to extend the ride."

Quinn brushed a line of sweat from above his eyebrow. "I'll let the decision up to the women." He gently pushed his shoulder into Kylee.

"We should probably head back," Kylee whispered and pointed to Gabbi who was snuggled against her, fast asleep.

"I'm going to go for a swim. Want to join me?"

The green of Kylee's eyes deepened and he watched her swallow.

He knew exactly where the hesitation was coming from. "You can still do your job. Serve a few drinks. And take a dip."

Kylee glanced at Angie like she was seeking advice.

Angie gave Kylee a verbal push. "Seize the chance to unwind because once you get back to Dallas it's going to be textbooks, tests and laundry."

Kylee thinned her eyes like she was calling Angie a traitor. "Swimming, it is."

Angie put her hand up to Quinn for a high-five.

Kylee tightened her squint.

"What?" Angie asked innocently. "I'm just thanking the man for getting you out of my space for five minutes."

"It's settled then. Angie gets her space. And we get to swim."

* * *

"Do you really need your space or were you just being a brat?" Kylee pulled two swimsuits from the drawer where she'd stashed her belongings.

"I've altered my opinion of His Royal Highness. Quinn's not a sleaze ball. He has the capability to be a sleaze ball, but when he looks at you his face softens."

"No it doesn't."

"It does. Don't get me wrong, he still wants to toss your panties over his shoulder. But I think he wants more than just a one night stand."

"Based on the way he looks at me?" The sarcasm was dry and pithy.

"Yep."

"Not buying it."

"Aren't you the one who says that psychologists are supposed to think in shades of grey? Yet when it comes to Quinn you seem to need hard evidence." At Kylee's sneer, Angie laughed outright. "You know what I mean. You're looking for a guarantee that he won't walk away after he gets what he wants." She sat on the edge of the bed and motioned for Kylee to do the same. "What I'm trying to say is that you should enjoy the weekend, enjoy each other, explore that chemistry and those hot looks. Don't think about the future, give yourself the moment."

"I wish I could be that casual.

Angie couldn't be serious if her life depended on it. "I heard if you don't consistently use your lady parts, they shrivel up."

They looked at each other and cracked up laughing.

"If that's true, I'm in big trouble." Kylee sighed. "I'm trying to hold onto my convictions – and my lady parts – but it's getting old, even to me."

"Then do something about it."

"Can I please bellyache about one more thing? I swear you won't have to listen to me anymore this weekend."

Angie mocked her with an eye roll. "Get whatever it is off your chest."

"Quinn drinks too much."

"Actually, he doesn't. When I'm working he does more flirting than drinking." Angie scrunched her face like she realized the impact of that proclamation. "You know what I mean, he's social."

"I've seen him intoxicated twice." Kylee wouldn't address the fact that he was a flirt. She'd whined enough and Angie's ears needed a break. Sometime they would discuss that Quinn had attended two very public charity events this week with a different woman each night. "My brain twists when he's around, Ange'. I want to run for cover but my feet won't move."

"There's only one solution to the madness. Let yourself have him, if only for a weekend. You'll regret it if you don't."

"I'm pretty sure I'll regret it if I do."

Angie's phone plinked with an incoming text message. She ignored it.

"Aren't you going to check who it's from?"

"It's Charlie. He's been texting me all day. He says we need to talk."

"So you really do need your space."

Angie lifted her shoulders. "Sort of."

"Why didn't you say so? You let me ramble on when you should've told me to get lost for awhile."

"You needed to talk and I'm your bestie."

Kylee kissed the top of Angie's head. "Charlie's your bestie too. Is everything okay between you two?"

"Couldn't be better. I think he's missing me and wants to talk dirty."

"Ahhh. Got it." Kylee inched off the bed. "I'll get out of your hair." She held up a black one-piece swimsuit. "What do you think?"

"Too mom-like."

"I'm a mom."

"You're also twenty-seven. Wear the pink bikini with the white polka dots. It goes great with your skin tone."

"My boobs are too big for that bikini. They try to escape."

"Be proud of those puppies. Show them off."

"The black one, it is."

* * *

She was baaaack. Quinn felt himself sneer; maybe not outwardly, but inside he was scowling big.

Tori lazed in the sun one chaise away. Quinn stirred his sweet tea with his straw. If she came back to ruin what was turning out to be a good day, he'd help her pack and personally drive her home. "I thought you were going to Houston."

"Halfway there I asked Henry to turn around."

He cocked an eyebrow. "Whyyyy?"

Tori messed with her floppy hat and pushed her sunglasses

higher on her nose. "I think it's obvious."

"Not to me," he said with more bite than he intended.

"Calm down. This isn't about you and me."

Quinn trailed his finger through the moisture beading around his glass. "Jake, huh?"

Tori squirted sunscreen on her arms and smeared it around. "I think he wants to warm up to me, but I sense he's holding back. Maybe he's waiting for your blessing."

Quinn removed his sunglasses. "Do you want me to speak to him?"

"Noooo. Don't even think about it. This has to develop naturally, or not at all."

"Give my seal of approval but don't talk to him?"

"Right."

"I'm confused."

"Men. If you don't have a schematic in front of you, you're lost." She crossed her feet at the ankles. "Start by dropping little hints that he and I would make a great couple."

Quinn moved from a half-reclined position to sit up straight. "That request is more than a little whacked, even for you. I'm your ex and you want me to slide subtle hints to one of my best friends that it would be a good idea for him to hook up with you."

"It's not whacked at all."

"You're a candidate for the loony bin."

"Possibly. Will you do it?"

"Tori, if you and Jake hook up because of me and then unhook because you drove him up a wall, that'll put a strain on our friendship."

"I won't be mad at you."

"Not *our* friendship, me and Jake's."

Tori's mouth plumped into a pout. "I'd do it for you."

No you wouldn't. "I'll see what I can do."

"That's all I'm asking."

Quinn sucked on the last ice cube from his glass. "I need more tea."

"Where's Kylee? Aren't you paying her to wait on you?"

"Toriiii," he warned.

"Well, aren't you?" she asked curtly.

Quinn jerked when someone shadowed over him and kicked the end of his chair.

"Hey, slick. I made it." Nancy Reeger grinned like a Cheshire cat. "I should've been here twenty minutes ago but my GPS kept saying 'when possible, make a legal U-turn'. I almost turned the darn thing into a Frisbee." A line of confusion creased her forehead when she became aware of Tori.

Tori sighed.

Quinn laughed.

He liked Nancy. She was easy on the eyes, articulate and didn't suck up to him. If anything, she did the opposite of suck up. "Glad you're here."

Tori's sigh morphed into a snicker of derision. "What is it with you trying to widen our circle?" She stood in a huff, threw her sarong over her shoulder instead of tying it at her waist and left without actually acknowledging Nancy.

Quinn frowned after Tori. "Don't mind her. She's in constant battle. With herself. You know, angel on one shoulder, devil on the other. They're always mixing it up."

"No worries. I work in a hospital, remember? It's more of an insane asylum most days and I run into people like her all the time."

"You work in the heart unit."

"Loons have heart issues too." She stepped in place. "Man it's hot. I think my flip flops are starting to melt. If you don't mind, I'm going to get situated in my suite and then catch up with Ty and Maggie."

"Sounds like a plan. Talk those knuckleheads into coming

to the pool."

Nancy gave him a mock salute. "Will do. And thanks for widening your circle." She gave him another silly grin.

"No way would I leave you out."

Her blue eyes sparkled. "Good to know, slick. By the way, I saw a white van slow down in front of the resort and when I looked directly at the driver, he sped away. I thought you should know."

"Maybe he wanted a better look at you."

"You incorrigible tease."

"I'm serious."

"Sure you are."

The van possibly belonged to paparazzi. The news media occasionally stalked him but they were more focused on Ty these days. They went nuts when he was named CEO of Vincent Oil. "Did you make any stops before you got here?"

"Since my GPS was being a pain, I stopped at a gas station to get directions. Come to find out I was just a mile away."

"Well there ya go. You drew attention with your sexy self."

She kicked the end of his chair again. "Tori's not the only one with an angel on one shoulder and a devil on the other."

"Yeah, well."

"Anyway, I'm not getting any cooler standing here. I'm heading in. And you'd better get out of the sun too before you get heat stroke."

"Always the nurse."

"You know it."

Quinn watched her walk away. He'd invited Nancy to the resort because she'd been a fun part of Ty and Maggie's wedding *and* because he'd seen Trigg fall all over himself every time she came near. You just couldn't buy that kind of entertainment.

From the corner of his eye he caught movement; five feet-five inches of well-built movement, to be exact. Dressed in a thirsty resort robe was the luscious woman who set his body on fire with just a look or a laugh. Hell, all she had to do was blink and he was aroused.

The robe was three sizes too big. It hung to the middle of her shins and she had it pulled up high around her neck like she was afraid to show some skin. Kylee cinched the robe tighter. "Where is everybody?"

"The wussies are hiding from the heat. It's Texas. It's supposed to be hot."

Wiping the back of her hand across her forehead, Kylee loosened the front of her robe from around her neck. "Can I get you a gin and tonic, or a beer?"

Quinn shook his head. "No alcohol for me today. Or ever again."

Kylee's generous mouth split into a smile. "How about a bottle of water?"

Quinn was out of the chaise and by her side in a flash. "Toss that hot robe. Let's go for a swim."

Sweat trickled down her temples.

"Come on before you pass out."

Kylee still hesitated.

"Don't make me do it, Steele," Quinn warned.

Kylee's eyes widened. "Do what?"

"This." He picked her up and tossed her in the pool, robe and all.

Kylee spit and sputtered to the surface. "Ohhhh, you are going to pay, big time." She shrugged out of the robe while she was still in the water and dragged it to the edge of the pool. She handed the soggy garment to Quinn and then chopped the water to splash him.

Quinn borrowed Nancy's comment. "I couldn't let you get heat stroke."

Kylee splashed him again.

He rung the bulk of the water from the robe and tossed it

across the back of a chair.

Quinn baited her by extending his hand. She grinned wickedly and he knew what was coming. He counted on it.

With one tug, he was in the pool.

When he broke to the surface, she was almost to the other side. Catching up with her involved no more than a few breast strokes. Just as she had a foot on the ladder to climb out, he wrapped his arms around her waist. To his surprise, she used that foot to kick out and they both flew backward and went under the water.

Advantage: Kylee.

Kylee swam to the middle of the pool. With her eyes just barely above the waterline, she watched him.

Quinn inched his way toward her. "Truce?"

The water was eight feet deep and Kylee was moving her arms and legs to stay afloat. She ducked beneath the water and then popped back up laughing. "Truce."

"Good. I didn't want to have to dunk you until you gave up." He motioned for her to close the small gap between them. "Come here you beautiful water nymph."

This time there was no hesitation.

Quinn circled her waist with his arm, bringing their lower bodies together. Kylee drew in an abrupt breath and engaged in a series of rapid blinks; either from nervousness or to clear the droplets of water bound for her eyes. "It feels so good to hold you, sweetheart."

To his surprise, she moved forward to flatten her breasts against his chest. It was his turn to suck in a breath.

"It feels good to be held."

The hunger that had been building all day, exploded. A hot collision of mouths was accompanied by groping hands. Quinn kissed her hard, savoring the warm fullness of her lips. She tasted like raspberry lip balm and chlorine. His body came alive in every form of the word. He wanted her. God, he wanted her.

He could tell she felt the same by the way she kept pressing into him so he could feel the hardened points of her breasts and the softness that lay below her waist. He dropped a hand to her bottom and gently squeezed.

Kylee broke the kiss and laid her mouth against his ear. In a voice filled with quiet sexual rasp, she whispered, "Oh, Quinn."

Quinn put their foreheads together. "There's something powerful going on between us, Kylee. I feel it every time we look at each other." He played with the strap of her swimsuit, finally pushing it from her shoulder. "I'm in a constant state of arousal when you're around."

"I'm afraid, Quinn."

"Me too." It wasn't a line. He was afraid of hurting her by taking what he wanted and then walking away. He'd have a hard time, but he *would* walk away. He'd have to make that abundantly clear. First, he needed to kiss her again. In one fell swoop, he connected their mouths with all the passion of a man on the fringe of fear and ecstasy. She moaned and he moved to her neck and suckled her damp skin. He progressed to her shoulder blade with gentle nips while pushing the other swimsuit strap from her shoulder.

Kylee elicited a sound of satisfaction.

In the fog of lust, he thought he heard her say, "Quinn."

He stopped kissing to meet her eyes. Those magnificent green orbs were wide with alarm.

"Quinn." There it was again but it didn't come from Kylee.

The voice he didn't want to hear this weekend made him put some space between him and Kylee. "What are you doing here?"

"I wanted to congratulate Ty on becoming CEO of his grandfather's company." Weston Randel's gaze snapped back and forth between, Kylee and Quinn.

His father didn't make a three hour trip to congratulate Ty. He came to badger him about his choice of companions.

Kylee swam away from him and clung to the edge of the pool.

Why was it that every time things started to get good with Kylee, someone or something got in the way? Karma catching up with him?

Quinn grudgingly swam to the shallow end, dried off with a towel and made the introductions. "Dad, you know Kylee Steele. Kylee, this is my father, Weston Randel."

His father's piercing eyes darted between Quinn and Kylee like he was trying to laser some sense into them. Quinn was used to the look. Kylee wasn't. He saw her draw herself tight. His dad was doing to Kylee what Quinn had done to Maggie when they first met. It *was* karma coming home to roost.

Kylee smoothed her wet hair from her face. "Nice to meet you, Mr. Randel."

A clumsy moment of silence lapsed. "Did Mom come with you?"

"No," his father replied tersely.

Damn. No buffer.

The lack of real conversation made Quinn tense. "I'm going to take my father to see Ty."

"I need to make sure Gabbi's up from her nap anyway, or she won't sleep tonight."

"We'll catch up at dinner. Okay?"

Kylee threw the soggy robe over her arm. "Sure."

Quinn watched Kylee walk away and was awestruck by his first real look at her in something other than street clothes. The bathing suit was modest but the stretchy material hugged all the right places.

When she was well away he laid a bead of anger on the elder Randel. "Let the ass-chewing commence."

Chapter Eight

Kylee wandered to the shady side of her hacienda and sat on the wooden bench just beyond the patio. She couldn't go inside yet because she hadn't been gone long enough to give Angie and Charlie enough time to catch up. Or talk dirty. Or whatever the heck they were doing.

A few monarch butterflies that hadn't migrated north, congregated on a patch of purposely planted milkweed and two dragonflies flew tandem, mating in the air over a wooden half-barrel ensconced into the landscaping as a small water pond.

Kylee took a deep breath and exhaled just as strongly, determined to let the serenity of her surroundings override the sweet and not-so-sweet tension that was stressing her out. The newest tension came in the form of Weston Randel. His sudden appearance had caught Quinn off guard. Quinn immediately tensed up and couldn't get away from her fast enough. Due to being caught in intimate circumstances? A strained relationship with his father was a real possibility too. Weston was painted in the newspapers as a handsome devil with a ruthless edge. The handsome part was accurate. She'd seen a hint of ruthless too in the angry set of his jaw and the iron grip of his look. Both were aimed at his son. Kylee refused to consider that she might be at the center of Weston's visit. She didn't have the brain space to obsess over another Randel.

One was plenty.

She noticed some flower gardens tucked in the shady area between haciendas. One held just tiger lilies. The other, Texas sage and Mexican petunias. Kylee plucked a lily and took it back to the bench with her. She twirled the flower and felt a measure of peace almost right away. Tiger lilies were her Zen. They took her back to a simpler, carefree time. As a kid, she and her mom fussed over a patch of lilies in their backyard. Her mom had called them ditch lilies. She'd said they were the underdog of flowers; a hardy variety until they were under extreme stress. Kylee was struck how those flowers were like her and her mom. They were both hardy, yet a little wilted.

"There you are."

Kylee bristled at the voice that was all too familiar. "Hey, Tori, what's up?"

"I knocked on your door and your roomie glared at me."

To Kylee's surprise, Tori's haughty nature seemed tucked away. "She's catching up with her boyfriend. If you know what I mean."

"I think it has more to do with me doing the same thing to her when we first met. I had it coming. You might want to knock on the patio door and let her know you're alive. I might've sent her into a panic when I said I couldn't find you."

Kylee shuffled to the patio and rapped on the glass of the door. She gave Angie a small wave and a smile to let her know she was fine. Angie smiled with the phone still glued to her ear.

Tori had taken a spot on the opposite end of the bench. She was crossing and uncrossing her ankles and flicking her fingernails at the same time.

Kylee was beyond curious. "Why did you come looking for me?"

"To get advice," Tori stated point blank.

Holy mother of surprise! "You came to me for advice?" Kylee was having difficulty processing the alien creature sitting a few feet away.

"Don't look so shocked."

"I don't mean to seem flabbergasted, but frankly, I am." Kylee had no problem being straightforward with Tori. She remembered telling her at breakfast that she wasn't a wimp or pushover. Where that had come from was still a mystery. Although, it was true. She wasn't spineless. Until it came to matters of the heart. Then she turned into a jellyfish.

The noise of fingernail flicking increased.

"I guess if you were the one coming to me for advice, I'd be more than shocked. As cruel as I can be sometimes, I'd probably laugh in your face." Tori squared herself in front of Kylee. "Thanks for not laughing in mine."

"You're welcome." Kylee gave her a bona fide smile. Despite Tori's haughty nature she wasn't a lost cause. "What kind of advice can I offer?"

Again, Tori took the direct approach. "You seem to have a way with men. I could use some pointers."

Give Tori tips about men? A maniacal laughed formed in Kylee's belly. To squelch it, she keyed on the amber of Tori's eyes. She was used to seeing condescension and anger. This time she saw something close to angst. Oh sweet Lord, the woman was serious. "What makes you think I have a way with men?"

Tori released an exaggerated sigh. "You have Quinn eating out of your hand."

Do not laugh or roll your eyes, Steele. While Tori wasn't a lost cause, Kylee still didn't trust her any farther than she could throw her. 'I think Quinn and I have a connection but I don't have him eating out of my hand."

"Go on."

"I'm myself when I'm with him." That was mostly true. She was also a mass of nerves but the way she responded to him was all her. "I'm a klutz and a dork and weird things come out of my mouth at the most inopportune times, but that's who I am. I wish I was polished and poised but I'm more a ditch lily." Kylee started to smile but chose a more serious look to make her point.

"What's a ditch lily?"

Kylee sidestepped the question. "The only advice I can give regarding men is to be you. Don't be afraid to show your strengths but also your flaws. If you don't know what they are or who you are, then dig deep and find out. Guys will respond to the real you." Yeah. That sounded like a heap of rubbish, even to her.

"What makes you think I'm not being real?"

Kylee reached over to touch Tori's shoulder. "I can tell by your eyes."

"And you call yourself a psychologist?"

Kylee wasn't offended by the remark. She identified it as part of Tori's self-defense mechanism. "I'm not a psychologist. I'm working hard to become one but I have a long way to go."

"I didn't mean to mock you. I can't seem to shut it off."

"Do you want me to continue?"

"Yes. Please."

"I'm not going to sugar coat anything."

"That's fine. I'll resist the urge to get snippy."

Kylee handed Tori the lily. "Here's what I see. You're beautiful, Tori." At Tori's raised eyebrows, she reiterated the thought. "You are. You have gorgeous eyes, perfect hair, great taste in clothes; yet you don't seem to be comfortable in your skin." The lifted brows gave way to a frown. "You come off as bitchy, but you don't want to be a grouch. You even said so a minute ago. I think you guard yourself so tight that you mechanically respond to people in a negative way."

"Hogwash."

"See what I mean?"

Tori looked thoughtful. "So you're telling me to bite my

tongue and let the world see who I am?"

"I'm not telling you to do anything except discover who you are."

"That's classic textbook mumbo jumbo."

Kylee nodded. "It's also solid advice. Let the real you come through. Some people will love you, some never will. That's just the way of it."

"I wanted advice *specifically* about men."

Kylee grinned but kept it small. "I haven't taken that class yet."

Interest fired in Tori's eyes and she broke into a laugh. "I don't want to like you, Kylee, but I can't help myself."

"Ditto."

Could the day get any more bizarre? Quinn had kissed her like they were lovers and fanned her desires so hot that she could've easily forgotten where she was and given herself to him, right there in the pool. Weston showed up with enough frost to temporarily reduce the fire to smoldering embers. And now she was giving Quinn's ex advice. Holy crap! She needed a stiff drink.

* * *

The muscles between Quinn's shoulder blades were knotted and if he held himself any tighter there was a good chance his back would crack. Dressed in a black pin-striped Armani suit with a cranberry colored tie, he walked behind his dad to the long table decked out with candlelight and crystal vases of black-eyed Susans. The formal attire madness belonged to his dad. 'Dinner is something special, Quinn. You're not going to wear shorts and a t-shirt, are you?' Quinn could've easily pointed out that he was footing the bill for the informal weekend and if wanted to come to the dining room in casual wear, or naked, he would. He'd save that battle for another day.

Quinn had sent Kylee a text advising her of the dress code. Hopefully she could read between the lines and understand that he didn't deliver the message in person because his dad wouldn't let him out of his sight. Thank God his father was headed to Brownsville and would be leaving right after dinner.

Each time he heard the cylinder of the restaurant door make its unique noise, Quinn tensed even more. He couldn't wait to meet up with Kylee but he dreaded the thought of her coming in direct contact with his dad. Who knows what the old goat would say, especially after the stern talking-to Quinn had given his father instead of the other way around. His dad came to verbally-muscle him into a better choice of companions. As soon as Quinn heard those words he flew into a blue-faced rage. He defended Kylee to the hilt. Quinn argued with his dad all the time. This was different. The fight that had been coming for a long time finally arrived. After a knock-down drag-out exchange of words where Quinn stood his ground about his choices and his life in general, his father conceded. Quinn didn't feel the least bit triumphant or happy to have won. When two people who loved each other exchanged blows, there were no winners. His dad promised not to poke his nose into Quinn's affairs. Quinn felt liked he'd clipped his dad's wings and he hated it. He'd hugged his dad, told him he loved him and that he would always welcome his *opinion*. He hoped his father would honor the boundaries that were now in place. Hopefully he wouldn't step over them one last time.

Trigg and Nancy arrived, deep in conversation.

Jake showed up alone. Not surprising. He'd been trying to dodge Tori all day.

Ty and Maggie came in with a dreamy aura of contentment surrounding them.

Tori finally made an entrance with an out-of-character smile. She scanned the room until she located Jake.

Run, buddy!

The waiter from breakfast sidled next to Quinn. "The package has been delivered to your room, sir."

"Thank you." Quinn shook his hand. "I left an envelope with your name on it at the head waiters' podium."

"Deeply grateful, sir."

"Same here."

The restaurant door opened again and Quinn's heart hitched. Kylee had arrived in a simple form-fitting, sleeveless black dress, cut at the perfect angle to expose a hint of cleavage. Her blonde locks fell in soft curls and she wore silver dangly earrings that sparkled when the light hit them. At her feet, a pair of sexy black heels that seemed to lengthen her already long legs.

Gabbi had come along and was holding her mom's hand. She waved excitedly when she saw Quinn.

In the heated discussion he'd had with his father earlier, it was mentioned that unlike Quinn's previous entanglements the one with Kylee came with complications. 'You and Kylee want different things', his father had said. 'You want to get her in the sack. She wants someone she can rely on. Need I remind you that she's been dumped twice; first by her father and then by the man who got her pregnant? As far as I know her mom is still in her life but there are too many miles that separate them. Kylee is beautiful. No doubt about it. I'm surprised she doesn't have guys lined up trying to get her to notice them. She's also strong, and that's alluring to any man. But I'm guessing that beneath the surface is a guarded mess. If you pull away her barriers and then break things off, you'll be widening her wounds. Don't do that to her, Quinn'. Quinn had fought his dad over those words, but now they embedded in his brain. Dammit.

Gabbi tugged at Kylee's dress and pointed to Quinn. A cautious smile tipped the corners of Kylee's mouth when their eyes met.

Quinn hadn't noticed that Maggie joined him until she bumped him with her hip.

"Don't leave them standing there," Maggie said.

"I won't. I just need a minute to deal with everything going on in my head."

"Ty told me your dad came to steer you away from Kylee because he doesn't think she's right for you. No disrespect to him but matters of the heart shouldn't be decided by a third party. They should be decided by the two people involved."

Quinn studied the dark-haired, blue-eyed breath of fresh air. He liked Maggie. She didn't have a snobby bone in her body and she always said what was on her mind. "I'd hug you right now but your husband would probably deck me."

"I love that about him."

"You're making me ill."

"Uh-huh. Sure I am." Maggie winked. "Now go get Kylee and Gabbi."

"Yes, ma'am."

Maggie inclined her head toward Kylee. "Your father beat you to her."

Quinn let out a heavy breath, tried to crack his neck by dropping it to one side and then the other, and charged to the entrance to either rescue Kylee...or rescue his dad. Kylee had donned her Kevlar this morning with Tori. She possibly had it on right now under that sexy black dress.

The fine hairs on Kylee's arms prickled when Weston Randel clouded her space and offered his hand for a shake.

"We got off to a bad start, Kylee. I wanted to apologize and let you know that it wasn't personal."

So, those angry looks hadn't been aimed solely at Quinn, and the reason he was there might have everything to do with her. Kylee refused to falter at the possibility. If it was about her she sort of understood his concerns. The Randels were a well-to-do family who worked hard to maintain their lifestyle and a certain image. The Steele's – her mom, Kylee, and Gabbi – were a dysfunctional family trying to maintain some semblance of order in the confusion that had become their lives. She was fairly certain she understood Weston without knowing having spoken to him until now. He had big expectations for Quinn. He wanted his son to marry within his wealth-class and he didn't want him to be saddled with a ready-made family. She understood. Sort of. Who wouldn't want the best for their child? She wanted the best for Gabbi. Hot tears gathered behind her eyes and she fought to keep her voice from breaking. "It's fine."

Gabbi tugged Kylee's dress again.

Kylee smiled in spite of her sudden desire to be someplace other than the restaurant. "Weston, this is Gabbi."

Gabbi grinned up at the tall, grey-haired man. What happened next shocked Kylee to the core. Gabbi let loose of her hand and grabbed Weston's. "My mom said even though you're a grouch you have remarkable eyes."

Kylee gasped. In that moment she wished the floor would open up and swallow her. She'd discussed Weston with Angie while Gabbi was still asleep. At least she thought she was asleep. She could remember exactly what she'd told Angie about Weston. The gist of it was that he was a grouchy S.O.B. with daggers for eyes, but if you got past them, they were remarkable. Kylee held her breath. If Gabbi added the S.O.B. and daggers part, Henry would be driving them back to Dallas before they ate supper.

Weston's mouth dropped open.

Kylee felt lightheaded and sick to her stomach. "Gabbi, honey, don't bother Mr. Randel."

"It's all right," Weston said, without returning eye contact. "It's nice to meet you, Gabbi."

"Nice to meet you too, sir."

"How old are you?"

With her free hand, Gabbi held up three fingers. "Soon to be four. I'm having a party and you're invited."

Kylee put her hand to her mouth to stifle another gasp.

Weston slanted a quick glance at Kylee. "She's very bright."

"Thank you." Kylee heard the quiver in her voice.

"Are you hungry, Gabbi?" Weston asked.

"I am, sir." Gabbi motioned for Weston to bend down so she could whisper, "Mom says we're having grilled asparagus. I don't like asparagus. Do you?"

Weston's smile started small but it grew into a full grin. "I don't love it but they tell me it's good for me. I bet if we ask the chef nicely he'll fix something else for you. What do you like?"

"Green beans."

"Well then, let's go find him." Weston straightened. "Do you mind?"

"Not at all." Kylee's fears subsided but the tears she'd fought to keep back were dangerously close to exposing her weak side, and for more reasons than screwing up Weston's first impression of her. Watching Gabbi take to Weston so easily made her feel like she'd short-changed her daughter in so many ways. No dad. No special relationship with her grandparents. No little buddies to play Legos with. The list was endless.

God, she needed a good cry. Or a gallon of straight alcohol. All the guilt and frustration for the things that weren't right in she and Gabbi's lives, started to close in.

"I'm getting green beans," Gabbi announced joyfully. She tugged Weston toward the man in the starched white hat.

Quinn sidled next to her. "Where are they going?"

Kylee wanted to melt into Quinn's strength but with his father close by, she decided to rely on self-strength; what little she had left. "To discuss green beans with the chef."

"I'm sorry I didn't run interference."

Kylee tried to collect herself. "I made a mess of things, Quinn."

"No you didn't."

Quinn leaned into her and Kylee wished he'd put his arms around her. She needed those arms. "I expressed my opinion of your father to Angie and Gabbi overheard. She just shared the information."

"Whatever you said couldn't have been too bad. The old man's smiling and holding hands with your daughter."

"He wouldn't take his anger out on a child."

Quinn took her by the shoulders. "What did you say that was so bad?"

Kylee dropped her head and Quinn brought it back up by lifting her chin. "I said that he's a grouch but he has remarkable eyes."

Quinn pulled her close and kissed her forehead. "Is that all?"

She would lie. "I actually called him a grouchy S.O.B. with daggers for eyes. I said if you got past the daggers they were remarkable. I'm sorry, Quinn. I don't know him well enough to say those things."

"Some days I don't either. But I know if he was pissed he wouldn't let your daughter charm her way into getting green beans." Quinn tucked a wisp of hair behind her ear. "You didn't screw up." He turned her so they could both watch the billionaire and the miniature version of Kylee negotiate for something other than asparagus. Quinn squeezed her hand. "Most of the time he is a grouchy S.O.B. with daggers for eyes. But beneath that rigid exterior is a kind and loving man. Few people know that about him."

None of this was real. She wasn't at a posh resort with Quinn by her side. Weston Randel and Gabbi weren't trying to switch asparagus for green beans. She hadn't called Quinn's father an S.O.B. and any moment she would wake up with Gabbi's feet in her face. She could only hope.

Chapter Nine

Quinn waited until the black limousine took a curve in the road and was out of sight before he stretched his neck from side to side. "That was interesting." His father had given him a fierce hug and told him to enjoy the rest of the weekend. The shift from testy to pleasant took him by surprise. In part it was due to Quinn finally getting through to his dad that he wouldn't bend about Kylee. He had a feeling Gabbi played a bigger part. She'd easily and effectively won over his father. The old man seemed to mellow in an instant. Quinn wouldn't have believed it if he hadn't witnessed it with his own eyes. He ran his hand across his chin. Weston Randel had been tamed by a three year old.

With his dad headed south to Brownsville, it was time to rock the resort and give Ty the party he deserved.

Quinn found Ty, Jake and Trigg in the shallow end of the pool splashing and dunking each other. Maggie, Nancy, and Tori were parked under the shade of an umbrella table with a pitcher of margaritas. Kylee was alone in the gazebo, sorting through a stack of CD's.

"It's time to toast Ty on his new position as President and CEO of Vincent Oil. Come on guys, out of the water."

Ty and Trigg belly bumped. Jake was the first one out of the pool. He flicked the women with water as he walked by.

Kylee delivered the two bottles of rose champagne Quinn had handpicked earlier and sprinted to retrieve a tray of crystal stemware. The resort was eco-friendly and shunned plastic.

Quinn noticed six glasses. "We need one more. You're going to join in the celebration."

Kylee gave her head a subtle shake. "This is something special between you and your friends."

Quinn raised a bottle of champagne. "I'm not popping the cork until you get a glass." He smirked when she raised her eyebrows and said, "So bossy," under her breath.

Ty wrapped his arms around Maggie from behind and laid his chin on her shoulder. "Lurking beneath that quiet façade is a sassy woman, Quinn. She reminds me of your mom."

"Oh yeah?" Quinn brushed off the notion but he assessed Kylee from across the pool. She was a lot like Vera Randel. Bright. Beautiful. Unafraid to call him bossy. There were more similarities but at the moment he was distracted by her incredible backside.

When everything was in place, they formed a circle around Ty. Quinn made the first toast. "To Ty Vincent, a great friend. We've been down many roads together; some have been fun, some have been bumpy. May this particular road be smooth and filled with love and success. Love ya, buddy." Each person followed with a personal message. Quinn especially liked Kylee's tribute.

"To Ty and Maggie: this promotion belongs to both of you. There will be times of joy and times when you want to pull out your hair, but as long as you have each other – and this great group of friends – you'll do just fine."

It had been pointed out on a few occasions that Kylee wasn't one of them; at the moment, she more than fit in.

The champagne was shoved aside and the party turned into a diving-splashing-whooping it up, extravaganza. Kylee kept the margarita pitcher filled for the women and served ice cold beer to the guys. She kept the sweet tea coming for Quinn.

Kylee popped a Metallica CD into the player and all four guys played air guitar. The women danced to Maroon Five, Kenny Chesney, The Fabulous Thunderbirds, Katy Perry and the Beach Boys. When Kylee popped in Gary Allan's CD, Quinn's head snapped around and their eyes met over the expanse of the pool. *Smoke Rings in the Dark* stirred memories of the steamy kiss and groping hands from the night before. He wanted both to happen again. Right now. He ran his tongue over his lips; thirsty for her mouth and hungry to hear her moan when he kissed her neck, breasts and all other body parts. He wanted to announce that the party was over so they could slip away. Since it was only nine o'clock and everyone was still keyed up, the pleasure of Kylee would have to wait a little while longer.

Quinn towel-dried the excess water from his hair and chest and blotted what he could from his swim trunks. He grabbed his key card and worked his way to the gazebo. "Do you have a minute?"

Curiosity flashed through her deep-green eyes. "What's up, boss?"

Boss? Was she trying to backtrack from where they'd been with a subtle reminder that she was his weekend employee? "I have something for Gabbi."

Kylee leaned toward him, lending him a whiff of something exotic and spicy. "That's sweet of you. What is it?"

"Let's go find out." Quinn didn't give her a chance to say no. He circled her wrist and waved to the others who had congregated near the diving board. "We'll be back in a little bit."

"If you're not back in fifteen, we're coming after you," Trigg hollered.

Quinn put his hand behind his back and gave Trigg the finger.

When they reached his room, Kylee gave him a suspicious smile. "Was that just a ploy to get me to your room?"

Quinn bobbed his head up and down, but said, "No." He grabbed a yellow plastic bag from the dresser. "For Gabbi."

Kylee peeked into the bag. "I don't understand."

"I was mostly out of it last night but I remember Gabbi being upset about not having her Little Mermaid DVD."

Kylee's mouth dropped open but she closed it right away. "There are at least ten DVD's in here."

"I had Henry pick up a variety."

Kylee put her hand to her mouth. "Quinn, this is so nice. Gabbi will be ecstatic."

Quinn didn't know how to deal with the weird happiness flowing through him. "I also remember her saying 'we're here to help'. Kylee, she's a great kid. I'm ashamed that she saw me in that condition."

Kylee laid a hand on his chest. "This is going to sound a little out-there, but seeing you like that wasn't all bad. It made you seem like an ordinary person instead of an always-guarded, uber-rich guy who could buy a small country."

"I'm not always on my guard." Kylee inclined her head and swept her lashes across her eyes as if to disagree. "Okay, maybe I am. It comes with the territory. There are people who make a living by reporting where I am, who I'm with, what I had to eat, if I smiled or frowned. If I stop by a department store to pick up something, they blast me for being a cheapskate. If I'm seen coming out of a five-star restaurant I get blasted again."

An impish grin lit Kylee's expression. "I'm sure it's hell."

"You mock me, woman."

Kylee stretched up to peck his cheek with a kiss. "I should probably get these to Gabbi while she's still awake. Thank you for being so sweet, Quinn." She paused at the door. "Will you be here or at the pool?"

Quinn tried to play it cool even though his body was

pulsing with anticipation. "At the pool, I guess."

* * *

Gabbi dashed across the room dressed in her nightgown with her hair still damp from a bath. She threw herself into Kylee.

Kylee hugged her tight. "What have you and Angie been doing?"

"Playing Uno. She beat me three games in a row." Gabbi whispered, "I pretended to be mad and it made her cry."

"No, honey, you didn't make Angie cry." Kylee smoothed a strand of hair from Gabbi's face. "She probably had something in her eye." Angie wasn't a crier. Even when she was wracked by fluctuating hormones thanks to PMS, she didn't cry. Sad movies didn't bother her. If Gabbi was right about Angie giving into tears, something was seriously wrong.

The yellow plastic bag holding the DVD's was still looped on her arm. "Mr. Randel wanted me to give you these."

Gabbi opened the bag and let out a squeal. "Aaaaariel!" She clutched the DVD like most kids would hug their blanket.

Kylee pulled back the comforter and ran her hand over the luxurious linens. Tomorrow the lavish digs would be no more than a memory; one she would cherish for a lifetime. She tucked Gabbi beneath the sheets. "Should I pop Ariel into the DVD player or would you rather go right to sleep?"

Gabbi countered with the cutest grin. "You shouldn't tease me like that."

Kylee tickled Gabbi below the chin.

The first glimpse of Ariel on the big screen TV brought a whoosh of joy and contentment from Gabbi. Minutes later her eyelids began to droop. Ahhh. That DVD was magic. Kylee kissed Gabbi's cheek and whispered her love.

Kylee found Angie on the patio with her phone in her lap,

staring blankly into the sunset.

Contrary to Gabbi's claim, Angie didn't show signs of crying. No watery or puffy eyes. No red nose. "I stopped in to check on my baby. Has she been good?"

"She's been a peach."

"I heard you kicked her butt in Uno." The statement was bait.

"Three times." Angie's mouth cranked into a half-smile. "I should probably let her win every now and then, but if I played the wrong card on purpose she'd be on to me. That child is too smart for her age."

"That's for sure." Kylee nudged Angie with her flip-flop. "Quinn did the sweetest thing." What Quinn had done finally caught up with her and found the soft, squishy part of heart. He'd gone out of his way to make Gabbi happy. *Big points, Randel.*

"Yeah?" Angie said, barely connected to the conversation.

"He had Henry track down some Disney DVD's. Gabbi now has The Little Mermaid in her possession." Kylee braced for a sermon that Quinn was a wily dog who knew all the right moves to get what he wanted.

Angie snapped out of whatever funk she was in to say, "His Royal Highness has been a surprise."

That was it? No lecture?

Kylee eyed her best friend, trying to get a feel for what was going on. "I don't say this often enough, but I appreciate you so much, Ange'."

"Back at ya." Angie spared a milli-second glance and went back to staring into space.

"You're awful quiet. Did all that talking dirty wear you out?"

Angie moved around in the lounge chair until she was facing Kylee with a small smile. "I am a little tired."

That's all she was going to offer? Kylee winced. A crowbar

and pliers were useless when it came to Angie. You couldn't pry or pull anything out of her until she was ready to share. She stood to leave. "If you need to talk, Ange', I can stay."

Angie put a hand on Kylee's forearm. "Tomorrow over coffee, we'll talk."

"I'll hold you to it." Kylee lifted her wrist to expose her watch. "I have to go. Quinn is paying me big bucks to play barmaid. From mom to mixologist." *And possibly more before the night's over.*

* * *

Quinn cleverly yawned.

Maybe not so clever since no one seemed to take the hint.

He yawned again.

It was almost one o'clock in the morning and his friends were still going strong. Nancy was showing Trigg how to do the Macarena. It was the funniest damn thing since Trigg was about as coordinated as a stick. Nancy finally gave up and pushed the clod into the pool.

Trigg ducked below the water to make Nancy laugh and then worked his way in front of Ty and Maggie who were sharing one chaise lounge. They were copping feels of each other when they thought no one was paying attention.

"Get a room, you two." Trigg made his way out of the pool, delivered a wicked grin and bombed them by doing a cannonball. Before he got his bearings, Ty and Maggie were in the water waiting for him.

"We'll get a room after you and Nancy get one." Ty wrapped his arms around Trigg from behind and Maggie took the honor of pushing his head underwater.

Quinn was pretty sure Trigg and Nancy's relationship hadn't progressed far enough to get a room.

Jake stood at the edge of the pool, beer in hand, rooting

Ty and Maggie on. "Dunk him again."

Tori slinked next to Jake.

Jake tried to ease away. Tori moved with him. The poor guy was fighting a losing battle against Tori's hormones and pheromones that seemed to be stuck in high gear. He'd spent the evening trying to get them unstuck with an amusing game of not-in-this-lifetime.

Quinn kept an eye on his friends while also keeping his radar locked on Kylee. He'd gotten a firsthand look at just how hard she worked. As soon as someone sat an empty bottle or dirty glass down, she was there to snatch it away. She constantly wiped off tables and fetched food orders from the kitchen. She'd done it all with a smile. He told her a few times to let the hooligans get their own drinks and food. She was quick to remind him that he'd hired her to wait on them. He almost slipped up and said that the money was just to get her there.

Kylee left to use the Ladies room.

Quinn drummed his fingers on the table, trying to rein in on the anticipation of spending a few hours alone with her. He couldn't wait to continue what they'd been doing off and on since they met. He wanted to taste that luscious mouth again and explore those phenomenal curves. Nothing would happen though until his friends called it a night.

Kylee returned, talked to Maggie for a few minutes and resumed her spot on a bar stool in the gazebo.

Quinn couldn't wait any longer. He stood, crossed his arms at his chest and let out a loud, lengthy yawn that was impossible to ignore.

Ty quirked an eyebrow.

Voila! Finally.

Ty scooted from the chair and extended a hand to Maggie. "Come on, wife." They walked hand in hand to Quinn. "Thanks for the great party, man. You're the best."

Maggie pecked Quinn's cheek with a kiss and inclined her head toward Ty. "What he said."

Quinn shook with a laugh. "You're an amazing couple."

Maggie kept her voice low. "I can't wait for you and Kylee to be an amazing couple too."

"I'm not sure that's in the plan."

Maggie smiled with her eyes. "Put it in the plan."

"Careful, beautiful, or you'll end up in the pool," Ty advised.

Quinn nodded in agreement. "I don't discriminate when it comes to pushing people in the pool."

Maggie looped her arm through Ty's and lifted her chin like she dared Quinn to lay a hand on her.

Quinn slapped Ty on the back. "You have your work cut out for you, my friend."

"Yep." Ty drew Maggie closer. "We'll see you in the morning." He waved goodbye to the others.

Trigg followed Ty's lead. He pushed his fist into his solar plexus. "Too many spicy chicken wings." He bumped Quinn with his shoulder on his way inside. "See you at breakfast."

The dominoes continued to fall, one by one.

Nancy excused herself from the party stating her twelve hour shifts at the hospital had caught up with her.

To Quinn's surprise, Tori tied her sarong around her waist and mumbled, "See ya," as she walked past. There were notes of defeat in her voice.

As soon as the coast was clear, Jake sprung from his chaise. "TV time."

"Jake – 1, Tori – 0," Quinn said.

Mischief beamed from Jake. "Something like that. See y'all when the sun comes up."

And then there were two.

Quinn went around to the tiki torches and put out the flames. He caught up with Kylee at the far side of the pool. She had a plastic pan propped against her hip and was clearing the last of the empty bottles and margarita glasses. "I think everyone had a good time." He was close enough to catch her sexy scent. Mmm. She smelled good. Quinn wanted to lay his nose against her flesh and take a big whiff. Soon. Very soon.

"You did a great job, Quinn."

"*We* did a great job." He put his hands on her shoulders. "I don't know what I would've done without you."

"You would've paid someone else to bartend. At half the money. Thanks, Quinn. Your generosity came in the nick of time."

That awkward feeling he got from both Kylee and Gabbi, filled his chest again. He didn't know what to make of it or how to deal with it." He slapped his neck. "Darn mosquitoes are trying to have their way with me."

Kylee's eyebrows lifted ever so slightly and Quinn held a chuckle inside. The mosquitoes wanted to have their way with him. He wanted to have his way with her. Sweet circle of life. He took the plastic pan from Kylee and set it aside. "I wanted us to check out that fireplace tonight but the mosquitoes are trying to siphon a pint. We can finish cleaning up in the morning. Let's go inside." He led them along the dimly lit path to their haciendas. "I'm not tired. Want to come in?"

Kylee pressed her lips together and slowly blinked. "Sure."

Hot adrenaline rushed through Quinn. In a rash move, he backed Kylee against the wall and pressed close until the tips of their noses touched. "I've waited all night for this," he said.

"Me too." Kylee wrapped her arms around his neck.

Quinn placed an arm around her waist to draw their lower bodies closer. With his free hand he cupped her face, his fingers went behind her ear. Kylee took a small breath and closed her eyes. Quinn tilted his head, closed his eyes too and moved in slowly, brushing his lips across her mouth. She quivered under his touch and he took it as a sign he was doing things right.

With just a light kiss and her closeness, Kylee put him in a full state of excitement. “Sweetheart,” he said, positioning himself so she became aware of what she’d provoked. “See what you do to me.”

Kylee replied by arching her back and crashing his mouth with a hard kiss. She sucked his lips, drew away and went back for more.

Quinn trembled with anticipation. His body wanted to buck wildly but he had to let her set the pace.

Kylee parted her lips in invitation and Quinn RSVP’d by sliding in for a taste. She moaned and it urged him on. He glided his hands over the swell of her breasts until she moaned again. The blissful sounds were almost his undoing. If they didn’t make love soon, he would embarrass himself.

Kylee dropped her hands to his butt and guided him closer.

Quinn kept one hand on her breast; with the other he fumbled to get his key card in the lock. A few frustrating attempts later, they were inside propped against the door mouth to mouth, bodies pressed so close it was hard to tell where one began and the other ended. Quinn lifted the bottom of her shirt and his fingers moved stealthily up her silky flesh until they reached her bra. He slid his fingers under the satin garment and ran his thumb across her nipples. Kylee gasped against his mouth. “Mmm, Kylee,” he said.

Her tongue darted out to wet her lips and he did the same to his.

Quinn pulled her shirt and the cup of her bra up so he could give hot, moist attention to her breasts. He lowered his head and seized her taut nipple. He sucked it and teased it with his tongue.

“Quinnnnn.”

He pushed the bra higher to give him even better access

and repeated the sensual assault to her other breast. At the same time he worked his hand under her denim skirt until he found the elastic of her panties.

She called his name again.

Quinn tugged at the elastic and he felt her tighten up. He struggled to ask the dreaded question. "Do you want me to stop?"

Kylee sounded like she was on the verge of panic. "Nooo, I don't *want* you to stop. I'm just not sure it's a good idea to keep going."

"Oh honey," he said, "it's a great idea. I want you sooo much." He moved to her earlobe and touched it with his tongue.

Kylee's breaths were heavy and erratic. "I want… I need… I'm afraid, Quinn."

Those three words were as good as a stop sign in the middle of a busy freeway. He heard the stomping of brakes and screeching of tires.

"Me too, Kylee." He wasn't lying, but their fears probably weren't the same. "I promise I'll be gentle."

"That's not it," she said, sounded even more frantic.

Quinn dropped his hands and leaned back. "Then what?"

Kylee put her face in her hands.

The sound of a fifty car pileup on that freaking lust-freeway was almost too much to bear. "Kylee, talk to me."

Still with her face in her hands she shook her head. "I'm afraid I'll get pregnant."

"I'll use protection. Let me love you, Kylee."

Kylee met his eyes while she pulled her bra and shirt down and smoothed her skirt.

Tonight was a perfect opportunity for them to get to know each other in the best way possible, but the look in her eyes said it wasn't going to happen. "Why did you get me so turned on only to wimp out on me?"

Tears framed her eyes. "This isn't a good time to talk about Asher, but I have to. So you understand." She sniffed. "He used a condom but I still got pregnant. I can't take the risk."

It was the first time Quinn had heard the bastard's name. He fisted his hands and wanted to track down this Asher guy and beat him senseless. He groaned and Kylee flinched.

They had been on the brink of ecstasy. So close. So damn close. Quinn was angry and desperate to make it happen. He almost offered to wear two condoms. "Aren't you on the pill?"

Kylee pressed her lips together and lowered her eyes. "No. I'm not."

He could not get a freaking break.

Quinn ran his hands through his hair.

"Don't be mad, Quinn. Please. Don't be mad," Kylee begged.

"That doesn't begin to describe what I'm feeling. If you had no intention of letting me have you, why did you kiss me back? And touch me? And grind those sweet little hips into mine? Why, Kylee?" He was shaking and she was crying, and he felt like an ass; a giant, furious, self-absorbed ass. He turned away to get himself under control.

The sound of the door opening and closing made him even angrier…with himself. He'd put forth more effort to win Kylee than he'd ever done for any woman. But he mishandled things from the start. He lusted after her shortly after his breakup with Tori. Lured her to an exclusive weekend at a high-end resort. And repeatedly informed her that he didn't want any part of a wife and kids. Who could blame her for an eleventh-hour ditch when all he wanted from her was a night of hot sex?

Chapter Ten

The desk lamp was barely enough light for Kylee to see. She pulled clothes from the drawers and tossed them into the suitcase.

A groggy voice cut through the semi-darkness. "What are you doing?"

"Packing our things so we can leave as soon as it's light out."

"Uh-oh." Angie heaved a sigh.

Kylee tried to keep the tears that were streaming down her face from reaching her voice. Quinn had put her in a fight or flight situation. Sadly, she chose flight. "There's no uh-oh. Everything's fine. I'm just too keyed up to sleep."

"Liar."

"It takes one to know one." Kylee dropped onto the bed and stretched out beside Angie.

"You've got me there," Angie said.

Kylee had been right, something was bugging Angie. She closed her eyes and rubbed the space between her eyebrows. "Are you ready to tell me what's going on?"

"Nope." Angie volleyed the question back to Kylee. "Care to tell me why you're packing your bags in the middle of the night?"

"Nope."

"Okay then. Quit making racket and let me get back to my beauty sleep or we'll both look like a fright in the morning."

"It is morning." Kylee rolled to her side to check the time on the clock-radio. "Four o'clock, to be exact."

"You're killing me, woman. Close your eyes and I don't want to hear another peep out of you until noon." Another loud exhale indicated the conversation was over. Kaput. Finished.

Kylee had to respect her friend's need for sleep, even though her own was elusive. She buried her face in the pillow and muffled a tearful, "Peep." The misery she tried to fend off crashed into her like a continuous tidal wave; hitting her hard, withdrawing and hitting her again, wracking her chest with sobs. So Angie could sleep, she had to lay still and silently withstand the agony.

Her thoughts were as turbulent as those tidal waves. If she just would've given herself to Quinn she wouldn't be face down in the dark, crying like a lovesick fool. But she couldn't in good conscience sleep with him knowing that she had a high probability of getting pregnant. It happened once. It could happen again. Quinn had made it more than plain that he didn't want a family. It was wrong to take the risk. He'd been forthright with what he wanted and didn't want. She should've been upfront with him as well. Now everything was a big, fat mess. This misery. This angst. All her fault. She knew Quinn's pursuit of her was about getting her in bed, yet she couldn't stop his good looks and charm from turning her brain inside out. She enticed him. She gave him hope that it was going to happen. She let him pay a phenomenal amount of money to get her to the resort. And then, bam! When the time was right for him to make his move, she cut him off at the waist. She wanted to go across the hall, knock on his door and beg for forgiveness. What would it change? Not a thing. She still couldn't sleep with him.

* * *

"What do you mean she left?" Quinn stormed from the front desk without giving the clerk a chance to answer. In a few long strides he was outside and headed to Kylee's hacienda to personally verify that she was gone. He'd knocked on her door earlier to discuss what happened last night; or rather, what didn't happen. When she didn't answer, he was mad all over again – not that he'd fully cooled off to begin with. Now he was being told that she'd checked out of the resort. "Bullshit. She did not."

Halfway to her hacienda, he put on the brakes. The desk clerk wouldn't mess with him. Kylee *was* gone. Without one word, she'd taken off. "That takes a lot of effing nerve, Steele," he gritted between clenched teeth.

He fished his cell phone from the pocket of his shorts and dialed Henry.

Henry answered right away, like he had his phone in his hand waiting for Quinn to call.

"First question," Quinn said tersely, "is the privacy window up?"

"Yes, Mr. Randel."

"Second question, is Miss Steele in the car?"

Again, yes.

Anger blasted Quinn with so much force he expected all his blood vessels to burst. "Tell me where you are."

Henry never got rattled. He was the kind of person who took one breath at a time, one step at a time and was genuine to the core. "Dallas," he replied.

Quinn had known the answer before he asked the question. Hearing Henry confirm it only made his rage skyrocket. "How can you be in Dallas? It's only nine o'clock in the morning, for God's sake."

"Yes, sir, that's correct. It's nine o'clock."

"Dammit," flew from Quinn's mouth. "*Why* are you in Dallas?"

"Because, Mr. Randel, I find it difficult to refuse a woman in distress."

Quinn wanted to throw his phone. "How do you know she was in distress?"

"Red, puffy eyes are a good indicator that one is emotionally under siege."

"Under siege?" Quinn repeated.

Henry continued the conversation in Kylee's favor. "I'm a sucker for someone who's hurting, sir."

"You're a sucker all right; for drama queens."

"Regardless, I made the decision to assist Miss Steele. In hindsight, I should've cleared the trip with you."

The self-regulating quality in his driver's voice told Quinn that Henry would do what he thought was right, even if it meant defying his boss. "You're a pain in the ass, Henry."

"If I've displeased you, Mr. Randel, I'll tender my resignation later today."

"I don't want your resignation. I want you to turn the limo around and come back to the resort." He was convinced that women were put on this earth to drive him berserk.

"As soon as I drop the ladies off at their door, I'll head back."

Quinn walked from the pool area to the front of the main building. "Do. Not. Drop. Them. Off."

"Mr. Randel, I will not participate in kidnapping."

"Kidnapping?" Quinn shouted. "What the hell, Henry? You're not kidnapping them. They entered the vehicle voluntarily. Am I right?"

"I won't argue the point, sir. I *will* drop the ladies off and then I'll drive back to get you."

"Don't bother. I'll fly back with Trigg." Quinn gave into his anger and threw his phone against a giant rock etched with the name of the resort.

* * *

Kylee watched the foothills disappear and the busy highway leading into Dallas come into view. Her head was throbbing from all the crying she'd done in the wee hours of the morning and her eyes were as sore as blisters. Fishing a bottle of Tylenol from her pocketbook, she popped two in her mouth and washed it down with a sip of water. She longed for a cup of strong coffee, but it would have to wait.

Angie was seated next to her but avoiding conversation by taunting Gabbi with gummy bears.

Kylee knew exactly what Ange' was doing. She was giving her room to come to grips with the way she'd left things with Quinn. She didn't need room. She needed textbooks and tests, Legos and laundry. She wanted to chase and tickle Gabbi. She wanted to back the calendar up to when she wasn't stupidly in lust with a millionaire.

She rubbed her eyes and wondered how it was possible for her world to catapult from semi-chaotic to full-on madness in less than seventy-two hours. It felt as though she was on an amusement ride that tilted her upside down and then broke. Instead of someone fixing the ride, everyone went home, leaving her stranded with all the blood rushing to her head. The most disturbing part of the whole ordeal was that she was responsible. Letting Quinn kiss her and talk her into this weekend, equaled getting on that faulty ride and then freaking out when things went awry.

Gabbi snapped her out of her funk. "I need chicken nuggets."

It dawned on Kylee that in the haste to escape, she'd forgot to feed her daughter. "Honey, they don't serve McNuggets at this time of the morning." She frowned at Angie.

"And it's way too early for gummy bears. As soon as we get home I'll make scrambled eggs."

Gabbi whimpered, "Mom, my belly doesn't think it's too early."

"Yeah, Mom," Angie mocked. "Let's talk Henry into stopping for food."

Kylee shook her head. "We're not going to bother him. He's probably in enough trouble as it is for whisking us away. If he gets caught driving through McDonald's, Quinn might find himself a new driver."

"He won't fire Henry." Angie winked at Gabbi and then knocked on the privacy window.

"Angie, no," Kylee warned.

The window lowered. "Ma'am?"

Kylee tried to thwart the plan. "Sorry, Henry, we don't need anything."

"Yes we do. Poor Gabbi is in dire need of chicken McNuggets. Any chance you could swing by McDonald's?"

Kylee watched the limo driver's expression in the rearview mirror. His serious look changed to a smile.

"I could go for some food too, ladies."

Kylee made big eyes of annoyance at Angie. "Fine," she said resignedly. It was wrong to deny her daughter breakfast. Besides, it was three against one.

In a matter of minutes, Henry located the nearest McDonald's restaurant and had parked the long, sleek limousine lengthwise across four parking spaces.

"I love you, Henry," Angie teased.

Henry's eyes sparkled with complicity.

Kylee winced. "I love you too, Henry, but I thought we'd go through the drive-thru."

"I hate getting crumbs in the car, miss."

"I understand." That was the *only* thing about the whole weekend that made sense.

Henry pulled his wallet from a hidden pocket inside his suit jacket. "Breakfast is on Mr. Randel." He flashed a platinum credit card.

"No way."

"It's not up for debate, miss." Henry smiled at the cashier. "I know it's too early to order chicken McNuggets," he ruffled Gabbi's hair, "but it would mean the world to this little lady if you could make her some."

Before the cashier could respond, Gabbi put her hand in Henry's and blinked up at him. "I don't have to have McNuggets, Henry. I also like sausage and hash browns."

The surprise on Henry's face was priceless. "Me too, Gabbi."

Kylee's heart swelled with affection for her daughter. Gabbi was polite and willing to compromise. She couldn't ask for more. Everything that burdened Kylee's soul took a backseat to a special kind of joy.

A grey-haired lady crowded beside them. "Randel? As in Quinn Randel?"

Kylee stiffened.

Henry stiffened too.

Angie chuckled.

And Gabbi innocently opened the spigot of information. "He's my friend."

Kylee placed her order to keep from freaking out. "A large black coffee, please." She was tempted to say a pot of black coffee but it would draw even more attention.

Angie jabbed her with an elbow. "Aren't you going to eat?"

Kylee pretended to ponder the menu. "I'm not hungry."

Angie spoke to the cashier. "She'll have a sausage, egg and cheese biscuit and hash browns. I'll have the same."

From her peripheral, Kylee watched the grey-haired woman bear down on her with intense inspection. "You're the one from the newspaper."

Kylee tried to remain polite. "Excuse me?"

Humor twinkled in Angie's eyes. "She sure is. The one from the funny papers."

The woman didn't catch on that Angie was joking. "Noooo. She's the one who's almost in a lip lock with Dallas's most eligible hunk." She retrieved a folded newspaper from a tote bag and opened it to reveal a profile photo of Quinn and Kylee in the pool, pressed together in a tight embrace, their noses touching and lips just a breath apart.

Kylee's mouth gaped open. That was her all right. The picture also showed water droplets trickling down her face, the straps of her swimsuit off her shoulders and her staring at Quinn like she was madly in love with him. "You think that's me?" She scoffed. "I wish." She gestured down the length of her. "Do you really believe Quinn Randel would bother with this?" It was a fair point. She had a bedraggled look going on with torn jean shorts, a plain white t-shirt and camo flip flops. Her hair was pulled up in a messy pony tail and she was minus makeup.

"Don't sell yourself short, dear. Quinn would be a fool to pass you up."

Such sweetness from a complete stranger improved Kylee's mood. "Thank you."

"I *know* this picture is you, hon." She patted Kylee's arm. "I'm thrilled to know the Randel boy is finally dating someone with substance. For once the paper got it right. You *are* a down to earth kind of gal."

Kylee was thrilled too because their food was ready. "Again, thank you. You made my day. And your breakfast is on us. Right, Henry?"

On the way to find a table, Angie didn't miss a beat. "The glamorous life of a debutante."

"I'm glad you find my situation amusing."

"You need to lighten up before those lines in your forehead become permanent." Angie stopped at the beverage station for ketchup and more napkins. "The way I see it, the only situation you have going on is where a hot guy finds you desirable and you're too big of a chicken to let it happen."

"It's more complicated than that."

"Only because you're making it that way."

"The secret you've been withholding, is *that* complicated?"

"You're a brat."

"So is my best friend."

Gabbi chose a table far away from the breakfast crowd.

Kylee waited for Henry to catch up. "Is there any chance we could make one more stop before you take us home?"

Henry had a keen intuition. "I'm sure we can locate a newspaper, Miss Steele."

"You're an incredible man, Henry. After we locate a newspaper maybe you can help me locate my brain."

Chapter Eleven

Quinn sat in the webbed lounge chair with his Rangers ball cap pulled low over his eyes.

"She just up and left?" Ty took the chair next to him with a tall glass of orange juice and half a bagel.

So much for having time alone to get his anger under control. "Looks that way." How did everyone know about Kylee leaving? Trigg had cornered him by the Men's room just off the lobby and asked why she'd high-tailed it out of there. Jake didn't ask questions but said, 'Sorry man', when they passed in the hallway. Now Ty was invading his space and would annoy him with a million questions. "Let's talk about something else."

Ty evenly distributed the cream cheese on his bagel with his finger before taking a big bite. "You're going to spill your guts whether you like it or not."

Quinn threatened with a lethal sounding growl.

"Remember when I was in no mood to talk about Maggie, but you made me?" Ty continued ripping into the bagel while waiting for an answer.

Quinn slunk further into the chair and pulled the bill of his hat even lower.

Ty chuckled. "You can't hide from the questions, Quinn."

"Go step in front of a bus."

"I don't see any busses." Ty stuffed the last bite of bagel in his mouth and washed it down with a long guzzle of juice. "We can talk here or while we play golf. You pick."

"I've destroyed my phone. Do you think it's wise to put a golf club in my hand?"

"You have trouble hitting the ball. What makes you think you can hit me?"

Quinn pounded his fist on the arm of his chair. "Anger improves my swing."

"Wouldn't that be a picture for the newspapers, you and me going at it with nine-irons?"

Despite his black mood one corner of his mouth pulled into a slight smirk.

"Come on. Let's go beat up on some golf balls."

Quinn pushed his hat up so he could see. "I really don't have much choice in the matter, do I?"

"Nope."

After changing from flip flops to golf shoes, Ty swung by the main building with a golf cart. The second Quinn was seated the grilling began. "Did you say something stupid to Kylee? Or did you do something to hurt her feelings?"

"None of the above," Quinn answered in such a thin voice it was barely audible.

"Women." Ty let the word hang there.

Quinn went back to hiding his eyes with his hat. "Why do we bother?"

"Rhetorical question, right?"

"It's not rhetorical. Why do we put forth so much effort for them?"

"Did you put forth a lot of effort for Kylee?"

Quinn hissed like a Western Diamondback rattlesnake ready to strike.

Ty snorted a laugh. "Didn't think so." He stopped the cart short of the first green. "What exactly is your relationship with her?"

"We don't *have* a relationship." Quinn muttered the f-bomb and flung his hat onto the fairway.

"Then why are you so bent out of shape?"

"Because she left."

"Someone you don't have a relationship with left the resort and you're pissed. That doesn't make sense. Any chance you have feelings for her even though you don't have an official relationship?"

"Don't be an idiot. I haven't known her long enough to have feelings for her. Besides, aren't you the one who told me to take time to adjust to being single again?"

Ty drummed his thumbs on the steering wheel. "Sounds like me." He turned toward Quinn. "Instead of going back to square one where I tried to persuade you to stay away from Kylee, let's progress to last night. When Maggie and I headed in, you and Kylee seemed fine. What happened between then and now?"

"Nothing happened."

"You're going to play it like that, huh?"

"I'm not playing anything. What did or didn't happen between me and that blonde-haired pain in my neck is none of your business."

"Wow. We're supposed to be best friends and you won't let me in. You expect me to spill my guts when something happens but when the shoe's on the other foot, you clam up."

"Stop whining. You sound like Trigg."

"Fine. Deal with your shit by yourself." Ty started the golf cart and directed it toward Quinn's hat.

"Run over it. I dare you."

Ty stopped the cart again. "Stop being a jerk."

Quinn went after his hat and slumped back in the cart. "This is all you're getting, nosey. Kylee's hot. I tried to get her in bed. She has issues. I'm an ass."

Ty was quiet for an overly-long amount of time. It felt like an hour but was probably closer to a minute or two. Finally, he spoke. "You know, Quinn, it's not healthy to constantly degrade who you are."

"Here we go. Lecture time." Quinn made air quotes. "You're going to tell me that I can be so much more."

Ty punched him in the arm. "You're already so much more but you tell everyone you're an ass so no one expects anything from you. It makes people keep their distance."

"Yeah right," Quinn replied with monumental sarcasm, although the analysis was dead-on. He *did* use self-deprecation as a tool to make people back off. Kylee sure as hell backed off last night and again this morning when she left. She'd stated her reasons but there had to be more to it than fear of getting pregnant. Maybe the implied red X of stay-away that he wore on his chest had something to do with it.

"Tell me I'm wrong," Ty prodded.

"You're wrong." Quinn kept his tone lifeless and dry to hide that Ty was making more than just anger surface.

"You're in denial."

Quinn yawned on purpose. "Whatever."

Ty winced and started up the cart. Instead of driving to the first hole he went in the opposite direction.

"Where are we going?"

"Driving range. We're going to hit a hundred balls while we sort things out."

"There's nothing to sort out. I made a move on Kylee. She freaked out. End of story."

Ty brought the cart to a halt at the small building the resort used to dispense clubs, tees and golf balls. He hopped out, grabbed some clubs and a bucket of balls and grinned like a mindless fool when he climbed back in. "You think this is the end of you and Kylee? Guess again, lizard. It's just the beginning."

"You're on something." Quinn wasn't joking when he said he'd put forth effort for Kylee. He'd gone above and beyond what he would've done for most women. Since she passed on a good thing she was history.

* * *

Kylee laid the Lifestyle section of the newspaper on the kitchen table and smoothed out the creases that ran across the photo of her and Quinn. She crossed her arms and glared at the caption – *The Rich Boys Are Keeping It Interesting! Quinn Randel and Kylee Steele: In Love? Or Passing Fancy?* "Passing Fancy," she quipped with soulful acceptance.

She dropped her chin to her chest and thought about the kisses they'd shared in the pool, and the foreplay that took place in the hallway and in Quinn's room. The magnitude of their desire had been off the charts. It still was. She could almost feel the warmth of his lips and the tenderness of his touch.

A sound similar to a sob broke from her chest.

Kylee closed her eyes. It was silly to get so worked up over someone she barely knew. She didn't know Quinn. Not really. She had no idea what his favorite color was, if he played sports in high school, what his job involved. There were just too many missing puzzle pieces regarding His Royal Highness that she should've already put together before she gave him one of her puzzle pieces – her heart. The irony was that Quinn got the opposite of what he wanted.

A small snore filtered from the bedroom off the kitchen. Gabbi was deep in a nap. Kylee traipsed to the box fan she'd placed in the entrance to the bedroom and turned it so it wasn't blowing air directly on Gabs. The window-unit air conditioning was running full boost but the apartment was still hot and stuffy. She was surprised Gabbi was able to fall asleep.

Shuffling to the sink, she filled a large glass with water and dropped in some ice cubes. After a few refreshing sips she went back to the newspaper picture. For appearances sake, she and Quinn looked like two people madly in love. Another weepy sound rolled from a deep, cavernous, well-guarded place – most likely her soul. She set the glass of ice water aside and steepled her hands over her nose and mouth and began compiling a mental check list of the things she *did know* about the guy who, whether he wanted it or not, was the owner of her most fragile part. The first thing that came to mind was that Quinn's blue-grey eyes were his best feature; although, when he was using his lips, they took the number one spot. And when he dressed in simple jeans and a white shirt, he couldn't be dreamier. She'd noted at the resort that he liked his steaks medium-rare…and his women blonde. He was a loyal fan of the Texas Rangers and Dallas Mavericks. Around his friends, Quinn was confident and cocky. In private he seemed to soften and was maybe a little unsure of himself. He drove a Corvette convertible and wore sunscreen with a hint of coconut. He had no problem flaunting his wealth, but he did amazing things with it too, like buy a little girl a dozen Disney DVD's because he wanted to make her happy. And he'd paid for a nanny so that little girl wouldn't be away from her mommy all weekend. Quinn Elias Randel was a great guy but he was no saint, not by a long shot. She shuddered at the memory of him throwing up. Thank goodness Trigg had been there to set the record straight that Quinn seldom drank too much and he couldn't remember the last time his buddy had gotten sick.

She gave Quinn big points for listening to the music of Gary Allan, when he was clearly into heavy metal.

Gabs let out another snore and Kylee thought about the picture Quinn had brought to the resort. She could deal with him being rich, good looking and cocky, but eccentric too?

She wrinkled her brow when the other eccentric Randel

popped into her thoughts. Quinn was a carbon copy of his father, at least in looks. Same hair. Same eyes. Same cocky behavior. Weston was a well-known billionaire snob. Quinn was a well-known millionaire skirt-chaser. Contrary to their personalities and lifestyles, they were world-class philanthropists who raised tons of money for charity. Quinn was easy to be around when he wasn't trying to get her in bed. Weston, on the other hand, kept an aura of intimidation surrounding him so you wouldn't want to be near him for very long. Together, the Randel men were a lot to take on.

Her cell phone plinked with an incoming text message from Angie. 'Moose Tracks on the way. I'll be there in five.'

As soon as the limo driver had dropped them off, Angie cut out of there to pay Charlie a visit instead of telling her what was going on over coffee like she'd promised. She'd been gone for almost four hours and now she was bring home ice cream. When Ange' brought home Moose Tracks is usually meant things were a mess with Charlie. There was a good chance their on-again off-again relationship had resumed off-status. Poor Ange'.

It was going to be a tough week. Ange' would whimper over Charlie and she would try not to whimper over Quinn. Kylee wondered if he sped back to Dallas or if was still at the resort. Did he blow a gasket when he found out she'd left or pull out his little black book to see who was next on his list? He wasn't one to mourn a breakup that was for darn sure. After he and Tori split, he wasted no time moving on. He'd flirted with her right away. A few days later his picture was splashed all over the newspapers with Olivia DiSalle and Tawny Billington.

Angie arrived with the ice cream. She plopped a plastic bag on the table beside the opened newspaper and twisted her mouth as she hawkeyed the picture. "Are you going to frame it? Should I get the scissors?"

"You're a laugh a minute." Kylee started to wad up the

paper but smoothed it out again.

"That picture makes you feel things, doesn't it?"

"It's about to become a thousand pieces of confetti and then we're going to drive by Quinn's building and throw them out the window."

Angie's mouth twitched with amusement. "Bitching is therapeutic, isn't it?""

"If it is, I should feel really good." Kylee slumped down in a chair.

"Instead of throwing confetti, you need to drive to Quinn's condo and jump his bones. A few hours of hot sex would do you a world of good. You want to. So do it."

"A few hours? Sheesh, woman." Kylee puffed out her cheeks and let the air leak out slowly. "Yes. I want to jump his bones. But…"

"There is no but. Throw confetti. Throw your panties. Whatever. Just do us both a favor and do it soon. All that tied-up sexual tension is making you cranky. Sex will loosen you up." Angie moved her arms up and down. "See. It's made me really loose." She giggled. "And don't forget to moan real loud."

"Why should I moan real loud?"

"No reason. I thought I'd throw that out there."

"You're over the top. Thanks, Ange'. I don't know what I'd do without you."

Angie pulled two cartons of Moose Tracks from the bag and cradled one of the cartons to her chest. "Mine. All mine."

"You're not going to eat a whole carton of ice cream by yourself."

"Watch me." Angie retrieved two bowls and two coffee cups from the cupboard. She slanted Kylee a mischievous glance. "You can have a little bit from my carton."

"Thought so."

Angie scooped enough ice cream for four people into the

bowls and filled their coffee cups. Instead of taking a chair at the table, she anchored against the counter and spooned a hefty bite of ice cream into her mouth. She followed up with a piping hot sip of coffee. "We should probably have a cup of alcohol instead of coffee."

Kylee peered over the rim of her cup. "Why should we have alcohol?"

Angie tapped the side of her cup with her fingernails. "Because I need to tell you something."

Chapter Twelve

She was too much work. She had a kid. She was the most uptight woman he'd ever had the displeasure of knowing. She had no intention of sleeping with him from the beginning but she'd led him on for some stupid reason. She was a witch with a freaking halo instead of a broom. She didn't have time for him. She was a nut job.

Quinn sat out on the balcony of his condominium thinking of reasons why he needed to forget about Kylee Steele.

He sipped sweet tea and watched the traffic on the street below. It was as chaotic as his thoughts. Horns sounded. Taxis maneuvered. Drivers tried to beat the red lights. No facade of order down there. None ten stories up either. For a guy who usually thrived on commotion, it was getting on his nerves. Actually, he'd been biting heads off and scowling so much this week that people took one look at him and went the other way.

Quinn put his right hand to his left shoulder and rubbed his tight muscles, trying to get a bloom of tension to release. He did the same thing to his right shoulder. His whole body was a tangle of knots. He'd be smart to take advantage of the exercise room on the third floor or call down to the concierge and have him send up one of the massage therapists the condominium complex kept on staff. But he didn't feel like sweating next to someone in the exercise room who would want to bend his ear about the weather or talk about the best stocks to invest in. He certainly didn't want anyone touching him unless it was…

"Stop being a fool."

Quinn put his feet up on the wrought iron railing and sighed. Ty had warned him against involvement with Kylee. His dad practically brow beat him to stay away from her too. Sam had gotten in on the act. Even Tori had some insight on the subject. If he'd listened to just one of the four he wouldn't be holed up in his condo, brooding and feeling sorry for himself. He'd be out with Trigg and Jake, drinking beer and scoping out women. He'd be happy.

His eyes shot to the newspaper that lay in a heap beside him. He considered throwing it off the balcony. He should've thrown it away on Sunday when he saw the damn thing. Instead, he'd kept it close all week.

He went inside to refill his glass and purposely left the paper outside, hoping it would blow away. As soon as he got to the kitchen and started to pour more tea, he went into a mild state of panic. He clunked the pitcher on the counter and took off to the balcony like his feet were on fire.

The newspaper was exactly where he'd left it.

He couldn't keep acting like Kylee had done him wrong and he needed to stop beating himself up for being an idiot. Something had to give.

* * *

Quinn stood at the end of the long mahogany table meeting the steely-eyed looks of the Board of Directors with a razor-sharp look of his own. He was tempted to answer the unasked question behind those critical gazes. Yes. It really was him. He hadn't set foot in the Board room for awhile so he understood their silent criticism. As Chief Financial Officer it was his duty to keep them updated regarding the fiscal dealings of the company. He'd blown off the last few meetings and let the task fall to his dad.

After spending a week alone, he'd come to some hard fought conclusions about himself, about Kylee and about his future. Ty had been instrumental in helping him finally see the light. He'd have to thank him when he got a chance. Ty had been right about so many things, especially about him being much more than just an ass. This morning, in the shower, Quinn decided to stop being one for awhile. The first test of this new stance came the second he dropped into his high-back leather chair. His father shuffled into Quinn's office and said if he was planning to skip the Board meeting he should leave soon because members were starting to arrive. He shocked his dad by telling him to stop enabling his bad behavior. His dad's mouth had dropped open. Once the shock wore off, Weston Randel squinted with suspicion. "Who are you? And what have you done with my son?" Quinn explained that he was tired of being thought of as a privileged ass that did whatever he wanted, whenever he wanted, with a few other privileged asses. His father asked if this sudden change had anything to do with Kylee. Quinn's automatic response had been, "Don't be ridiculous", yet the question was still in his head, waiting for a real answer.

The last Board member arrived, took the seat closest to Quinn and looked around. "Did I miss a memo? Is this Bring Your Child to Work Day? "

"Freaking hilarious," Quinn muttered under his breath. He cleared his throat. Loudly. It was time to show his father and his constituents that he was a force to be reckoned with and that he was the financial gatekeeper of Randel Holdings. "It's great to see everyone." A few members mumbled that it was great to see him too. Right. They were as cool and unwelcoming as… Damn. They were as cold as he was to most people. The truth took him out of his game for a few seconds. He glanced at his father and received a subtle shoulder lift, which meant it was up to him to earn their respect; something he should've already had.

Quinn squared his shoulders, crossed his arms at his chest and hit each person individually with a firm stare of authority. He wasn't CEO but he was second in command and he would prove to them that he was *so much more* than their current opinion of him. He would prove the same thing to himself by taking direct responsibility, by managing the financial risks, analyzing data and challenging the company's strategy. He would show them he was his father's son. He held up a ten-page stapled document. "I've compiled a month by month report of the company's earnings for the past five years." Quinn pointed to the reports he'd placed on the table in front of each seat. "We have a lot to discuss, so let's get started." He took a deep breath, blew it back out and tried to look every bit the stern executive by narrowing his eyes to slits.

Everyone, including his dad, looked dumbstruck.

Yeah, well, he was dumbstruck too. It had taken a full week of solitude and reflection to figure out who Quinn Randel really was. Although he remained unhappy that the blonde goddess had left him hanging, he was no longer angry with her. As far as his mistakes, he identified the things he'd done wrong over the past several years and owned up to them; at least to himself. He felt bad for stringing Tori along when he didn't have any real feelings for her and now he was filled with regret for letting Kylee get away. In all that brain-cramping self-reflection, he found that he no longer wanted to be poked at or essentially be made fun of in the newspapers and tabloids. He decided to accept what his inner-critic had been trying to tell him all along, that he needed to shuck his who-cares attitude. Dodging his job had to stop too. The biggest revelation to come out of all that thinking shocked him more than he cared to admit. He wasn't ready to share what it was or act on it. He might never be ready.

***

Kylee stowed the last of the dinner plates in the cardboard box that also held her salt and pepper shakers and teapot. The pots and pans, silverware and utensils were next to be boxed up.

As predicted, it had been a tough week for more reasons than just losing her mind over Quinn. After she and Angie killed an entire carton of Moose Tracks, Angie tearfully opened up and shared her tightly guarded secret. She and Charlie weren't off-again. They were more than on-again. Charlie had proposed. Kylee was ecstatic that her best friend had found love. There was a catch that accompanied the news. A monumental catch. The reason Angie had been acting so weird was that the proposal came with an immediate relocation to Cleveland. Charlie had been promoted and his new position was in Ohio. Angie had been struggling with how to tell Kylee she was leaving – not in a few months or a few weeks, but a few days.

Today was the day. In an hour, Charlie and Angie would drive into the parking lot with a U-haul trailer and load up the boxes stacked by the door.

Angie, who rarely cried, bawled like a baby this morning when she emptied her dresser drawers. Kylee saturated a handful of tissues too, but she kept a lot of her tears inside. She didn't want to make things any harder for Angie than they already were.

Kylee glanced at her own stack of boxes. Never in her wildest dreams did she imagine that Angie's new circumstances would trigger some for her and Gabbi. While their apartment was nothing fancy, the rent was more than she could handle on her own. Kylee sniffed and blinked back another round of emotion. "Deal with it, Steele." She couldn't fall apart. Not now anyway. She had to keep it together at least until she and Gabbi got to Arkansas. From the corner of her eye, she caught sight of the newspaper clipping Angie had put on the refrigerator with magnets. The tears she'd been trying to hold back leaked out and ran down her cheeks. She shuffled to the fridge and stared at His Royal Highness until she admitted that the woman in his arms had fallen helplessly, hopelessly, carelessly in love with him. The educated, logical side of her brain rejected the conclusion. The soft, squishy, womanly side told the logical side to suck eggs.

* * *

Quinn watched Sam march to the back of the bar with a towel slung over his shoulder and his hands on his hips. Sam had warned a bride-to-be and the rowdy members of her bachelorette party to behave or he'd toss them out. So far, they hadn't taken his threat seriously. They were up on tables dancing with their cowgirl boots on and starting to peel off items of clothing.

"Get. Down. Now!" Sam shouted. A shirt flew inches from his face and one of the girls stomped hard on the wooden table. "Stop that!"

Quinn almost fell off the barstool when that same girl defied Sam and unsnapped her jean shorts.

"Last warning." Sam held up his cell phone. "Get down and put your clothes back on, or I'm calling the law."

Quinn wasn't interested in the tawdry behavior of the bachelorette party but he was enjoying watching Sam restrain himself. If it was a bunch of guys misbehaving, Sam would have no problem grabbing them by the shirts and singlehandedly throw them out to the street. Since it was women causing the trouble, he was trying a hands-off approach. Basically, he was talking them to death.

The view from the cheap seats was blocked when more ladies decided to join the mayhem. Quinn cocked his head. Get involved? Or get the hell out of there? He slid from the bar stool and headed toward Sam. Before he made it past the first booth, he reconsidered and did an about-face.

"Randel," Sam hollered, "help me out."

Quinn moved his head slowly back and forth. "I'm not touching them."

Sam grumbled a loud noise of frustration. "Then at least take care of my customers."

"You want me to bartend?"

"What part of 'take care of my customers' don't you understand, lame brain?"

Quinn snorted a laugh. "Chill. I'll be you for awhile." He wouldn't make small talk with the customers or listen to them bitch about their pathetic lives like Sam would. His whole reason for being in the bar was to talk to Angie but he hadn't seen her yet. "Where's your help?"

"Long story. Now get behind the bar and wait on my customers."

He mocked Sam with a salute. "Yes, sir."

Quinn easily switched hats from customer to bartender. Once he stepped behind the bar it was nonstop action with people wanting Lone Star beer, strawberry daiquiris, Buttery Nipples, whiskey sours and more. In a short time, he served a phenomenal amount of booze.

Sam managed to settle the bachelorette party down only to have to corral a group of guys who were getting out of hand by the billiard table.

A busty woman with red hair and freckles made eyes at Quinn. "Hey, sugar, y'all want to make me a Texas Tea?"

Y'all? Quinn started to look around but he stopped. There

was only one of him behind the bar but he didn't need to be sarcastic by pointing it out. Some folks said y'all when they meant you. *Y'all* was plural. *You* was singular. It was one of his pet peeves. But hey, he wasn't the grammar police. Besides, some people would say he was wrong and she was right. Whatever.

"Coming right up." Quinn checked the laminated drink guide that Sam kept chained to the beer cooler. He read the ingredients for a Texas tea out loud. "Tequila, rum, vodka, gin, bourbon, triple sec, sour mix and cola." That was enough alcohol to knock a six foot-five, two hundred pound man off his feet. How would this barely five-feet, well-stacked woman handle it? "Are you sure you want one of those?"

"Uh-huh." The thirty-something woman was a real looker and her thick drawl was sexy as hell. "I just broke up with my boyfriend and I'm fixin' to get soused. Y'all want to join me?"

"Tempting, but no. I'm on the wagon." He was on the wagon all right. He vowed to lay off alcohol *and* women until he got his head on straight.

"Well that stinks, hon."

Quinn shrugged. "I've drank so much sweet tea in the last week it's starting to come out of my ears." He handed her the potent drink. "Enjoy."

The redhead didn't wander away. "You look familiar. Do I know you?"

"I get that a lot. Must be my boyish good looks."

"Nothing boyish about you, handsome." Her eyes slid over him. "You're all man."

And you don't stand a snowball's chance in an oven. Usually he was the one teasing women with cheesy pickup lines and it was weird to have one used on him.

The red-haired honey tapped her long, painted fingernails on the bar with a thoughtful look on her face. He could tell when she put two and two together. "Well I'll be armadillo run over by a wagonload of melons. You're that high cotton Quinn Randel." The space between her eyes crinkled. "Why are y'all bartending? Did your daddy cut you off?"

High cotton. The term was used by some folks to describe snobby people of wealth. There was no edge of sarcasm to Red so Quinn wasn't offended. He stifled a laugh instead. In his eyes, he wasn't high cotton, just a lucky S.O.B. He inclined his head toward the ruckus in the back of the bar. "Sam's channeling his inner-brute. I'm channeling my inner-bartender by helping him out."

It was hard not to be thought of as high cotton when there was real news in the world but the newspapers wasted valuable space cataloguing his every move with pictures and sordid headlines.

Someone dropped a quarter in the juke box and Garth Brooks' song, *Friends in Low Places* revved up the crowd.

The woman stirred her drink with the swizzle stick. "I could use a friend for the night."

They both knew she meant a one-night stand with all the trimmings.

Quinn didn't want to hurt her feelings, especially since she was dealing with the sting of a breakup. He knew the feeling and it wasn't the split with Tori that stung. The determined look in the redhead's eyes made him lie. "Sorry. I'm taken."

"I know," she said dejectedly. "I saw that picture of y'all staring at the current peach in your life. I can't catch a break," she whined. "Oh well, if y'all have a weak moment I'll be over there."

Me and my current peach. He wondered what that beautiful, blonde peach was doing right now.

Sam brushed his hands together like he'd shown everyone who was boss. He uncapped a beer and most of it in one swallow.

"You okay?" Quinn asked.

"I am for now." Sam put a hand on the back of his head and one on his chin and cracked his neck. "I thought I was going to have to hog tie those women and then throw a few punches at the guys who were itching for a fight."

The guys had left. The women were still there.

"You handled things pretty good."

"I'm getting tired of the hassle. I'd sell the place but my dad gave it to me as a gift."

"You ungrateful bastard," Quinn said with a grin.

"There's a lot of that going around," Sam quipped.

Quinn stretched his grin bigger. "We're both wearing the same brand of ungrateful shoes. Sucks to be us."

"Some days I feel like I'm stuck between a rock and hard place. You know, wanting something else but your circumstances dictate where you are."

"I know exactly what you mean."

Intuition and curiosity beamed from Sam. "Want to talk about it?"

"Not really."

"Okay then. Any chance you could help me out until closing time?"

Quinn scanned bar. Currently, the place was standing-room only. "Sure thing. But later I want to hear that long story."

"Deal."

The next few hours involved a whirlwind of booze, line dancing, mechanical bull riding, billiards and beer pong.

At precisely three in the morning, Sam flicked the neon sign from open to closed and shooed out the last two guys who would stay there until the sun came up if he let them. "If I had to hear 'just one more beer' I was going to punch somebody."

Quinn sopped up the last of a spilled beer and tossed the wet towel in a plastic bin under the bar.

Sam pulled a beer from the cooler, chugged a few swallows

and sighed with exhaustion. "You saved me tonight, man. I don't know what I would've done without you."

"No problem." Quinn checked the coffee pot. There was at least a cup left. It was as dark as tar. He poured it into a cup and took a taste. It tasted like tar too. "I have a new respect for what you do, Sam." And for Kylee. "Bartending isn't for sissies."

"It's an acquired skill." Sam finished his beer.

Quinn's stomach rumbled. "Let's make some food."

"If you turn out all the lights with the exception of the ones directly above us, I'll rustle up some grub."

Fifteen minutes later they were seated in a booth with a grilled ham and cheese sandwich and a side of waffle fries.

Quinn yanked a pickle from his sandwich and popped it in his mouth. "Time for that long story."

Sam fished two envelopes from his back pocket and handed them across the table. "These will tell the story better than I can."

Quinn furrowed his brows.

"I'm getting another beer. Do you want me to make another pot of coffee?"

Quinn shook his head. He waited for Sam to walk away before he ripped open the first envelope and found a folded sheet of yellow tablet paper; the kind used in kindergarten and elementary school. Tucked inside the paper was the check he'd made out to Kylee. A few expletives fired through his tired brain.

He couldn't believe she'd returned the money since she was low on funds. In a way, he completely understood. She was a hard worker with a big heart and a big conscience. If she felt she didn't earn the money or that it was a handout, it might explain why the check was left un-cashed. Or...she might've thought it was payment for bedroom activities. "Lady, I don't pay for sex." Was the money a subconscious way to lure her between the sheets? His nagging inner-voice piped up with, "Duh".

Quinn flipped the check over a couple of times and lifted it to his nose to see if it smelled like the blonde goddess. To his disappointment, it smelled like paper. Laying the check down, he thrummed his fingers on the table. His eyes swept to the handwritten note that came along with the check. He wanted to read it yet he didn't. There was a good chance she'd told him to jam the money where the sun didn't shine.

He wasn't a wuss. He would read what she had to say and accept it.

'Quinn, thank you so much for the generous compensation for my bartender services. It's a bit much so I'm returning it. Actually, the stay at the luxury resort was more than enough payment. It was a once in a lifetime opportunity and I'm deeply grateful, so is Gabbi. She keeps talking about how much she enjoyed the pool and the carriage ride. Not sure if I mentioned it, but Gabbi has a special affection for horses. I would be remiss if I failed to also thank you for your thoughtfulness with the Disney DVD's. That was beyond kind and I promise to repay you for them when I can. I'm truly sorry about getting you physically worked up, only to walk away. Trust me, that wasn't the plan. I hope you can forgive me'. She simply signed it – *Kylee.*

A weird sound came from Quinn's chest. He recognized it as regret for letting foolish pride, anger and stupidity rule his world for the past week. Did he have a right to be pissed with Kylee? Yes and no. In the short time they'd known each other it felt like they were in a relationship-marathon. They'd pass certain mile-markers and she'd send him back to the starting line. She finally kicked him out the race altogether.

It had taken the entire week to push aside his anger. He involved himself with work to get back on track and to distract himself from the memory of those green eyes and to forget the pain he'd heard in her voice when she said it wasn't going to happen for them. At the time he was too pigheaded to understand her reasons. Now he wished he would've taken her in his arms and kissed away her fears. They could've made love without getting her pregnant. He'd wanted her so much. He still did, but he'd come to accept the consequences of chasing after her to get what he wanted. Kylee wasn't a weekend fling. She was a woman in need of so much more. He was fully aware that he couldn't have a relationship with her without changing his stance about the future.

He tore open the second letter. It held the check made out to Angie and also a note. He read what she had to say right away. *'To Quinn Randel: I didn't want to return your check. Since Kylee returned hers I felt compelled to do the same. Anyway, I wanted to thank you for the weekend at the resort. It was fabulous in every sense of the word. Kylee would knock me silly if she knew the rest of what I'm going to share. Here goes. Kylee has feelings for you. She does. I'm sure she'd deny it until she turned blue. You can take that information and act on it, or be a dork and ignore it. Again, she'd kill me if she knew I told you. There's more. You already know the reason she didn't sleep with you, but it goes deeper than the chance of her getting pregnant. She doesn't want to screw up your life. Asher (the moron) Hutten turned into a shouting maniac when she missed her period. He'd told her upfront he didn't want kids. And YOU told her the same. She went through a lot emotionally after Asher tried to get her to terminate the pregnancy and then again when he walked away. I thought you should know the particulars. With that being said, I should also inform you that I'm getting married, and that Charlie and I are moving to Cleveland. Long story short, by leaving I've put Kylee in a world of hurt. She can't make it on her own so she's moving to Arkansas to live with her mom. My gut says you want her in your life. If I'm right, you better hurry. Don't be a pinhead; do it right now. By the way, I'm sorry I called you 'His Royal Highness'. Yours truly, Angie.'*

Quinn sat back with a million thoughts racing through his head. He read Kylee's note again, and then Angie's. Blinding-white panic made him rush from the booth. His heart was pounding and he was shaking. He was almost to the door but impulsively made a right turn to the whiskey. He poured a shot and stared at it before dumping it down the drain.

Sam came from the kitchen with a bottle of ketchup and a shrewd grin. "What are you still doing here?"

Quinn squinted hard. "You knew all along what was in those letters."

"I had an idea. The look on your face confirmed I was correct."

Quinn considered himself to be a confident man. Some people thought he suffered from too much self-assurance. He wanted to be *that* guy, not the one unable to get his thoughts in line. "I'm not sure what to do, Sam."

"Waffle fries? Or Kylee? The choice should be easy."

Chapter Thirteen

Kylee cocooned herself in a blanket even though it was stifling hot in her apartment. She desperately needed the feel of something holding her tight. She preferred the corded strength of muscle but she'd settle for fleece.

Earlier, she and Gabbi had shared a round of tears after they said goodbye to Angie. They cried, ate the second carton of Moose Tracks ice cream, watched The Little Mermaid three times and cried some more. Around midnight Gabbi fell asleep. It was now almost four in the morning and Kylee hadn't been able to close her eyes for even a second. There was a good chance Gabbi would be awake before she got to sleep.

Instead of turning off the lamp, Kylee covered her face with the blanket to block out the light. She'd overloaded her eyes with so many salty tears in the past week that they felt swollen. Her chest hurt too. Was it possible for repetitious sobbing to crack a rib? It's what she'd done Sunday night and most of Monday and Tuesday. Wednesday her crying jags tapered off to just every once in awhile. Until today. Watching Angie and Charlie wave from the moving van had been almost too much to bear. She was happy for them. At the same time, she never felt so alone. Everyone she cared about, with the exception of Gabbi, had somewhere else they'd rather be. Her mom. Her dad. Ange'. Even Quinn. She wondered where the blond-haired, blue-eyed hunk was at that very moment. She sighed. He was probably fast asleep with a well-built, wealthy blonde curled up next to him.

She crisscrossed her arms tightly across her chest when another pile-driver of misery, insecurity, and desire for the guy who was clearly wrong for her in every way, came without warning.

The pain felt real.

Maybe she really did have a cracked or bruised rib. She could've unknowingly hurt herself when she helped carry Angie's bedroom furniture down three flights of stairs to the U-haul trailer. Or it might be stress coming home to roost. As a student of the sciences, she knew how harmful stress could be. Under certain circumstances it released hormones known to paralyze large portions of the heart. There was a name for it. Tako something. Tako… Tako… Takotsubo's cardiomyopathy. That was it. The condition was also called broken heart syndrome. Maybe she was suffering from a paralyzed heart. It primarily affected post-menopausal women, not those in their twenties. Still…

Kylee pushed the blanket aside and sluggishly worked herself from the couch. She began pacing back and forth in front of the TV that she'd put on mute after she tucked Gabbi in bed. How could she leave Texas for Arkansas? Seriously, how? Arkansas was a lovely state, but it wasn't home. How could she leave everything she'd ever known? She loved The Lone Star state. She loved its blistering heat. She loved the barbeque, the chicken enchiladas, the thick, chocolate cake donuts made only by Mustang Donuts. She would die if she didn't get to enjoy the spectacular sunsets that silhouetted the downtown skyline at the junction of I-30, U.S. 175 and I-45. The ruby red grapefruit alone was a reason to never leave. And no other place on earth had…Quinn Randel. Could she be any more pathetic? She swiped a fresh batch of briny tears from her cheeks.

She wasn't sure how long she paced. It could've been a half hour or just a minute or two. But she was spent. Collapsing into the recliner, her eyelids drooped and lashes fluttered. She chuffed out a weighty breath of fatigue and felt the last bit of resistance leave her body. Sweet sleep was finally knocking at her door.

She jerked. Was knock real?

Kylee dashed to the door and smashed her eye against the peek hole to see if Angie and Charlie had a change of heart. She drew back and leaned against the door to stabilize her sudden wobbly knees. Quinn was not on the other side of the door at… She glanced at her watch. It was four o'clock in the morning.

Another knock made her flinch.

She rubbed her eyes and shook her head. It was a dream. She was fast asleep in the recliner and her mind was doing what it was supposed to do – organizing the days' chaos into a neuro-folder that she could open at a later date. Another low rap made her scrap the folder malarkey. She took one more look to verify she wasn't sleeping and that Quinn was actually standing in the hallway with his hands shoved in the pockets of his jeans, dark circles under his eyes and his normally perfect hair was mussed.

"I hear you moving around, Kylee. Please answer the door."

Kylee went completely still. All week she hoped he would call or stop by so she could tell him she was sorry for taking off like a scared jack rabbit and for leaving him in physical state of discomfort. Now that he was there, she was afraid to let him in the door and back into her life. She wasn't sure her heart could withstand more Takotsubo's cardiomyopathy.

"I'm dog-tired, Kylee, so open up."

Kylee slowly slid the chain from the first lock and then took her time with the deadbolt. She cracked open the door enough to physically confirm what her heart refused to believe. Oh God! It *was* Quinn!

She threw the door open wide.

"Kylee." Quinn's voice was deep with rasp, possibly from lack of sleep. He barely had one foot in the apartment before he swung her against him. Wrapping her in a tight embrace, he repeatedly kissed the top of her head.

Kylee pressed her face into the comfort of his chest. "Quinn, I'm so sorry."

Quinn loosened his arms and worked his fingers through her hair. "I'm sorry too." His eyes drifted over every inch of her face like he was inspecting her for damage. Finally, they settled on her mouth.

He was going to kiss her.

A hot serum of excitement flooded her veins and the urge to cry was overwhelming, but this time it was from joy.

In one fell swoop, Quinn found her lips. He sucked them and kneaded them and drew a moan from somewhere close to her soul. He massaged the small of her back and dropped lower to cup her bottom. "I've needed to touch you and kiss you. I've missed you so much, Kylee."

Kylee could feel the broken bits of her heart slowly being taped back together. "I had a hard time this week without you too."

Quinn kissed the tip of her nose, then each eye lid. He brushed his lips across her cheeks before dropping to her chin to do the same thing. He slowly made his way to the tender spot just below her jaw line. Gently he suckled her skin.

One of his hands wandered from her bottom, glided around to her sweet spot and lingered there. Kylee tensed and Quinn whispered, "Sorry, baby, I can't help myself."

He moved to her chest.

Without removing his eyes, he repeatedly ran his fingers across the plump swell of each breast. He kept pecking her mouth but mostly he watched her reactions to his touch.

Kylee opened and closed her eyes with every delicious move. She let her head drop back when he manipulated her nipples with his thumb and forefinger. He gently squeezed. "Ohhhh, Quinnnnn." Red hot pleasure burned its way through her, singing everything in its path.

"My Kylee," he said, burying his face in her neck.

Quinn's breathing turned to panting gasps and his arousal pressed firm against her thigh.

In a shocking move, he released her with a hoarse groan.

Noooo. She didn't want him to stop. "What's wrong?"

"I have to stop or the thing you didn't want to happen, will." He put his palms up like he was fully prepared to leave the goods alone.

His words were blunt force trauma that projected straight to her heart. Did he purposely come to give her a taste of her own medicine? To turn her on and then back off, like she'd done to him? Kylee's emotions were ragged but she refused to cry. The backbone she seemed to be missing lately, stiffened.

Quinn ran a hand over his eyes and forehead. "I've decided to stop being an ass."

That was a random and odd comment when they were still breathing heavy.

Kylee steepled her fingers her mouth and nose and stared at Quinn over her fingertips. "You're not an ass." She wondered if he meant right now or overall. "You were just reacting to being turned down."

Quinn rubbed the back of his neck and caught sight of the mound of cardboard boxes placed near the end of the couch. "Oh sweet Jesus, you really *are* leaving."

Kylee swallowed hard. "It's complicated."

His face was already tight from sexual strain but now the lines went deeper. "Listen, woman, you can't start something with those incredible eyes and that scrumptious body and then just up and leave."

"Me start something? You're the one who started this, whatever this is. At Ty and Maggie's wedding you toyed with me as soon as you came to get a drink." Kylee closed the small gap between them and laid her hand at the base of his throat. Quinn had skillfully turned her on and was now accusing her of being the culprit who initiated their beginning. Was he teasing or serious? It didn't matter. He was there. And she wouldn't let him leave. If he made a move toward the door, she would rip off her clothes to make him stay. They could continue the discussion naked. In bed. Or on the kitchen table. Against the TV. It didn't matter where. But she wouldn't let him leave and she was willing to let her inner-hussy take charge.

The thought of flesh to flesh with Quinn blasted her with another round of heat. Her breasts tingled against the satin of her bra and explosive currents raced through her veins. She felt lightheaded and blissfully doomed. Completely. Wholly. Utterly doomed. Whatever Quinn wanted, was his for the taking.

"Maybe I started it." Quinn lifted an eyebrow. "Maybe it was fate at play. I clamped on to you and you clamped on to me. Neither of us have let go." He watched a range of emotions play across her expression. Without actually admitting he was right, she was letting her body language say it. The green of her eyes deepened in color and those long, sexy lashes swept across them with invitation. She'd sucked in her belly and thrust her chest out. Miss Kylee Steele looked determined and eager to have him. Even without those signs, the way she'd returned his kisses and the less-than-quiet sounds of pleasure she made was all the proof he needed.

Kylee darted her tongue out to wet her lips.

Quinn felt his pulse speed up again. Not that it had slowed down much. Excitement shot to his groin and the charging bull inside of him wanted to go for the good stuff. Fast. He wanted to kiss her senseless and carry out her unspoken wishes. There was only one thing stopping him. Those packed boxes.

He and Kylee had to talk.

Dammit.

Talking was overrated and it was the last thing he wanted to do, but this was a defining moment for them. In order to keep Kylee in Texas and in his arms, she had to speak her mind and he had to be part of the conversation. "Let's sit down." He slid his hand in hers and led them to the couch.

As soon as they hit the cushions, Kylee snuggled next to him and threw her legs over his thighs.

He was a fool for thinking they could talk. They were both too physically keyed-up. Quinn smoothed a lock of blonde hair behind her ear and gently tapped the side of her head with his finger. "I need to hear what's going on in there. I want to know where we stand and how I can convince you to stay." He planted a soft kiss on her forehead. "Don't hold back."

"I don't want to talk. I want to kiss."

She wasn't going to make this easy.

Quinn caressed her thigh.

Kylee looked at him from beneath lowered lashes. "You really want to talk?"

Hell no, I don't. "Yes. We have to. Since we can't seem to keep our hands off each other, let's start the conversation there. I need to know what you're thinking."

Kylee sighed and shifted so she could face him. "All right. Here goes. We have strong chemistry, Quinn. There's no denying it. When you're around I want to kiss you, run my hands all over you and feel the strength of…" She cleared her throat. "…every last inch of you."

Quinn widened his eyes. "Kyleeee," he warned, "that's not the kind of talking I meant." Although, he preferred it.

She grabbed his arm. "This isn't sex talk. I'm trying to put everything out there."

Quinn nodded. "I'll try not to ravish you until we're

done." He motioned for her to keep going.

"Here's the thing..." She paused. "The thing is..." Kylee still had a hold of his arm. She loosened her grip. Tightened her grip. Loosened. Tightened. "I have a hang-up about sex." She hesitated again as if waiting for a reaction.

Quinn kept his face void of expression but inside he was grumbling. Of all the things she could have a hang-up about, why did it have to be sex? Why wasn't it clutter? Or not letting her peas touch the potatoes on her plate? He had a hang-up about people messing with their phones at the table. Why couldn't it be something like that?

"My issue isn't with making love." Her eyelashes fluttered and she made a noise similar to a moan. "Making love is heaven."

She was doing it again. Maybe on purpose. Maybe not. But she was provoking the beast to full attention.

"The difficulty... No. Not difficulty. My problem stems from fear." She released his arm and picked at her fingernails. Her voice dropped to just above a whisper. "I got pregnant even though we used protection." Kylee laced her fingers and dropped them in her lap.

Quinn was struck by a sudden awareness that Kylee was always in motion. She never seemed to relax, which had to come from constantly having a thousand things to take care of.

He almost chimed in with his thoughts about Asher, which involved substantial meanness and four letter words. Instead, he let her talk.

"I don't regret the pregnancy because being a mom is the best thing that's ever happened to me. I love kids. They're amazing little creatures. At the same time, having another baby and raising it by myself scares me to death." Her voice shook with emotion. "This is going to sound sad and pathetic but it's what eats at me and what drives me to do certain things. Here it is in a nutshell: My mom got pregnant. Dad walked away. I got pregnant. Asher walked away."

"Kylee..."

She put her hand up to cut him off. "I was an oops. Gabbi was an oops. I can't continue the pattern. I have to be responsible. "

"Kylee, you're not an oops. Neither is Gabbi." Quinn took her hands and wrapped his around them. "You're a beautiful woman with a big heart. Gabbi is a beautiful child with a lot of love to give too." He held her soft gaze. "All this is unfamiliar territory for me and there's a good chance I'm going to say something stupid. So don't get hurt or mad. Okay?"

Kylee pulled her lips in and nodded.

"I can't fix what your dad did. I can't fix what Asher did. I can only take care of what goes on between you and me. I want to make love to you. You want to make love to me. We'll be good together and we'll use protection." Quinn winced. "Can I guarantee a hundred percent that you won't get pregnant? No. There are no guarantees. All I can promise is that I won't turn my back on you if it happens."

Kylee was off the couch before he drew his next breath. She clenched and unclenched her hands at her sides and gave him a fierce look before fleeing to the kitchen.

Quinn was hot on her trail. "What did I say?"

Kylee put the kitchen table between them. "You didn't say anything wrong. It's just that if we act on all this chemistry, it'll make moving to Arkansas that much harder."

"*If* we act on all this chemistry? I hate to tell ya, but we've been acting on it for a couple of weeks now. We just haven't taken it to the last level." He tried to slide a few steps forward without her noticing, but damn, she noticed and took the same amount of steps away. "Whether you sleep with me or not, I don't want you to move to Arkansas. Keep your butt firmly planted on Texas soil. Please?"

"I don't have any choice."

Quinn tried again to get closer. Kylee thwarted him by placing a chair in his path. "Is it money? I can help with that." He gave her a firm look. "You should've kept the check you earned bartending."

"I didn't earn ten thousand dollars."

"It was worth ten thousand to have you there."

The falter in her green eyes said she was on the ropes. At least he hoped that's what they were saying.

"Thanks. I think." She yawned behind her hand. Quinn noticed the dark circles under her eyes. His probably looked the same. "Quinn, it's more than just money. I can't work, go to school and raise Gabbi on my own. With Angie gone, I can't get the logistics right. I can't be with Gabbi and bartend. I can't afford to send her to daycare. My mom has offered to let us stay with her for awhile."

"You can't leave."

"Staying isn't an option. I wish it was, but it's not. Besides, I miss my mom and Gabbi misses her grandma. It's time we reconnected with family."

Family was important. He couldn't imagine not seeing his mom or fighting with his dad on a daily basis. Still, he was afraid if she left he'd never see her again. "I'll pay for a live-in nanny."

"Ohhh no. I won't let you. Gabbi and I are not your responsibility."

Quinn threw up his hands. "You're just going to leave."

Kylee looked down at the floor.

"Dammit. Look at me."

Kylee slowly lifted her head. The tears leaking from the corners of her eyes crippled his anger in an instant. He remembered telling Jake he was immune to tears. Turns out, he was as weak as the next guy. He'd also told Ty that he had a perfect life and didn't want to muck it up, but at the moment he was trying hard to do just that. With purposeful long strides, he stormed around the table and shoved the chair out of the way. He didn't touch Kylee but only a few inches separated them. "For years, I was happy being a shallow, self-centered pain in the ass who didn't give a rip about anything. Since I met you I want more from my life. I know that sounds silly, but it's true. Ask Ty."

Kylee blinked at him through dewy lashes. "I don't have to ask Ty. I believe you. I also believe that part of the reason you want me is because I'm not easy. I don't mean that in the physical sense."

Quinn gave her a half-smile. "You're definitely not easy. You're the complete opposite of easy, but the difficulty factor isn't the attraction."

"Then what is it about me that you like?"

"Besides those amazing eyes?"

Kylee's mouth cracked into a grin.

"I love everything about you, Kylee. You're genuine and have an awesome sense of humor. You're not afraid to tell me how you really feel. In my world, that's rare. So many people suck up to me. You don't. You see through the B.S. I dish it out and you dish it back. We're good together. And I know when we finally make love it's going to be epic!"

"I've thought from day one that we were in synch, but being in tune with each other doesn't fix my life." She smiled again but this time her mouth quivered. "If you want to come to Arkansas to see me occasionally, I wouldn't mind."

"I'm not driving to another state to date you."

"Then I guess we should kiss and say goodbye." The tears in her eyes matched those in her voice.

Check mate.

Quinn was out of moves.

He dropped his arms and walked to the counter with his back to her.

A squeal cut into the heavy air surrounding them.

"Quinnnnn." He turned and Gabbi threw herself into him. The blonde pipsqueak wrapped her arms around his thigh and grinned up at him. "I'm so happy to see you," she said so freely and innocently.

Quinn was blown away. The joy he saw in Gabbi's eyes was the same joy he felt for her and her mom, and there was no way he could let either of them slip out of his life.

He knelt down and folded Gabbi in a hug. "I'm happy to see you too."

Quinn glanced up at Kylee. She had her hand across her heart and her eyes were closed. In that moment, the tears he thought he was impervious to, lined the bottom of his eyelids. "Gabbi, I wondered if I could still help you celebrate your birthday in a couple of weeks."

Gabbi's smile took over her whole face. "That would be awesome. You'll have to come to my grandma's house though."

"What do you think about celebrating your birthday at my place? Or maybe at the resort?" He didn't miss Kylee's sharp intake of air.

"Quinn," Kylee said, "you shouldn't offer something like that without clearing it with me first."

"Sorry. Let me rephrase the question. To you." He stood up, put Gabbi's small hand in his and met Kylee eye to eye. "Kylee, will you…" His voice caught in his throat. "and Gabbi, move in with me?"

Kylee's mouth fell open and the size of her eyes doubled. "No," came out right away. "We won't move in with you. You're panicking *and* thinking with the wrong part of your anatomy, Quinn."

"I'm not thinking with my…" Okay, maybe he was. Nothing else explained being that impulsive. "I don't want you to leave Texas and I'm willing to share my digs to keep you here. Plus, it would be great waking up to you every morning."

Kylee shook her head adamantly.

"Just think about it before you decline." His stomach growled loud enough to make Gabbi giggle.

"Sounds like you have a monster in your belly. Don't throw up, Quinn."

"I'm not going to throw up. I need pancakes."

Gabbi's face lit up. "I could go for some pancakes too."

"I know a place that's open twenty-four hours. They make every flavor of pancake you can think of." He smiled at Kylee. "Can we go?"

Gabbi tugged on the bottom of Kylee's shirt. "Say yes, Mom."

"I don't know. I need a shower and a change of clothes."

"You're perfect just the way you are. Besides, it's four-thirty. Not too many people are out and about this early. We can slide in for pancakes and slide back out when we're done. It will give you time to think about my offer and then we'll discuss it tomorrow."

"It's already tomorrow."

"You know what I mean."

Gabbi grabbed Kylee's hand. "I love pancakes."

"You're outnumbered two to one, Kylee." Quinn winked at Gabbi. This was not how he expected things to go. Not even close. But hey, he'd take it.

* * *

You could've knocked her over with a string. Quinn had invited them to move in. Kylee couldn't wrap her head around the generous offer. It was clear the millionaire had no grip on reality and how three toothbrushes in his bathroom, instead of one, would seriously crimp his lifestyle and reputation.

Kylee chuckled behind a forkful of pancake. A few days of stepping on Legos, moving baby dolls out of the way and having The Little Mermaid take over his DVD player, Quinn would be cussing under his breath. Or out loud. He might even hire a hit man to take him out.

Quinn signaled the waitress to bring more coffee by lifting his cup. He grinned at Kylee and at Gabbi, who'd insisted on sitting next to him instead of her. "If my dad could see me now," he said.

"Speaking of your dad, he and Gabbi seemed to hit it off."

"He's a brute most of the time but he has a soft spot for kids." Quinn gently nudged Gabbi with his forearm. "The half-pints win him over with just a smile."

Certain newspapers and tabloid magazines painted Weston Randel as a one-dimensional heartless tool, while others sang his praises as a champion for charity. Kylee had seen at least two sides to Weston in their short acquaintance. She discounted the one-dimensional bit. He'd been angry and uppity upon his arrival at the resort, but when he met Gabbi he seemed like a decent man. The fact he'd raised a pretty great son said a lot about him too. She couldn't help but wonder why the Randels didn't have more kids.

Quinn dragged a bite of multi-grain pancake through a puddle of syrup. "Aren't you going to ask?"

Kylee almost had another bite of pancake to her mouth but laid the fork on her plate. "Ask what?"

"Why I'm an only child."

Holy mackerel, they *were* in synch. "Are you comfortable with me asking something so personal?"

"You can ask me anything."

A warm feeling invaded Kylee. It was different from the heat of his touch or the kind he stirred with his eyes. This was a sweeter, more target-specific warmth that went straight to her heart.

Quinn reached across the table and laid his fingers across hers but quickly removed them to fish his wallet from his back pocket. He flipped it open to reveal his driver's license in one slot and a wallet-size photo of him in the opposite slot.

"It's the same picture you had on your nightstand at the resort."

A sad look covered Quinn's expression, but it didn't linger. "That's not me. It's my little brother Jamie."

"Where is he?" Gabbi asked.

Quinn mussed Gabbi's hair. "He's my guardian angel."

"Oh Quinn," Kylee said softly. "I'm so sorry." She placed her hand across his like he'd done to her.

"Does he have wings?" Gabbi asked.

"Gabs." Kylee wasn't quite sure what to say.

"It's okay, Kylee." Quinn smiled tenderly at Gabbi. "He does."

Kylee was glad the waitress arrived with a freshly brewed pot of coffee. She and Quinn's eyes met briefly. In that millisecond moment he conveyed that he was glad the coffee was there too and when the time was right they would talk again about Jamie.

"How are those pancakes, young miss?" The waitress asked Gabbi.

"They're almost as good as my mom's."

The waitress shot a cheeky grin, first to Quinn and then to Kylee. "Your daughter is adorable."

Kylee started to explain that they weren't a family. Quinn stopped her. "Thanks," he said, pushing his cup over for a refill. "She's three going on thirteen."

"Soon to be four," Gabbi spouted.

"Well I hope you have a nice birthday, sweetie."

Kylee moved her cup so the waitress could top if off. In the process, her fingers brushed Quinn's. Their gazes meshed and she knew that they could no longer deny their feelings or forgo making love. If they held back much longer, they'd both go insane.

Chapter Fourteen

"Drop what you're doing and meet me at Sam's." Quinn ran a bath towel over his hair while holding his cell phone to his ear.

Ty sounded groggy like he just woke up. "Who is this?"

Quinn held the phone out and glared at it. "You know who this is. It's eight o'clock. Get your lazy keister out of bed. We need to talk."

Ty handed the phone to Maggie. "Quinn Randel what are you up to?" she asked.

"Mornin' to you too, Maggie." Quinn chuckled. "Don't worry. I'm not up to anything illegal or rotten. I just want to borrow your husband for awhile."

"We're picking out new furniture this morning."

"Sooo it's a no?"

Quinn heard muffled conversation in the background.

"What do you need and how long will it take?" Maggie asked.

Quinn burst out laughing. "Already cracking the whip, Mrs. Vincent?"

"Better than crackin' skulls," she laughed. "I can lend you this handsome beast for two hours. Three, max."

Quinn had a light-bulb moment. "I want to borrow you too, Maggie."

"Shh. Ty is right here."

"You goofball. I don't want to borrow you in that way. Ty would have my head on a platter."

"Marriage does that to ya. You should try it sometime."

"Ha. Ha. You're very funny early in the morning, Mrs. V. Anyway, could you and Ty meet me at Sam's? I have some things I need to run by you. Oh, if you could have Nancy join us too, that would be helpful."

"Does this have anything to do with a certain green-eyed blonde?"

"Come to Sam's to find out."

"He doesn't open up until eleven."

"Technicality."

"Do you want to meet somewhere else for breakfast?" Maggie asked.

"Normally, I would say yes, but I'm full of pancakes right now."

Maggie mocked him. "Sooo it's a no?"

"Touché."

Maggie giggled into the phone. "We'll meet you at Sam's at eleven. Now quit bugging us. We're newlyweds, ya know."

"Have fun." Quinn tossed the phone on the bed. He changed into a clean t-shirt and jeans and grabbed the phone again. Scrolling through his phone contacts, he located Sam's number.

Sam sounded tired too. "The bar better be on fire or I'm going to knock you silly when I see you."

Quinn felt bad for disturbing Sam's sleep. "I need Angie's phone number."

Sam shared a few expletives before asking Quinn if he'd lost his freaking mind.

"Come on. Dole it out."

"What are you up to, Randel?"

Quinn snorted a laugh. "Same question I got from Maggie."

Sam let out a lengthy yawn. "I assume this has to do with Kylee."

"Again, same thing I got from Maggie."

"Stop bothering people so early in the morning, meathead. I'm going to hang up now and you'd better not call me again until I've had a few more hours of sleep."

"Or what?"

"Or I'll rip your head from your shoulders and use it for a bowling ball, that's what."

Sam was capable of making good on that threat so Quinn got down to business. "Remember what you said last night about owning the bar?"

"Dude, can't this wait?"

"No. It can't." Time was of the essence and he wouldn't waste a minute.

* * *

Kylee looked at the stack of boxes every time she walked past them, trying to decide whether to start loading them into the car or hold off until Quinn came back. When he dropped them off after breakfast, he said he might be gone for awhile but he begged her to stay put. He made her promise.

After a nap that lasted past lunchtime, she perched lengthwise on the couch and read about theories of psychotherapy and counseling. Heavy stuff for an already overcrowded brain. She had to read the chapters twice for the information to sink in. A not-so-easy online test followed. She composed an email for the members of her study group letting them know she might have to drop out for awhile, but she couldn't quite hit the send button. For now it was in draft status. A phone call to her mom was next. They talked about her impending trip to Little Rock and the available job opportunities. Kylee tensed up every time she thought about leaving Dallas. By the time Gabbi was awake, she was a knotted with anxiety and ready to climb the walls. "Road trip," Kylee said, piling them both into her bucket of rust with four wheels. They headed straight to McDonald's drive thru, and then to Lee Park where they dined on their chicken McNuggets and strawberry milkshakes under the comfort of a shade tree. After they ate, they strolled around the park. Gabbi was fascinated by Turtle Creek that ran along the park. Finally, they took a much needed walk on the Katy Trail. Gabbi checked out every flower, bird and stick along the way. By the time they were finished, they were happy, hungry again and a little sunburned because they'd forgotten sunscreen. Kylee glanced at her watch. How could it be dinner time already?

On the way home, traffic on I-635 narrowed to one-lane and there were red brake lights for as far as the eye could see. All eastbound traffic had ground to a halt. Being stuck in traffic was nothing new. Neither was being wedged between two semi-tractor trailer rigs. If you didn't get stuck or wedged once in awhile it meant you seldom left home.

Kylee chewed her thumbnail while they waited. If Quinn showed up and they weren't there surely he'd send her a text asking where they were. She could easily send one to him but she didn't want to seem clingy.

Gabs wanted to sing the alphabet and made Kylee join in. They sang it three times. Counted to fifty twice. And played I-Spy until they covered everything within the visible radius of the car. Kylee popped in Gary Allan's Greatest Hits CD and together they crooned and seat-danced to *Smoke Rings in the Dark*. Had another car been beside them they would've gotten some strange looks. But hey, quality time with her daughter didn't always involve a cushy chair and a story book.

Twenty-five minutes later, the tear in traffic was mended and they were on the move. Kylee pressed the accelerator like a woman possessed while keeping the rust bucket at the posted legal speed. She couldn't afford a speeding ticket or another time delay. She and Gabbi both had to pee so bad the whites of their eyes would soon be yellow. They took the nearest exit ramp, found a gas station and held hands while they ran inside to use the restroom.

Kylee smiled when she recalled making another mad dash for the restroom; the one involving a fight or flight reaction. Today's dash had a little fight involved. It was a combination of milkshake, bottled water and jumpy, eager nerves for the man who turned her knees to jelly and her brain to grits. She must've frowned for a second because Gabbi latched onto it.

"What's wrong, Mommy?"

"Nothing's wrong, sweetheart. Everything is great. Better than great." It was weird coming to that conclusion in a gas station restroom.

Her phone rang from the pocket of her jean shorts. "Hello," she said a little too excitedly.

"Whatcha doing?"

It wasn't Quinn but it was still a call she was happy to receive. "Gabs and I are on our way home from the Katy Trail."

"Lucky ducks. Charlie and I are in Louisiana. We're sitting along I-20 near Shreveport with a flat tire. We ran over a board in the middle of the road with a bunch of nails in it. Charlie isn't a happy camper. He called AAA and they're sending out a repair truck. I thought now would be a good time to catch up with my peeps."

"We're not chickens. Well, sometimes we are."

"We're not roosters. Right, Mom?"

Angie heard Gabbi's question and cracked up laughing. "I miss that little pipsqueak already. I can't wait to hug her neck."

Kylee thought she heard a strange sound in Angie's voice. Did that mean something was amiss? For once she wished Angie would say what was on her mind and get it over with.

Maybe she was having second thoughts about marrying Charlie.

Kylee propped against the restroom sink while Gabbi washed her hands. How was a person supposed to know if they were in love? Your head could tell you one thing while your heart said something else. Your body couldn't be trusted to give you the right answers. The only true wisdom came from the soul. If you felt something soul-deep it had to be love. She thought about her feelings for Quinn. They were deep. Really deep. Soul deep? Maybe.

"Other than a flat tire, how are things going?"

"Greaaaat."

Way too much exuberance. Angie's odd behavior was mostly likely caused by car claustrophobia and caffeine. "How much coffee have you had?"

"Enough I should be bouncing off the walls."

"Cars don't have walls."

"They sort of do. Oh crap. The repair truck just showed up and Charlie is motioning for me. I have the AAA card. I'll call you later." Angie ended the call.

"Ange' sends her love, Gabbi."

Gabbi stared up at her. "Will we ever see Angie again?"

"Of course we will, she's our bestie."

"I'm getting sad again, Mom." Gabs bobbed her head up and down. "This calls for ice cream."

Kylee refused to get weepy over the real likelihood that it would be months before she saw Angie. "Moose Tracks, here we come."

* * *

Quinn bounded up the stairs instead of using the elevator. By the time he reached Kylee's apartment he was out of breath. He knocked and listened for the shuffle of feet. Not hearing anything, he cracked his knuckles and knocked again. He couldn't wait to see Kylee's face when he shared everything he'd done today.

Still no response. He laid his ear against the door and knocked a third time. "Kylee."

The door to the next apartment opened just enough for Quinn to make out a short woman with glasses. "They left," she said in a frail voice.

Quinn rejected the idea. "No they didn't."

"I used to babysit for Gabbi. Today, they drove away."

Quinn fisted his hands at his side. Was Kylee so hell-bent on getting out of Dodge and starting a new life that she couldn't hang around long enough to say goodbye? He'd gone without sleep to put some things in place to keep her in Texas. And she just up and leaves? Again. He was instantly pissed. He started to heavy heel it to the elevator but backtracked to ask the woman if she'd actually seen them load up their car.

"No. I think Marjorie down the hall saw them go. She said they were on their way to Kansas or Nebraska."

"Arkansas." Quinn was no longer fully connected to the conversation. He was already thinking about the quickest way to get to Little Rock.

"Maybe it *was* Arkansas. My hearing isn't what it should be."

"So you didn't personally see them pack up and drive off?"

She shook her head.

Quinn rubbed his forehead. "Thanks for your help." Now what? Realistically, he was too tired to track them down and bring them back. He hadn't slept in over twenty-four hours. A whoosh of exhaustion and frustration rolled from his chest. After the discussion he and Kylee had earlier, he thought he'd convinced her to stay.

The elevator dinged open and a familiar head with blonde pigtails peeked out.

They hadn't left! They were still in Texas and still in his life.

Quinn's anger vanished and he hurried to Gabbi who was now flouncing toward him. He crouched to envelope her in a hug. "I'm glad you're home." His eyes searched and his pulse went into hyper-mode waiting for Kylee.

When she didn't come to them, they went to her. Kylee was busy putting groceries in the crick of her arm because the plastic bag she'd been carrying had split open at the bottom.

Quinn stooped down to help. "I was so worried," he whispered.

Kylee looked frazzled. "Me too." She started to explain that they'd gone out for McNuggets and to stretch their legs and…

Quinn took the groceries from Kylee and laid them back on the floor. He pulled her into his arms and placed a series of kisses on her mouth. Between pecks he said, "I need you, Kylee. And I need Gabbi."

"We need you too, Quinn."

Gabbi leaned into them and the three of them embraced. Gabs got her fill of the gushy love stuff and reminded them they had ice cream. Quinn laughed. If someone would've told him a few weeks ago that he'd be head over heels for a blonde with a ready-made family, he would've given them the bird. But here he was, heart-deep, in that exact scenario. He had serious feelings for Kylee and her daughter, and the thought of them messed with his head. "Come on, ladies, we have ice cream to eat."

Kylee pushed into him with her hip. "Dinner first. We're having tomato soup and carrot sticks. I didn't restock the cupboards or fridge because we were leaving."

"I love tomato soup." It didn't matter what they had as long as they were together.

Kylee searched the few items she hadn't packed. She'd purposely left out the can opener but it was nowhere to be found. The packing process had involved tears and tape, not markers and organization. There was no way to determine which one held the can opener and she wasn't about to start pulling off tape to find the blasted thing. "We might have to order pizza."

"You can't go wrong with pizza." He pulled his cell phone into view. "I'll take care of it." He walked to the far end of the living room and in a hushed tone placed the order.

Odd. He hadn't asked what kind they liked. It didn't matter though. If it came with onions and anchovies she and Gabs could pick them off.

Quinn wandered back and put his hands on her hips. "It should arrive any…" A knock on the door made his eyes sparkle and his lips curl into a smile. "….second."

Kylee quirked an eyebrow. "You have clout, Randel, but not enough to have pizza delivered at the snap of your fingers."

Quinn started for the door. Kylee stepped in front of him and opened it to find Ty and Maggie, Trigg, Nancy, Jake and Tori. "Umm…" She tried not to show her surprise but she couldn't stop her face from scrunching with confusion. "Come in."

Trigg carried in several pizza boxes. Ty had a case of Coke. Jake had a twelve pack of Lone Star. Maggie had a plastic grocery bag hanging from her wrist that held paper plates, Dixie cups and napkins.

"Good thing I couldn't find the can opener."

From beneath one of the couch cushions Quinn produced the opener. "You mean this one?" He smiled like he pulled a fast one.

"How in the world?"

Gabbi giggled. "Quinn and I tricked you. When you weren't looking he tiptoed to the couch with the opener."

"Nark," Quinn teased but gave Gabbi a high-five.

Kylee pretended to be irked by closing her eyelids halfway, but the corners of her mouth went up on their own.

Maggie gave Kylee a hug and shared some truth. "You

have to watch him every minute. Next he'll be hiding your underwear."

Kylee deliberately tugged her jean shorts a little higher. "Thanks for the tip."

Trigg sat the pizza boxes on the coffee table and was about to take a slice from the box marked deluxe.

"Drop it, Sinclair."

Trigg laughed and took a bite. "Who's going to stop me?"

Nancy wrinkled her nose with amusement. "Quite the bunch, aren't they?"

"They are," Kylee said, still curious as to why they were there.

"Everyone back away from the pizza," Quinn ordered. He lifted his wrist to expose his watch. "The others should be here anytime now."

"The others? Quinn, please explain." Kylee crossed her arms. Quinn remained tight-lipped. "Are you staging an intervention?" She looked to Maggie for answers. If anyone would give it to her straight, Maggie would.

Maggie turned an imaginary key at her lips and pretended to toss it over her shoulder.

Nancy lowered her head so she wouldn't be coerced into giving anything away.

Tori lifted her chin and looked away.

Kylee got the same sealed-off, don't-bother-asking expressions from Ty, Trigg and Jake.

Last but not least, she used her forefinger to motion Quinn closer. "Tell me what this is or…" She poked his chest and dropped her voice so Gabbi wouldn't hear. "…I won't let you hide my panties."

Quinn opened his eyes wide. "Hold that thought."

A noise outside her door sounded like a herd of cattle coming through.

Trigg smashed his eye in the peek hole. "They're here."

Kylee begged. "Please. Tell me."

Quinn spoke softly. "Trust me."

"I do."

"Then take a deep breath and let this happen."

"Let what happen?"

"Deep breath."

Kylee pulled in enough air to fill her lungs and blew it back out.

Quinn nodded to Trigg. "Let them in."

Kylee's mouth dropped open when Angie and Charlie walked in. "Ange'?"

Like they were on a runway, Angie blew her a kiss and pulled Charlie aside to make room for Sam. "Sam?" Kylee put her hand to her forehead and moved her head back and forth. "Oh sweet Jesus!" rolled off her tongue when Weston Randel entered with a strikingly beautiful woman who Kylee assumed was Vera Randel. No wonder Quinn encouraged her to take a deep breath. The room was closing in with so many people standing around looking at her, waiting for some kind of reaction. The only show they were getting was her mouth dropping open and then snapping closed. She was probably turning white too from getting lightheaded.

Gabbi broke the awkwardness by running full speed at Angie. "I've missed you so much, Ange'."

Angie scooped Gabbi up and planted kisses all over her face. "I've only been gone for a day."

"It seems like forever."

Kylee met Angie's eyes. "There's no way you were in Louisiana."

"Yeah. About that."

Quinn put a finger across his lips to shush Angie. He slid his hand into Kylee's and gave it a squeeze. "I can't wait for you to meet my mom, but first we have one more guest set to arrive."

"I feel dizzy, Quinn."

"Buck up, sweetheart."

Trigg opened the door a little wider to give entry to the last visitor.

Kylee felt the muscles in her legs loosen and she swayed into Quinn. If she was blown away before nothing compared to now. "I don't know what to say."

Quinn held her steady. "How about you introduce me to your mom and I'll introduce you to mine."

Kylee hurried hand-in-hand with Quinn across the room. "Mom." Quinn dropped her hand so she could wrap her mother in her arms. "It's so good to see. I'm a little mystified as to why you're here but we'll sort that out in a little bit." She squeezed her mom again. "I've missed you so much."

There were tears in both their eyes and her mom clung to Kylee like she was getting a quick daughter-fix. "I've missed you too, honey." She fished a tissue from her pocket and dabbed her eyes. "I've been a little weepy without you."

"Same here." Kylee sniffed back a splash of emotion and slanted Quinn a look of appreciation. "You play dirty when it comes to getting what you want, but I'm glad you do."

Quinn gave her a small nudge and cleared his throat.

"Oh sorry." Kylee looped her arm possessively through Quinn's. "Mom, this is Quinn. Quinn this is my mom."

Quinn took Kylee's mom's hand and planted a chivalrous kiss on top. "Happy to meet you."

"Likewise."

Kylee watched her mom blush. What was it Nancy had said about Quinn at Ty and Maggie's wedding? Oh yeah. 'Too smooth for his britches'. Truth.

"I can't wait to get to know you better," Quinn said.

"Kylee, this one's a keeper," her mom declared.

"He's a keeper all right. Of secrets."

Her mom smiled. "Most men are."

Quinn swept across the room to get Gabbi and bring her to them.

"Grandma," Gabbi said shyly.

"Hey, punkin." Kylee's mom held out her arms and Gabbi instantly filled them.

Kylee's heart squeezed. Gabbi needed to know her grandmother. Without moving to Arkansas it would be difficult to give Gabbi that special relationship known only between a grandchild and grandparent. A whimper crept up her throat but she muffled it in time.

"Ladies, it's time to greet my parents." Quinn put an arm around Kylee and the other around her mom who was holding onto to Gabbi like she'd never put her down.

Weston and Vera Randel had taken a place on the couch and were patiently waiting to be acknowledged.

Quinn dropped his arm but clutched Kylee's hand and gave it a squeeze. "Dad. Mom. Thanks for coming."

Weston stood up without a speck of intimidation. He helped his wife from the couch.

Kylee's palms started to perspire and a salty bead of sweat dotted her upper lip. She wasn't anxious about meeting Quinn's father again, but when it came to meeting his mom she was beyond nervous. Vera Randel was a gentle force in society. According to the newspapers she made things happen but shunned the credit and tried to escape the limelight. Nice or not, Vera would run down a mental checklist to see if Kylee passed inspection. That's just how it was. As a mom herself, Kylee knew it would be intense even if Vera smiled the entire time.

"Kylee, you know my dad."

Kylee nodded. "Nice to see you again, Mr. Randel."

The lines etching Weston's eyes crinkled. "Weston," he said.

"Weston," she repeated.

"And this is my mom, Vera."

Kylee imagined Vera clicking her pen, ready to start making check marks and X's on that invisible checklist. "Pleased to meet you, Mrs. Randel."

"I'm delighted to meet you too, Kylee. I've heard a lot about you. I'd be tickled if you'd call me Vera."

She'd heard a lot about her? From Weston? Yikes. "Thank you, Vera."

"And this is your mother."

Kylee drew her mom forward and made the introductions. The two women clicked right away. Her mom mentioned seeing Vera's picture in the newspapers and that she was lovelier in person. Vera made her mom feel at ease too by saying she could see where Kylee had gotten her good looks.

From her peripheral, Kylee watched Quinn. He was homed in on both mothers.

Vera's gracious smile stretched as wide as her mouth would allow. "So this is the sweetheart that Weston went on and on about." She extended her hand to Gabbi. Kylee held her breath. With kids you never knew from one minute to the next what they would do.

"You have pretty eyes," Gabs spouted and gave Vera's hand a hearty shake.

Weston leaned into his wife. "I told you she was bright."

Kylee and Quinn's eyes locked; so did their smiles.

"Why thank you, Gabbi. Yours are pretty too."

The place became a buzz of conversation. Vera and her mom wandered to the kitchen table with Gabbi. Ty, Jake, Trigg and Sam popped open a beer. Maggie, Nancy and Ange' opened the pizza boxes and passed out paper plates. Tori didn't move from her perch by the front door and kept her eyes glued to Jake. Quinn headed down to his car to get another case of beer from his trunk and Kylee used the opportunity to head to the bathroom. She closed the door and sagged against it. For all practical purposes, this seemed like nothing more than a gathering of friends and family. Kylee knew better. Quinn was either hosting an intervention like she'd suggested or he was staging a coup.

Kylee splashed cold water on her face, blotted it with a towel and looked in the mirror. No one would believe that sitting in her small, stuffy living room was one billionaire and seven millionaires. Holy crap. Even she didn't believe it. She opened the door just enough to peek out.

Her mom and Vera were laughing at something Gabbi had said.

Everyone else, except for Weston, was crowded around the TV watching the Texas Rangers play the Seattle Mariners. The game was tied. Trigg accused the umpire of trying to rush the game by making bad calls. Jake claimed the runner was safe. Sam mentioned that it was only the second inning and that they shouldn't get their panties in a bunch.

Weston tapped the top of his beer can with his thumb while repeatedly glancing at the door. His solemn expression changed to a half-smile when Quinn returned.

"Kylee," Quinn hollered above the noise.

Kylee removed the elastic tie from her pony tail, gave her hair a quick brush through and let it hang down around her shoulders. She wished she was wearing something other than a drab olive-colored t-shirt and cut-off jean shorts that had a few wayward strings that needed snipped with scissors. She inhaled a stout breath and headed for the living room.

Quinn had his hands behind his back and a serious look on his face. "I need to ask you something, Kylee." He pulled two small boxes with silver bows into view.

Kylee's heart squeezed and the air caught in her lungs. There was no way. This was not what it looked like. It couldn't be.

Chapter Fifteen

What had he been thinking by inviting everyone there to witness a possible rejection? He hadn't considered that Kylee would say no until now. Her green eyes were huge with surprise and she was biting down hard on her bottom lip.

Quinn handed the boxes to Ty.

"Gabbi, can you come here?" Quinn lifted her in his arms, pecked her forehead with a kiss and then stood her beside him before he dropped to one knee.

Quinn felt Kylee tremble when he took her hand. "Kylee," he said, swallowing a lump the size of a coconut. "From the moment I laid eyes on you I knew something was going to happen between us. I didn't think it would be this." He smiled. "But I chased you until you caught me. Boy did you catch me. Three weeks ago I was a guy dead- set against marriage. Almost everyone here can vouch for that. I was completely in charge of my life and what I wanted and didn't want. And then I met you." He huffed out a breath and watched Kylee blink rapidly with dewy lashes. "What I'm trying to say, is that something has changed inside of me. That sounds corny, but it's true. You've changed everything and I want to keep you in my life. I want Gabbi there too. I have to give you fair warning though. I've adjusted my outlook on a few things, but I'm still me. There will be times that you'll want to tear your hair out because I can be an insufferable…," he almost said ass. With Gabbi there he changed it to, "…donkey."

A muffled comment from the peanut gallery made Quinn look over his shoulder. Ty shrugged. "What? All I said was true that."

Quinn gently squeezed Kylee's hand. "Despite my flaws I hope you want me because I want you. Marry me. Be my wife."

"Quinn," Kylee rasped tearfully, "I want to say yes but I can't easily forget that you said you didn't want to be married and you didn't want kids. You made that perfectly clear on a few occasions. I have a child. And as much as the fear of me getting pregnant has stood in our way, at some point I want another child. Gabbi deserves a brother or sister."

Gabbi spontaneously said, "Sister."

"A sister would be great, Gabbi." Quinn dropped his head, swallowed hard and looked up at Kylee with tears blurring his vision. "There's something you should know; something I should've told you from the beginning." He sniffed to try to hold his emotions in check. "When Jamie died it hurt so much. It was excruciating and I never wanted to go through that again. He had a congenital heart defect and I didn't want to risk fathering a child with a similar issue and then losing them. My own heart wouldn't survive if that happened."

He lost the battle with his tears. They rolled down his cheeks.

Kylee had tears leaking from her eyes too. "I didn't know."

Quinn looked away to compose himself. He heard sniffs from others in the room, possibly his parents. Reminding them of their loss had to be painful but hopefully what he was about to do would bring them a measure of joy.

"Today was incredible, Kylee. I got answers to a lot of questions. I discussed proposing to you with Ty and Maggie. Maggie surprised me by asking what took me so long. She apparently knew we'd be right for each other." Quinn's thoughts were all over the place. "Did you know Maggie and Nancy are nurses in the heart unit at Carriage Memorial?"

Kylee nodded.

"Well, I picked their brains. Nancy explained that a congenital heart defect isn't necessarily a genetic disorder. My mom explained the same thing a long time ago but I must've been too distraught to listen. The reason I'm telling you all of this is so you understand why I said I didn't want a wife or kids. When I thought I was losing you to Arkansas, I realized that I had to put my fears aside to keep you in my life. How do I say this without sounding desperate or like a whack-job?" He exhaled loudly. "Falling for you has realigned my brain. Ask my dad. Instead of being an anchor to his hard work I'm trying to be a sail. I want to be a man you'll be proud to have by your side."

He heard Angie say, "Aww."

"I want you by my side. If you'll have me. Together we can do good things. A little birdie," he looked at Angie, "told me today that you give part of your hard-earned tips to food pantries." He got choked up at the thought of Kylee barely scraping by but faithfully giving back to an organization that helped her when she needed it the most. "I want you to know that together we'll continue to give our support." He cleared his throat. "You've been working your butt off to keep everything in balance while trying to get your degree. As my wife, you'll have time to study and time to spend with Gabbi. If you're as fertile as you claim, we're going to have a lot of little Randels to tend to. It might be chaos but I'm up for it. I love you, Kylee. I know we haven't been together long, but I love you. I do. Before I grovel like a pathetic dweeb tell me you love me too and that you'll marry me."

Kylee pulled Quinn to his feet and placed a hand on his chest. Her voice was thick with emotion. "I've protected my heart for so long because the men in my life have tossed me aside. But I let my guard down for a little while and you found your way in. I love you too, Quinn," she said softly. "I'm giving you my heart. Please handle it with care."

"Oh God, Kylee!" Quinn wrapped her in a tight hug and kissed her with everything he had. "I love you so much," he said close to her ear. "I'll handle your heart with care, and Gabbi's too. You don't have to worry about me tossing you aside. I'm keeping you. Forever."

Kylee was beside herself with joy. Her pulse was thumping hard and she could barely breathe but she couldn't imagine being happier than she was at that moment.

Ty handed Quinn the small wrapped packages he'd held for safekeeping.

Kylee's hands shook when Quinn handed her the first package. She carefully untied the silver satin bow, lifted the tape from the wrapping paper and opened the box. Gleaming up at her was a dazzling white gold ring with a brilliant-cut round diamond in the center flanked with a thin row of pave-set diamonds on each side. "It takes my breath away, Quinn." Her hand shook when she handed Quinn the ring so he could slide it on her finger.

"Angie helped me pick it out."

Kylee's gaze flew across the room to Angie.

Angie put her thumb and forefinger together. "Little white lie about being in Louisiana. The flat tire wasn't a fib though. We got it just outside of Dallas. After we got it fixed we decided to spend the night in a hotel. This morning Quinn called."

"Thanks, Ange'. For everything." Kylee blew her a kiss then smiled at Quinn. "You're an amazing man, Quinn Randel."

"I couldn't have pulled any of this off without help." He held up the second box and handed it to Gabbi.

Gabbi squealed with delight and wasted no time tearing

the bow and paper off. "It's a diamond necklace that looks like your ring!" She mimicked her mom. "You're an amazing man, Quinn Randel."

Everyone cracked up laughing including Kylee, but she was also on the verge of tears again. Sheesh. For a woman who pulled all-nighters studying and taking tests that stretched the limits of the brain, worked full shifts at the bar, spent time with her daughter and kept the apartment relatively tidy, she was a weepy wimp when it came to love. She stretched up to kiss Quinn. "Thank you for including Gabbi."

"We'll never leave her out."

Any latent doubt she might've had about Quinn vanished before the next pump of her heart. The happiness she felt went…soul deep.

"Woo-hoo! Time to celebrate!" Trigg came through the door with an armload of champagne bottles.

"Where'd you get champagne?" she asked.

"Quinn stashed it outside your door."

Kylee flashed a smile at Quinn. "You've thought of everything."

Trigg popped the corks and Tori passed out paper cups. When she reached Kylee and Quinn, she shook her head. "I'm not sure how you did it, chick, but you managed to take this big lug out of his comfort zone and he seems to like it. Quinn and I were square peg-round hole from the start, but you two are a perfect fit. As hard as it probably is for you both to believe, I'm happy for you." She gave them each a hug.

"Thanks, Tori. That means a lot," Quinn said.

Kylee gave Tori a second hug and whispered, "If you feel strongly about Jake, don't give up."

Weston, Vera and Kylee's mom worked their way over with a bottle of champagne. "This is an remarkable day for all of us," Weston said, filling their cups.

Ty whistled to get everyone's attention. "Quinn, I knew

the moment you set eyes on Kylee that you were a goner. You said Kylee realigned your brain. Well, Maggie realigned mine. It's one of the side effects of love, my friend." He raised his Dixie cup. "To Quinn, Kylee and Gabbi: may today be the beginning of a lifetime of happiness. Cheers." After a swallow of bubbly, he added, "Half of our little group has fallen fast. Jake. Trigg. You're next."

Jake rolled his eyes. "No one's realigning *my* brain."

Trigg swiveled toward Nancy with a goofy grin. Nancy lifted an eyebrow. "Back away, Sinclair." Quinn and Ty roared with laughter. Jake shook his head and spilled his drink.

Sam took a step forward. "I have to get going. My temporary help is probably overwhelmed right now. Nevertheless, I wanted to offer my congratulations. I also wanted to thank Quinn for coming up with a plan regarding the bar. As most of you know, I've wanted to step away from the bar for quite awhile. This morning, when I was trying to get my beauty sleep, he bugged me until I wanted to swat him upside the head. In the end, I'm glad he did." He zoomed in on Kylee. "Your mom and I have a surprise for you."

Kylee's mom moved next to Sam. "Sam has made me an offer I can't refuse. Your stepdad and I are going to manage the bar."

Kylee put her hands over her nose and mouth in shock. "Really?"

"Really." She hugged her mom and did the same to Sam before throwing herself into Quinn. "This means the world to me, Quinn." She was smiling with tears spilling down her cheeks.

Her mom's eyes were a watery mess too. "Every time we talked on the phone I was crying in the background. When Sam offered the job, your stepdad and I jumped at it."

It dawned on Kylee that her stepdad hadn't made the trip. "Dad's not with you."

"He's so excited to be moving back, Kylee. He stayed behind to pack up our things. He should be here mid-week."

"How did you get here?"

"Trigg came and got me. I got to ride in his plane. Pretty cool, huh?"

"Technically, the plane belongs to my dad," Trigg said. "I tell everybody it's mine."

"I owe you, Trigg. Thank you so much," Kylee said.

"You don't owe me a thing. You're one of us now." He bent and kissed the top of her head.

Jake refilled their cups with more champagne. "You and Quinn have some kind of strange magic between you. I never would've believed it if I hadn't seen it with my own eyes. I'm tickled for you two. I mean you three." He winked at Gabbi. "I want to offer my services with planning your wedding. Quinn knows I'm a person with an eye for detail."

Kylee pressed her lips together and turned to Quinn. "You and your parents have lots of family and friends, but I really don't go for a lot of pomp and circumstance. Would it be okay if we had a small wedding?"

"If you want small, we'll do small," Quinn said.

"It's okay with us too, dear," Vera said. "You and Quinn can have whatever size wedding you're comfortable with. Afterward, Weston and I can throw a huge party with our friends to celebrate becoming grandparents. We were the only ones without grandchildren." Vera beamed a smile at Gabbi. "Now we have a beautiful little granddaughter."

"Sorry, Jake," Kylee said.

"I can throw together something small but elegant. All you need to do is name your wedding party, pick out dresses and tuxes, and show up. I'll take care of the rest."

"You're on, Jake. But what about flowers and a cake?"

"The cake will be simple. Three layers. White. Chocolate. Yellow. And the flowers are no problem either. Angie said your favorite is tiger lilies."

"Ange', you're the best."

"Can you have it all pulled together by next Saturday?" Quinn asked.

"What?" Kylee started a chain reaction. The question echoed around the room.

"Next Saturday," he repeated. "It's Gabbi's birthday." He softened his voice. "I'm giving her a dad for her birthday." He leaned into Kylee to whisper, "I'm also giving her a horse, but we'll keep that quiet until then."

Chapter Sixteen

How had he gotten so lucky?

Quinn eyed his bride from his perch by the main fountain at Lee Park while he sipped sweet tea from a crystal champagne flute. Kylee was beautiful and smart and madly in love with him. She and Gabbi were standing a few feet away getting their pictures taken to grace the cover of a magazine published by Jake's family. The exclusive photo shoot was Jake's wedding gift to them. He said it was a good way to properly introduce the newest additions to the Randel family.

Jake sidled next to Quinn. "It's going well, I think."

"Understatement." Quinn gave Jake a manly half-hug. "Thanks for everything, buddy." An outdoor wedding with all the trimmings was hard to pull off even with a year of pre-planning, but Jake made it happen in a handful of days. They'd said their vows under a stately shade tree and had a delicious meal under a white wedding tent set in the middle of the park. They dined on grilled Atlantic salmon with mango citrus chutney, butter poached filet mignon, and something with cornmeal and bacon. Quinn couldn't remember what they were called but he'd scarfed them down and had the server bring more to the table. They also had blistered tomatoes in a puff pastry. He'd shoved his aside. He wasn't about to eat anything blistered.

"No thanks needed. We're friends. Besides," Jake nodded toward the photo shoot, "those pictures will sell a ton of magazines. I imagine the newspaper editors and tabloid bosses are going to kick some reporter and paparazzi ass for missing out."

So far they'd managed to throw the news media off course. Thanks to Jake. He'd put out a rumor that Quinn and Kylee were getting married in Bali. There would be a few ticked off reporters when they found out differently. Quinn also knew that before the reception was over, someone would tip them off and they'd show up at the park. "Those goons will go absolutely berserk."

It was true that the Garrison publishing empire would make a fortune from those pictures, but Jake's heart was pure. He'd set the photo shoot up because he knew it would make Quinn happy. Jake was an all around good guy; a quiet people-pleaser. There was only one person Jake wasn't out to please – Tori. She'd cast her net and he kept swimming in the opposite direction.

The caterer motioned for Jake.

Quinn slapped him on the back. "When it's time for you to tie the knot, I'm there for you."

"No tying of knots for me, thank you very much. I'm happy being on my own."

"Uh-huh. We'll see."

"Kiss my pasty white ass, Randel," Jake said, laughing his way over to the caterer.

From behind, someone used their knees to buckle Quinn's.

Quinn tried to keep from falling. He turned to find Ty smiling like he didn't have his right mind. "Hey, knot-head."

"Hey, dork-face." Ty tapped the white gold bank on Quinn's left hand. "You did it."

"We did." Quinn's gaze drifted to Kylee. His wife. The woman he would soon have in his bed. The woman he loved.

"Wasn't it you who said you'd never be caught with a ring through your nose?" Ty arched his eyebrow high to heckle.

"It's on my finger, not my nose."

"When I was going gaga over Maggie I distinctly remember you ribbing me about having a ring through my nose." Ty took a drink from his engraved beer stein and smacked his lips. "A ring on your finger and one in your nose. Accept it, Randel."

Quinn smiled. "With just a few words I went from bachelor to husband to father to son-in-law."

Trigg joined them. "Let's lay odds. Who do you think will be the next to fall? Me? Or Jake?"

Quinn and Ty both said, "Jake."

"Ha! Guess again. It's going to be me." Trigg hawk-eyed a certain blue eyed blonde that was standing close to the photographer. "All I have to do is convince Nancy to go out with me." He used his hand to make a wave. "It'll be smooth sailing from there."

"I'm thinking choppy seas. What do you think, Ty?"

"Rough waters, for sure."

"I hate you guys." Trigg snorted a laugh. "But you're probably right. Reeling in Miss Nancy Reeger won't be easy, but then, nothing worth having ever is."

Quinn and Ty shared a look of amusement. "Ring through his nose," Ty quipped.

Nancy was on the move and Trigg was a few steps behind her.

Ty shook Quinn's hand and went to refill his beer stein.

Quinn watched Gabbi lean against her mom, giving the photographer fits. The photographer's assistant made her stand straight, adjusted her small bouquet of ditch lilies and fixed the white ribbon that was trying to slide off her head."

Ditch lilies. Of all the beautiful flowers in the world, Kylee's favorite was ditch lilies. That said a lot about her. She was down to earth and didn't have an ostentatious bone in her body. He, on the other hand, liked the better things in life. Would that cause problems later on? Maybe. But he'd never let it tear them apart.

Gabbi caught Quinn watching and waved. Kylee followed suit with a small wave.

Vera Randel nudged Quinn with her shoulder. "Gabbi's excited to spend a few days with us while you and Kylee are on your honeymoon. Your dad's excited too. He's going to take her to the office and show her off. I haven't seen him this happy for a long time. He's going to love being a grandpa, Quinn, and I already love being a grandma." She lowered her voice. "We're happy for you, son."

"Thanks, Mom. Kylee and Gabbi are what I've needed for a long time."

"I know. They've needed you too. By the way, did you get Gabbi a horse?"

"We've decided to hold off on that for awhile. Gabbi's a bright kid but she's only four and we've thrown a lot at her these past few weeks. We're going to give her some time to get used to her new life."

"Probably a good thing."

"You've said all along that it takes strong women to put up with Randel men. Kylee will have her work cut out for her. Gabbi too. So I'm only going to make them deal with one horse's ass at a time."

Vera smirked. "Keep that sense of humor, Son."

Angie stepped from the tent and clapped her hands. "We would like everyone to join us for a few minutes."

The photographer nodded that he was finished. Kylee gave him a swift hug. Gabbi followed suit.

Quinn scooped Gabbi up and looped his arm through Kylee's. "Let's go see what Angie needs."

As soon as they were under the tent, the small crowd

serenaded Gabbi with "Happy Birthday" and then parted so she could see what was waiting for her on a far table. Gabbi's face sparkled like Christmas. Her eyes grew to the size of quarters and her smile couldn't stretch any wider.

Quinn put her down and Gabbi took off like her feet were in roller skates. When she saw The Little Mermaid cake, she squealed. "Ariel!" She looked back at Quinn and Kylee. "Mom. Dad." She pointed to the cake. "Ariel!"

Dad. Just like that. She called him dad. It took a lot to make him cry but he felt tears collect in his eyes. Being a father would take some getting used to, but he was ready for it. More than ready. And being a husband... Awesome!

Kylee slid her arms around his waist. "I love you, Quinn."

"I love you too, Kylee."

She gave him a slow, seductive grin. "After cake, can we can say our goodbyes and get started on the honeymoon?"

Quinn's pulse went into hyper-mode. He dragged his lips across her forehead and then to her ear. "I thought you'd never ask."

* * *

Kylee climbed into the limousine, kicked off her heels and lowered the zipper of her form-fitting, stretchy red dress just enough to expose a hint of cleavage. Tonight, she and Quinn would finally give in to all that fire that had been building since they met. They almost gave into it the night they got engaged. Sunday, it almost happened again. The few times they were alone during the week, things got to the combustible stage but they backed off before it was too late. They didn't purposely get each other revved up only to leave things unfinished, they just couldn't help themselves. A glance or a smile was a good as striking a match to kindling. They'd slam into each other, kiss until they were panting and explore each other with their hands and mouths. Quinn had been the one to keep his head. He'd pull away fully aroused and barely able to breathe. "We can wait," he'd said. Kylee wasn't sure if he was trying to convince himself or her. She had to admit, it had been more than difficult to power-down after being powered-up, but she understood his reasons for wanting to wait and they made her love him that much more. He was determined – for her sake – to break the pattern of *oops*. If she got pregnant right away, he wanted it to happen when she was officially Mrs. Randel.

Finally, it was time to stop backing off. Kylee grinned wantonly and lowered the zipper a little more.

Quinn said a few words to Henry and climbed into the limo. The second he spotted cleavage his eyes all but popped out of his head. "Kyleeeee."

Obviously, he approved.

Quinn's eyes danced over her, making Kylee take a deep breath. He slid across the seat and brought the heat. He gathered her in his arms and kissed her with so much fire they could've easily melted the expensive leather seats. He sucked her lips, parted her mouth and went in for a deeper, more sensual invasion.

Kylee voiced her appreciation.

Sliding her zipper down to give him better access, Quinn pushed her bra up to expose the fullness of her chest. In one fell swoop he was on her breasts with his tongue and lips, kissing and pulling, teasing and tantalizing. Her nipples stood erect and happy. He trailed his tongue to the swell of her breasts, lathering them with warm, moist attention. He kissed and nipped her skin while sliding up her thighs with his hands. He whispered his love against her tender flesh while he sought the treasure under her dress.

All that pent up sexual need burst forth. "Quinnnnn," she called in a raspy voice, trembling from so much want. Hot. Delicious. Want.

Quinn's fingers glided across her belly to hook his thumbs in the elastic of her lacy panties. He slowly tugged them down until they were off. Tossing them aside he laid his mouth against her neck and gently suckled while his fingertips sought her sweet spot. When he found it, Kylee instinctively arched. "My woman," he whispered, and continued to brush across the distended bud that had eagerly awaited his touch. She quivered at the onslaught of pleasure taking over her body. In a matter of minutes – maybe seconds – white lightning struck. It sizzled its way through her veins; crackling, singeing, scorching. She cried Quinn's name again and again. Her breaths came in scatty gulps until the lightning settled to small tingles. "Ohhhh, Quinnnnn."

"I know, baby, and there's more to come. Lots more."

She didn't want to crimp the moment by thanking him, but she wanted to say it repeatedly. His careful manipulation of her body was unlike anything she'd ever known. The few times she'd been with Asher, he'd never made her feel loved or this out of control.

Quinn had given her a taste of heaven and she was excited to return the favor. She straddled him and crushed her mouth against his. She sucked his lips in the same way he'd done to hers. Instead of shoving her tongue in his mouth though, she teased him by darting it in and out, stoking the heat until he was panting hard and straining to say her name. She unbuttoned his trousers and wrapped her hand around the evidence that he wanted her as much as she wanted him.

The fantasy is usually better than reality surfaced from out of the blue. When she first met Quinn she leaned on that possibility as a way to stop drooling over him. She chuckled inwardly. In Quinn's case, *reality was so much better than the fantasy* and she couldn't wait to experience all the reality they could fit into their first night together.

Quinn groaned from the low knock on the privacy

window. "Noooo. Not yet." Kylee's hands of satin had his body and mind pulsing hard to reach the pinnacle of fulfillment. He was a few seconds away from that spectacular moment of bliss.

Damn limo drivers.

Kylee moved from his lap with a smile. While he tried to get his breathing under control he lifted her hand to his lips and planted kisses across her knuckles. "We're going to have a good life, Kylee."

She swept her lashes slowly across her eyes. "I know, husband." She raised her eyebrows and tugged her zipper all the way up.

Quinn pecked her mouth with a quick kiss. "Seems a little silly to try to guard the goods now. Besides, you're minus your underwear." He gave her a toothy grin and lowered the privacy window.

"We've arrived at the private entrance to the hotel, sir."

"Thanks, Henry. We need a moment or two."

Henry nodded. "Knock when you're ready to exit."

Quinn raised the privacy window again. "Are you ready to take this inside?"

Mischief laced Kylee's green eyes. "More than ready." She ran her tongue over her lips and his body instinctively jerked from the sexual taunt.

Quinn retrieved her panties from the floor and stretched them between his two index fingers. With an equal amount of mischief, he hit the button to open the moon roof and tossed the panties out.

"You didn't!" Kylee poked her head out of the moon roof and Quinn joined her. He slid his hand into hers while they watched the undergarment catch a breeze and end up in the meticulously groomed hotel landscaping.

"I bought those for you," she said.

"Which means they were mine to toss. Do you have any

more you'd like me to throw out?" He placed his hand on the curve of her bottom. "You're not going to need panties for a while. Just sayin'."

Henry appeared in their line of vision. "Do you want me to chase those, sir?"

"Umm, no. We're good. Thanks anyway, Henry." Laughter roared from Quinn's chest but Kylee's face was coated with a fine shade of red. "We can be stuffy and proper when we're eighty," he whispered.

The corners of Kylee's mouth dimpled. "I have a feeling when we leave the hotel they'll be glad to see us go."

"That can only mean our honeymoon was awesome."

Henry opened the door and Quinn could tell the chauffeur was trying to keep a straight face.

Quinn extended a hand to Kylee. She scooted carefully across the seat, tugging her dress down to keep from revealing her state of undress. As soon as she was out of the car, he crushed her against him and kissed her deeply. "Our room waits."

"Thanks, Henry. We won't be needing a car for a few days." Quinn planned to whisk Kylee and Gabbi on a much-longer, much-deserved vacation when the dust settled. Kylee had classes to finish and he had work to do too. When the time was right, they would jet to the destination of Kylee's choosing. Or Gabbi's. They'd probably end up at Disney World. He was okay with that.

Kylee said something to Henry that made Quinn wonder where it came from. "You were right, Henry. Love is worth the gamble." She leaned away from Quinn so she could kiss Henry's cheek. "Give Rebecca our love."

"Will do, miss."

* * *

Kylee flicked off the bathroom light and Quinn's pulse

skirted through his veins. Slowly she walked toward him dressed in a sheer white negligee that protected the scenery without obstructing the view. Her dusky nipples poked against the fine fabric and with each step her heavy breasts bounced.

Quinn moved quickly off the bed and met her in the middle of the room. He put a hand on his chest and shook his head. "You are a vision."

Kylee smiled shyly and folded herself in a hug. "There's something I need to tell you, Quinn."

"What is it?"

"My body isn't…" She paused and lowered her eyes.

"Isn't what, sweetheart?"

"Perfect." She still had her eyes downcast.

He'd seen a good portion of her body and it was mouthwatering perfection. Quinn opened her arms and lifted her chin so they were eye to eye. "I have a four inch scar on my upper thigh. I was showing off while water skiing and hit the boat." He pointed to his left eye. "I have one eye slightly larger than the other. Don't get me started on my feet. They're just plain gross."

Kylee pressed her lips together and tried to look down again. Quinn still had his fingers under her chin and prevented her from leaving his eyes. "I have a few stretch marks," she said with a crack in her voice. "As silly as this will sound, they're special to me, but you might find them a little distracting."

"Never," he said tenderly yet forcefully. He knelt down and parted the sexy nightie to have a look. There were a few small, barely visible purplish colored lines below her belly button. He looked up at Kylee before planting soft kisses across them. "They're not distracting at all. Not even a little. But this string," he snapped the elastic of the thin piece of material that was supposed to be a thong, "is way too distracting. It has to come off."

Kylee jiggled with a laugh.

Quinn rolled the make-believe thong from her hips and down her legs and shot it across the room with his make-believe slingshot.

With the insecurities and antics out of the way, he stood up and drew her into his chest. He pecked the tip of her nose and then laid a powerful kiss on her mouth. She tasted like raspberry lip balm. The heady smell of musk met his nose.

Quinn scooped Kylee up and carried her to the bed. Laying her across the satin sheets he had a clumsy moment and literally fell on top of her. He started to laugh and so did she. "So much for being suave."

"Save suave for later. Right now I need you to make love to me, Quinn." Kylee raised her knees and opened them so he could position himself.

Quinn rushed to her mouth to kiss her hard and fast, then he moved to her breasts and elongated her nipples with his lips. She arched and made a sound that was pure joy to his ears. He moved lower and flicked her belly button with his tongue. She moaned and wriggled.

He moved back up and dragged his lips across hers.

"Now. Quinn. Now."

Quinn took a deep breath and in the span of his next heartbeat they joined. Neither one moved. They stared into each other's eyes. Finally, he moved carefully and Kylee moved with him. With each thrust the tempo increased, so did their breathing. Quinn made love fast to Kylee. He watched her amazing green eyes deepen and her lips purse. When she was close to reaching that spectacular moment where it was hard to tell where earth ended and heaven began, he was the happiest man alive. She called out his name, tightened around him and held on for dear life. "I loveee you," she said against his mouth.

"I love you too." His body trembled and strained. He spiraled upward to land on the same billowy cloud that held his wife.

Quinn had known that he was in love with her but at that incredible moment he understood the magnitude of his feelings. Keeping Kylee in his life was the best choice he'd ever made.

~ The End ~

About The Author

Jan Romes grew up in northwest Ohio in the midst of eight zany siblings. Married to her high school sweetheart for more years than seems possible, she's also a mom, grandmother and mother-in-law. Jan writes contemporary romance with sharp, witty characters who give as good as they get. When she's not writing, you can find Jan working as a part-time fitness trainer or with her nose buried in a good book. She also likes to grow pumpkins and sunflowers.

TEXAS BOYS FALLING FAST (Series)

Married to Maggie – **available**

Keeping Kylee – **available**

Taming Tori- **summer 2014**

Not Without Nancy – **winter 2014**

OTHER BOOKS BY JAN ROMES

One Small Fib

Lucky Ducks

Kiss Me

The Gift of Gray

Stay Close, Novac!

Stella in Stilettos

Three Wise Men

The Christmas Contract

Mr. August

Three Days with Molly

You can follow Jan here:

www.authorjanromes.com

www.jantheromancewriter.blogspot.com

https://twitter.com/JanRomes

https://www.facebook.com/jan.romes.5

71314381R00134

Made in the USA
Lexington, KY
19 November 2017